Linda (MacLeod) van Omme grew up the infamous 'middle child' on the family farm on beautiful Prince Edward Island, with her two sisters, her parents, and her grandparents, all in the same house. She trained for a career as an occupational therapist, married the man she loves, has three dear, and almost perfect, daughters (and now five totally perfect grandchildren) and worked for 42 years, all across Canada, with the delightful 'mixed bag' of Canadians who inhabit this great country. Her books, though fictional, reflect this experience.

This book is dedicated to all the hard-working, hard-boiled, and often quite hilarious people who created and grew up in the many small communities, settlements, and towns, which collectively became, and are, Canada.

It is also dedicated to 'the relatives', who have been so supportive, and loving, in this 'writing thing'.

Linda van Omme

GLIMPSES: ST. AGGIES

AUSTIN MACAULEY PUBLISHERS™

LONDON * CAMBRIDGE * NEW YORK * SHARJAH

Ordering Information
Quantity sales: Special discounts are available on quantity purchases by corporations, associations, and others. For details, contact the publisher at the address below.

Publisher's Cataloging-in-Publication data
van Omme, Linda
Glimpses: St. Aggies

ISBN 9798889106166 (Paperback)
ISBN 9798889106173 (ePub e-book)

Library of Congress Control Number: 2023921084

www.austinmacauley.com/us

First Published 2024
Austin Macauley Publishers LLC
40 Wall Street, 33rd Floor, Suite 3302
New York, NY 10005
USA

mail-usa@austinmacauley.com
+1 (646) 5125767

I would like to particularly thank the "storytellers" in my life and my travels, who have sometimes supplied the 'seeds' for my imaginings, the excellent, and very patient, staff at Austin Macauley Publishing, and my husband, who smilingly tolerates my middle-of-the-night writing urges, and my frequent 'hogging the computer'.

Table of Contents

GLIMPSES

Explanation

Most of the time, it's just glimpses you get into people's lives, at a bookshop, or a retirement home, or just on the street in some little town.

Sometimes, you wish you knew how things turned out for them, that you could see just a little bit more and, sometimes, you're glad you can't.

Sometimes, people's lives blend with yours, and they become more than just a snapshot in time to you.

But with most people, all you get are glimpses.

Author's Note

The St. Aggies of this book is a fictional place, and any resemblance to a real town, or a real church, or real people, is purely coincidental.

It is true though, that the words, actions, and thoughts of the people in this fictional place may, at times, have been inadvertently inspired by the memories—the 'spirits', if you will—of the words and actions of some of those I have encountered in my time so far upon this earth. I have therefore tried my best to treat these 'spirits' with the utmost respect.

And even though Saint Agatha is not a real town, it is real to me and, I am hoping, it will be real to you, for a while, inside the pages of this book.

Synopsis

A town is not just a collection of buildings. The buildings mean nothing.

Instead, a town is defined by the people who live in those buildings, work in them, pray, sing, love, struggle, and laugh there.

It is defined by its history, and its reasons for being, and by how all these things act together, and grow with each other, to make one town 'feel' different from another just down the road.

Here are some glimpses into the 'life' of one such town.

Main and Recurring Characters

Saint Agatha (the town):

- Agatha—who started it all.
- Bruce—a moose.
- Clive—who loves burgers.

Bill's Gas Bar and Beauty Emporium:

- Staff and 'family'.

Just out of town:

- Edon and friends (Henry, Charlie, Stefan), and 'Cousin Freddy'.
- Rebecca (Charlie's sister).
- Lexi.

St. Aggies (the church):

- 'The Rev'—Minister at St. Aggies.
- Hellie and Wellie – Caretakers.
- Mr. Rooney (who has only three legs), and Thug (his 'sidekick').
- Boomer—Just a dog.
- Mrs. Chadwell—Church organist.
- 'The Choir', including Lillian who cannot sing.
- 'The Youth Group'—A very aggravating bunch of teenagers.
- Mrs. Henley—A lonely old lady who lives with a cow.

The Mission:

- Frank—The chef.
- 'The guy with the red toque'.
- Martha Grey (a 'bag lady'), Gwynn, Molly, Rick, and others.

The RCMP station:

- Sergeant Bell (and family).
- Chief Superintendent Jacob.
- Constable Kaminski, etc.

OLIVER—The Musical:

- Cast, 'production team', and audience.

Saint Agatha Health Center (SAHC)

- Clients and staff.

Townspeople:

- Michael Jacob Gregory Findlay—Just a kid.
- Mrs. Winters—The crabbiest person in town, and Emily (her neighbor).
- Soldiers—Ed and Marty.
- 'Docky'—The town vet.
- Miss Emma—A brand new schoolteacher.
- Ellie—A very pregnant community nurse.
- Marylou—A child with a child.
- Malcolm MacPherson—who loves hugs.
- Uncle Jake—A cowboy.
- Nick—who almost got lost.
- Pete, of 'Pete's Burgers'.
- Marion and Ruth—Two retired teachers.

Introduction

"The old girl's looking a bit rough round the edges, wouldn't you say?"

He frowned as he ran his hands gently down 'the old girl's' flanks.

"Yeah well, what can you expect? She is 95 years old! You'll be a bit rough round the edges too, when you hit 95!"

"If."

"If what?"

"If I hit 95."

"Yeah, s'pose you're right. If we hit 95, you mean!" And he punched his brother on the shoulder and the two of them wandered off, bickering as usual, while 'the old girl' watched silently, as she had done for the past 95 years.

Saint Agatha wasn't just the name of the church; it was the name of the whole town. In fact, the two of them had grown up together, and hardly anyone in town really remembered which had come first.

The early settlers had slogged their way 'up north', mostly with ox carts or horse and wagons, through the mud, and the rain, and the fierce snowstorms, to establish a tiny 'Landing'; The place where the first cart had finally broken down beyond repair, and those particular settlers had decided this was 'as good a place as any' to stop and stay.

Once they had built reasonable enough shelter to get through until spring, they had all gotten together and built a church; a place to get gather, and share meals, and thank God they were still alive. They named it after the first baby born there, which was also, coincidentally, the name of some long lost saint, who likely would have been quite pleased to be thought of at all.

'St. Agatha's' had quickly, affectionately, been shortened to 'St. Aggies', and 'the old girl' had watched over them benignly for 95 years.

Agatha

"Dear God, help me. Dear God, help me. Dear God, help me."

She just kept repeating it to herself, like a mantra, as she struggled along through the gummy brick-red mud, one hand on the edge of the cart, each step an effort now.

She hadn't told her husband when her labor pains started. He had enough to worry about, and there wasn't anything he could do about it anyway. It would be a while. The women in her family had always had long labors.

She caught her breath, and stopped for a moment. "Dear God, help me."

They had come from Hungary. She had laughed when she found out the English word that sounded almost the same: Yes, they had been 'hungary' all right, all the time they were there. That's why they'd left. Left family, home, everything, all for this.

Every season had its ups and downs. She'd been glad when the winter snows had finally melted, but then came the mud, which built up in layers on your boots, so you gained inches in height as you walked, and the cart kept breaking down and getting stuck.

Then the bugs. She didn't know what they were. It didn't matter. Little black flies of some sort, but, apparently, they planned to feast on these puny humans; this unexpected treat.

The cart suddenly stopped, stuck, yet again, and the woman, bent over in a spasm, clutching the side rail of the cart, almost fell.

She looked up, a pleading look to the heavens, and she saw a light, rising out of the mist coming over the top of the hill in front of them, dazzling her. Like a vision; a vision of a person holding out her arms. She rubbed her eyes to make it go away and smiled at her foolish thought.

The man let go of the reins he had been holding, and moved to the ox's head. His legs spread, his hands on either side, clutching the thick leather harness fastened around the heavy, shaggy head, ready to tug, yet again, and he looked into his ox's eyes: One more pull? One more effort? One more little bit at a time. Just to the top of this rise here?

It was a good ox, and a good cart, but even the best of things can only take so much, and at the first go, just when the mud seemed to be losing its grip, the sound of a great crack shook them; The sound of the axle breaking in two.

Well. The man looked around him, at the little green slope, and the stream trickling by. Maybe this would be as good a place as any to make a new beginning.

He looked to his wife, to ask her opinion, and he realized his wife had other things on her mind.

"I'd like to call her Agatha."

"Agatha! What kind of a name is that?"

"I don't know. Just an idea I had." She glanced up, over his shoulder, at the sun peeking through the trees, on the top of the hill.

Her husband shrugged, and shook his head over the funny ideas of women.

"Okay. Call her whatever you like. I'll call her 'Aggie' then," and he gave her hand a squeeze, then turned to deal with the wagon, and the patient ox.

His wife watched him go, then looked down at this new little babe; this new 'Canadian', and she smiled up at the sky, and she whispered: "Thank you."

The Shepherd

Edon was a good shepherd, which was just as well, because he didn't know how to be anything else. His father had been a shepherd and, even when he was very young, Edon had followed his father about, determined to be a shepherd himself, when he grew up.

Then his dad died, and Edon had to grow up fast.

He never forgot that night when his dad appeared at the door, almost too weak to open it, with blood on the hands holding his head, and fell to the floor just inside.

A wolf, a loner, acting oddly and particularly vicious, had attacked him. It hadn't even seemed interested in the sheep, just the man. Edon's dad had eventually beaten the wolf off with his heavy stick, but not before he had been bitten in several places.

Edon's dad died, after days of worsening fever and weakness and, finally, yelling, screaming crazed words, holding his aching head. The doctor said it was from the rabies, given to him by the wolf, and Edon never forgot it.

When Edon's mom died, Edon was alone. Alone with his sheep. A quiet, lonely man. To the surprise of his neighbors, he one day announced that he was leaving. Leaving his homeland and immigrating to Canada, to make a new start.

His neighbors bought his sheep, and his farm. Not that it was worth much but they paid a bit more than they usually would have done, and they sent him on his way, shaking their heads about him, that evening over supper.

He settled in northern Saskatchewan. It reminded him of his home in Albania, and he worked wherever and whenever he could, and gradually built up a herd of sheep, until he felt like a shepherd again.

Neighbors in this new land were few and far between, but Edon didn't mind. He was a loner at heart.

He did meet them sometimes though, when he went to town for groceries and such, but he always seemed to find some excuse to refuse their invitations to a meal, or to the local, homemade, evening entertainments.

Every day Edon took his flock out to find the best places to graze, in this vast land, and every evening he brought them back to the paddock, outside the tiny cabin; more of a shack really, he considered his home now, and he talked to the sheep, and his voice calmed them, and they felt safe, because they knew he was a good shepherd.

Winter came quickly that year. Unexpectedly. Edon had taken the flock to a far off place, where he knew there was good grazing, because the sheep needed to eat, and get fat, before the long winter came down.

He hadn't expected it to come down that very day.

When the sudden snowflakes became a squall, and then turned to a whiteout, Edon herded his sheep toward the base of a hill, in the lee of the wind, to the middle of a rough circle of rocks, persuaded them all to lie down, then sat down himself, at the entrance to their rocky haven.

It was reasonably cozy there, considering the general situation, and he leaned back against the closest sheep, and pulled his heavy cloak around his head. The sound of the wind, and the warm nearness of the sheep, had lulled Edon almost into sleep, when another sound alerted him.

Not a good sound, and he lurched to his feet, as his eyes tried to adjust to the gray blur of snow and evening gloom. There was something else out there; like the shadow of a ghost, against the whiteness. Edging closer.

Edon yelled, and shook his stick at it, a long staff of heavy black walnut, usually used to guide the sheep, but a shepherd's weapon too, when a weapon was required.

The thing moved off. Edon knew it was a wolf. What else could it be? But it seemed gigantic against the blur of flakes and it was moving oddly, stiffly, as if there was something wrong with it, and it didn't move far. He could see its eyes, catching the light, there behind the snow, waiting for him to make a wrong move.

Edon swore. Edon didn't swear often, but he knew how to do it. In several languages. He swore at the snow, and the night, and even the sheep, whom he loved. He swore at this land, which had taken him in, and his former land, that had allowed him to leave.

He swore at his neighbors, who were not there to help him, and himself, for not even trying to be a neighbor to them. He swore at God, in Albanian, and in English, in case God couldn't understand Albanian, for taking his parents from him; for allowing him to think this was a good place, and lulling him into complacency, into thinking he could have a good life here after all.

And he swore at that wolf, out there, waiting to kill him, just like it had killed his father.

When the wolf finally attacked, Edon was ready: He swung his heavy staff, just as the wolf leaped into the air, and he knocked it to the ground, into the icy drifts, and he hit it again, and again, until it was surely dead.

Then he noticed the blood on his hand; not a lot of blood, but enough, and the teeth marks there.

The squall was settling, and Edon could see the sheep now. He called to them, and they gathered round and followed him, in a scraggly line, back along the trail.

Edon felt tired. Really tired, and his head hurt, like something was beating at it, from the inside of his skull, and, funny thing, he no longer felt cold. He felt hot.

"Hey! Edon!"

It was Henry, his closest neighbor, with Etienne and Stefan, a couple of other neighbors, who had all come to find him.

"Big wolf back there, ay? Never seen a silver one like that!"

"Sick-looking though, wouldn't you say? Moved funny." Edon wiped the sweat from his forehead.

"Nah, just old. Looked healthy enough. Maybe slowing down a bit. Not able to keep up with the others. Massive though! Likely the grandpa of the pack. I'd say he thought he'd found a nice easy snack when he saw those sheep of yours."

"Wasn't reckoning on such a tough shepherd though, was he?"

And they clapped Edon on the back, and helped him herd his sheep towards home. Edon smiled to himself, at himself. His headache had magically disappeared, and the heat and the weariness he had felt were gone.

He decided, the next time he was in town, when he met his neighbors, and they invited him to supper, he might just say: "Yes."

Also, it might be a good idea to stop in at the church they had just finished building there, if only to apologize to God for all that swearing, and to say 'Thanks', in English, and in Albanian too, just in case God couldn't understand English.

Bill's Gas Bar and Beauty Emporium

Saint Agatha, when it first came to be, was a bit of a 'Rootin'-Tootin'' town. Because it was out of the way (Some said: "In the sticks."), there were quite a few people who ended up in Saint Agatha cuz they wanted, or needed, to 'disappear' and, because nobody really wanted them around, they just quietly hopped on a CP train, and got off at the last stop.

Saint Agatha was the last stop.

It did give the town 'character', and most of the 'characters' eventually settled down to become solid citizens, and you would have never known, to look at them, what pain-in-the-necks they were before. But some of them never 'settled down'. William Good was one of these.

His last name wasn't actually 'Good'. He had changed his name, unofficially, when he came to Saint Agatha. He, more accurately, should have been called 'William Bad', cuz he had been involved in pretty well every criminal activity a 'bad dude' could be involved in, except for murder. Willie did draw the line somewhere, even if it was about as low as you could get on the page.

The RCMP had been closing in when Willie boarded the last car, on the last train, and ended up in Saint Agatha. And, to tell you the truth, the Mounties didn't put a lot of effort into finding him. They were just glad he was gone.

Willie, who was not without charm when he chose to display it, wooed and won a sweet little First Nation's girl named Lyla, but by the time their son William (named after his father) was born, Lyla had realized what a great big mistake she had made.

She stuck with it though, for the sake of her son, and also because Willie, who worked as a lumberjack – only because there was limited scope for his criminal talents in the area – was away from home most of the time.

Willie did have one redeeming quality; only one: He did love his son, or at least he never beat him, not very often anyway, and he passed on, to his son, the one legal skill he knew. So 'Billy', by the time he was 13, was working in the woods too.

When Willie was killed in the line of work (a tree fell on him), everybody agreed it was 'a shame', but not a lot of tears were shed, and Lyla and her son moved back to live with Lyla's family.

Young 'Billy' was happy. He loved his mother's family. He had never been allowed any contact with them before – and they folded him into their arms, and loved him back.

Billy had always cut his own hair, ever since the day when he was 4 years old and he got hold of a pair of scissors. But, you know, he did seem to have a seed of talent for it, so his family began to let him 'trim' theirs too. It was a chance to sit down and chat with the boy.

It was the lumber-jacking though, that brought in the cash to help support he and his mom.

As young Bill got older, his haircutting skills improved, which was a good thing, and by the time he was on his own, working full-time in the lumber camps, he was pretty good at it, and he actually made more money cutting hair for 'the guys' in the camp—as well as for the female wives, cooks, etc…who were part of camp life—than he did from cutting down trees.

Bill had inherited his father's size, but his mother's personality, so he was as social as his father had been antisocial, and because there was no one else who cut hair in Saint Agatha, Bill started to practice on his growing list of friends in town as well.

When Bill, like his father, fell in love and married a First Nation's girl (Although, to be honest, it was highly unlikely old Willie had ever had it in him to ever actually 'fall in love'), his new wife objected to him being away for long months in the camps, and Bill, who had had enough of lumber-jacking by that time anyway, agreed, so he decided to look for something else.

Cars had just made it to Saint Agatha—You had to have roads before you could have cars—and Bill was just as fascinated by the first car in town as the rest of them were. But cars needed gas, and the closest gas station was more than an hour and a half down the road. So, since Bill had saved all of his hair-cutting cash, in a tin box under the bed, he decided to 'blow it', and he built the first gas station in Saint Agatha, at the corner of 1st Street and Main (the only 2 streets in town), just down from St. Aggies, with an attached little building, to do haircuts, at the back.

And after he had gone 'down south' for a couple of months, to take a 'real' hairdressing and barbering course, he came back, hired Jim and Leonard

('Lennie'), whom he had met at hairdressing school, as managers, and he and his wife, officially, with cake and ice cream and the whole bit, opened up 'BILL'S GAS BAR and BEAUTY EMPORIUM'.

Bruce

There were some hazards to playing soccer in Saint Agatha. I suppose you could call them 'challenges', if you were kind. The first was the geese. Not really the geese themselves. They generally took off as soon as the team arrived. The issue was what they left behind.

The geese did love the soccer field. It was mowed in the spring, with a hay mower at first, and then, as the town grew, with a fancy big, ride-on lawnmower. It was great, cuz the new grass, which grew after each mowing, was like 'the best thing ever!' to a goose – maybe like lobster, or cheese curds from Quebec, or a Nanaimo bar, would be to us – and the geese came from miles around to 'savor the flavor'.

They made the ground 'slippery', which is a polite way of putting it.

Add that to the mud. Cuz it rained a lot in Saint Agatha. Enough that nobody even bothered to carry an umbrella; it was just too much trouble. Instead, they wore rain gear and 'Ducky boots', three seasons out of four, and just pretended it wasn't raining. It did work to a certain extent, and if it didn't work for you, you just left town.

So, all things considered, soccer was a 'challenge'. But just about everywhere in the world, kids grow up 'kicking a ball around', and since Saint Agatha was a 'company town', with people brought in from all over the world, living there, it was something everybody knew, and loved, so no matter what; goose droppings, mud, rain, it didn't matter, everyone played.

The soccer field was constructed early. Just after the church and the general store, on the only flat piece of land in town, between St. Aggies and the school. They had to clear some trees, cuz it was right up against the forest, to make enough space, but it was worth the effort.

Sometimes a bear or two would wander across the field, and the game would have to be put on hold to let them pass. But generally, the bears avoided the noise.

The first time the moose showed up was in the middle of a tournament; Italians versus the Finns. It was a hot tournament, and there was no way one moose, even a big moose, was going to interrupt it. So they just ignored him just like they ignored the rain, and they played on.

The moose appeared to like soccer—Not playing it. I can't imagine a moose playing soccer. Well, I can imagine it, sort of, but it's a bizarre thought.

He (They could see it was a 'he', cuz of the antlers) just stood at the edge, between the field and the forest, and followed the play. He didn't cheer—something I really cannot imagine at all—but he certainly did appear to be enjoying it, and, between games, he took a break and just hung around, like the rest of the spectators, only he nibbled grass while they drank coffee.

After a while, everybody just forgot he was there, and the next time they looked he was gone, until the next week, when he showed up again.

He showed up for every game; didn't seem to discriminate, no matter what the level of play. He was there for the 5-year-olds, the same as he was there for the 50-year-olds, and his attendance, after a while, got to be just a normal thing.

If the ball happened to come toward him, he backed off into the woods, and you could see him, peeking out from behind a tree, which was pretty funny really cuz he was a lot wider than a tree, until the ball was safely back in play.

It was one of the 6-year-olds who named him. One day when the ball was speeding his way, she yelled: "Kick it, Bruce!"

He didn't, but the name stuck, and 'Bruce the Moose', who grew bigger and bigger, until he was, by far and away, their 'biggest fan', never seemed to grow out of his love for the game.

They knew it couldn't possibly be the same moose, over all those years, but he always looked the same to them.

His son perhaps, or his grandson? Maybe his love for soccer was hereditary, or maybe he just handed it down, to the next moose in town.

Dang Cat

"It was that cat's fault! Anybody could tell you that. That dang cat's fault, right from the start! Came smack out of nowhere, and I swerved to miss it—I'm a cat-lover, you know, but I like dogs too—We were just out for a drive. My buddies and me.

"The stupid police are calling it 'reckless driving'– Oh yeah! Sorry! You ARE the police. But it was just a drive; just for fun, you know! Though I can tell you right now, there wasn't a lot of fun in that ride! Not that I can remember anyway.

"Oh! I forgot! I sneezed! I meant to tell you that! I saw one time on the TV, how you automatically shut your eyes when you sneeze, and I totally remember doing that, Officer. So it wasn't really my fault. I'm allergic to cats, you know.

"And then St. Aggies just sort of leaped out in front of us, right out of the fog, and we crunched right into her. It did make a lovely crunch! Not that that's relevant or anything, Sir—I should call you 'Sir', right?—It's just part of 'The Facts', I guess you could say.

Oh! Really? I could have sworn there was fog! Sure looked like fog to me."

"Name, Sir?"

"You know you have very nice eyes, Ossifer. No, that can't be right! 'Ossifer'…Hey you!" and he giggled.

"They're the color of, let me think now, periwinkles! That's some kind of a flower, isn't it, or maybe it's a shellfish. You know, I'm not sure. What were we talking about?"

"Your name, Sir."

"You first! What's your name, big boy?"

"Bell, Sir. Sergeant Bell."

"Well, ring-a-ding to you too!" and the man giggled again.

"Oh right. My name! Well. Isn't that funny? I believe it's just slipped my mind. I'm sure I must have it written down somewhere though. When do you need it? And, by the way, it is very nice how you keep calling me 'Sir'. Very respectful. I think ossifers are very nice people. Don't you? Always have been, as far as I'm concerned. You never can believe what you read in the newspapers!

"No Sir! I was NOT drinking! I NEVER drink! Bad for the liver. Yeah. A couple of joints maybe, that's all. Ages ago. WAY before that church hit us. No big deal. Harmless stuff. Just relaxes a person. Oh yeah, I was real relaxed.

"That is true, Officer! 'Good job no one else was around' is right! You are right on there! Somebody coulda got hurt! That's why we went out for a drive so late see, when nobody'd be around. 'For the good of the public', I suppose you could say.

"No, I don't think it was a black cat. To tell you the truth – I always tell the truth, Officer, just like my mother told me. It looked kind of like it was pink, and a bit fuzzy.

"Yeah! I'm sure now I think about it: It was a pink cat! No, that's true. You don't see a lot of those around. Shouldn't be hard to find.

"Took a bit of a chunk out of old St. Aggies, ay? Well, just a couple of bricks, really. Nothin' anybody'd notice. Sort of blends in with the rest, wouldn't you say? And it's not like the place is gonna tip over or anything. The old girl's pretty solid. Bin around a long time. Must be close to a hundred years now. Looks good for her age, don't you think? Yeah. The car is a different story. That is true.

"No. No, it's not mine. Well, I borrowed it for the night, from my Aunt June. She lent it to me, sort of. She doesn't really know she lent it to me. She's not home right now. She's up north, visiting my cousin Greg. Bit of a jerk, ol' Greg.

"You're right about that. She may not be too happy. I suppose I should get it fixed for her, ay? When I can get hold of some cold hard cash. To tell you the truth though—Yes, I do always tell the truth! Somebody told you that, did they? It looks like a write-off to me.

"It sure is good St. Aggies and the police station are so close together, ay? Heard the crunch, did yuh? So you could come straight away! Yeah, 'Caught in the act' and 'Scene of the crime', do sort of both seem to apply. You guys sure keep late hours. Too bad.

"Yeah, us too.

"No. That's okay. I'd prefer to spend the night in my own bed. Hey! Where is my bed anyway? Never mind. I'll find it. Not to worry! I'll just drive around a bit and I'm sure it'll show up.

"Oh. Right. You are accurate! My car, well Aunt June's car really, does seem to be a bit under the weather. Should I just let it stay there for the night then? Sort of a sleepover kind of thing? Oh. Okay. I'll just leave it for now. Kind of snuggled up into the corner of St. Aggies there, ay? Cozy-like. Might even be holding a couple more of those bricks in place too, so good idea to leave it where it is.

"Yep! I'm a-comin'! Kind of you to offer me a ride, Ossifer. My car was in an altercation. Yes, with a building. How'd you know that anyway? Oh, you heard.

"Don't forget to look for that cat, ay! Shouldn't be hard to find. All this is that cat's fault! Dang cat!"

'The Boys' and Mr. Rooney

When Hellie and Wellie were about 6 years old, they 'swore an oath' that they would "Never! Ever!" get married.

At various times in their long 6 years, they had heard adults speak of 'a horrible fate' and they decided that this must, obviously, be what all that talk had been about. 'This' being the day their 'Maiden Aunt', aged 24, got married, and they were invited to the wedding.

Apparently the groom, to the two boys' disgust and embarrassment, soundly kissed their aunt "in front of everybody!" at the reception, and they both decided this 'Horrible Fate' was "Never! Ever!" going to happen to them!

In fact, they would have given up on their aunt entirely except for the fact that she happened to make great gingersnap cookies, cut in shapes, sometimes with icing, which she freely shared with her nephews. Besides, they decided it hadn't really been her fault, as the disgraceful act appeared to have been initiated by her new husband.

This oath of theirs was accompanied by solemn words and, after sneaking their father's X-ACTO knife from his workshop, by the blending of blood from the little fingers of each of their left hands. Their mother had assisted with the application of the required Band-Aids, explained away by blaming the cat.

Their mother did wonder at the depth, and the perfectly matched positioning of the wounds, but, having already lived with two little boys for six years, she decided she really didn't want to know.

The X-ACTO knife was quite sharp, and this 'solemn oath' hurt quite a lot, and produced a fair amount of blood, requiring several layers of Band-Aids to staunch the flow, but they both felt it was well worth it. And they still wore their scars proudly, over 50 years later, and still abided by those weighty words: They had 'Never! Ever!' gotten married, or even had girlfriends, as far as anyone knew.

Everyone at St. Aggies thought it was cuz they were too shy, or maybe because of how they looked.

(Their cousin Ellie, who had the unfortunate habit of saying out loud whatever came into her head, said, "they never got married because they never got up the gumption to ask anyone, and just as well, cuz they're both dull as dishrags!"

Which wasn't actually true. They just kept their mouths firmly shut when they were anywhere near their cousin Ellie.)

They had retired early, moved into an apartment just across the street from St. Aggies, and, after a few months, found they were bored. So one day, the pair of them showed up at the church asking if they could do some volunteer maintenance work there, and the church board snapped them up.

The two men looked a lot alike, amazingly alike. And for good reason, since they were identical twins.

Their parents had christened them 'Harold' and 'Wellington'. Good, solid, noble names. Names that couldn't be messed with. So, of course, they grew up being called 'Hellie' and 'Wellie'. ('Hell' and 'Boot', at school, and still sometimes.)

It was only strangers in town who looked puzzled, sometimes even alarmed, when they walked by St. Aggies, and heard someone yelling: "Hell! Get down here, will yuh!"

Mostly, at the church, and around Saint Agatha, everyone just called them 'The boys'.

It was true Hellie was shy. Wellie, however, could 'talk the hind leg off a dog', and the joke around town was that this is what had happened to 'Mr. Rooney', their three-legged dog.

(In fact, it had been the fault of the pup's unfortunate encounter with an old-fashioned hay mower.)

Mr. Rooney had been found one morning, in a basket on the front steps of St. Aggies, and had gotten himself adopted by 'The boys', thus ensuring himself a 'dog's life', which was better than most humans.

Mr. Rooney had grown up to be a bit of a 'dog about town', in spite of his odd number of legs, and there were considerable puppies in the area who looked quite a lot like Mr. Rooney.

"I wonder how he does it?" Hellie was staring out the window one day, at Mr. Rooney and one of his obvious progeny, playing together on the front lawn at St. Aggies.

"Does what?"

(It was tax time, and Wellie was bent, muttering, over some forms on his desk in the church basement.)

"You know." Hellie pointed through the glass, at the two almost-identical dogs, except, of course, for their size, and their number of legs.

"Oh."

Wellie looked outside, to where a second Mr. Rooney clone had just joined in the fun, and he frowned, and ran his hand down his long scraggly gray beard for a moment, as he contemplated the sight. Then he shrugged: "Don't know. He does seem to manage it though!", and he went back to his papers.

The other odd thing about Mr. Rooney was the fact that he was totally silent: Not a bark to be heard. Not a growl. Not even a whimper.

The boys had wondered if this might be another result of the accident which had robbed Mr. Rooney of his leg, but 'Docky', the town vet, couldn't find any cause, and his other doggy senses seemed perfectly fine: He could clearly hear. In fact, he had an obvious preference for country and western music, and he came running whenever either of the boys called him.

And his nose worked. He could sniff out a peanut butter and baloney sandwich from at least 40 paces—blind-folded, they would have bet, though they had never actually proven this.

But not a peep out of him, ever.

That day the boys were watching Mr. Rooney through the basement window, the Rev was also looking out at the same scene. He had been trying to come up with a spellbinding sermon for the next Sunday morning, and was fiddling with the little gold cross, engraved with his name, which his family had given him at his ordination.

He always kept it on his desk, in a turned wooden bowl a friend had made for him, along with a couple of old pennies and his Remembrance Day poppy.

Usually he found fingering the little cross helped his concentration, but today, so far, nothing was on the page, so he sat staring out his office window, letting his mind wander.

The puppies were yapping and growling, as they play-acted their ferocious attacks on Mr. Rooney and each other, but Mr. Rooney, easily bumping the pups away with his nose, and rushing here and there to attack or repulse, was, as usual, not making a sound.

The Rev frowned: It was strange that. You'd think the dog would say something, sometime, if he could.

As he watched, two different people walked by, in two different directions, leading their own female dogs. Both dogs stopped dead, watching Mr. Rooney intently, and finally had to be dragged away, reluctantly, looking back over their shoulders, by their owners.

"Well," the Rev laughed to himself, "It does look like some ladies do prefer the 'Strong, silent, type'."

But there seemed to be no way, or at least no way he could think of, to fit *that* into a sermon.

Mr. Rooney had 'guy friends' too. He appeared to be a 'dog's dog', as well as a 'lady's man', and various other dogs came to visit him, to share the gossip from the Saint Agnes' canine community, or perhaps just to squabble over a particularly fragrant bone.

One of these was a solid-looking, low-to-the-ground Basset Hound named 'Boomer'—The name was written on a tag on his collar—who came to visit off and on, presumably whenever he was 'in town'. The other was a tiny Yorkie the Rev christened 'Squirt'.

Even on his hardest days, the sight of these 'three amigos', meandering down the sidewalk, or sitting together on the front steps of the church, as if they were surveying the scenery, or just keeping an eye on the place, never failed to make the Rev smile.

Thug

Nobody would have, ever, called Thug a 'sweet little pussycat'. For one thing, he had never been little: He was born a single, very large, kitten, almost as big as his mother, and she had barely managed to get him out of there, was apparently just relieved to be rid of the burden, and left him to his own resources as soon as it was possible.

He was also about as far from 'sweet' as any cat could ever be and, as he grew up 'on the streets', he developed into an aggressive, self-centered bully, dominating pretty well the whole 'cat kingdom' around St. Aggies.

He was mostly a coal black color, with long hair, matted into clumps around his ears and his tail, and everywhere else too, and the pleasant sight of him coughing up hairballs onto the sidewalk was a familiar one to the disgusted residents of the neighborhood.

Overall, he did not appear to contribute much, nor add to the 'positive ambience' of the area, and the locals would have been quite glad to run him out of town, if only they had been able to catch him.

But 'every cat has its day', as the old folks say, and Thug was slowing down.

He didn't know it though, and continued his sport of lying in wait for approaching vehicles, especially when it was dark and he was practically invisible outside of the lights, and then dodging out in front of them, at the very last possible moment, and laughing—if cats actually can laugh—at the resultant screeching of tires and the yelling voices, as he sneered – yes, cats can definitely sneer—and swaggered away up the sidewalk, with his tail straight up in the air, flicking in derision.

But one black night, Thug's favorite game didn't work out. His timing, perhaps due to a touch of arthritis in his knee, or a small decline in his vision on one side, was a bit off, and this time the car won the game. It clipped him on the right side, flung him up into the air, and, for once, the cat, or at least this cat, did not land on its feet.

Hellie and Wellie found him in the morning, in the bushes beside the front corner of the church. He didn't look too great, but then Thug had never looked that great, but at least he was alive, and the boys gathered him up, and wrapped him in one of their jackets, and took him inside to their workshop/boiler room retreat in the basement of the church.

"What is that anyway?" (The Rev had come down for a chat and a cup of coffee.)

"It's a cat. You never seen a cat before?"

"That's a cat? Prove it."

Just then, the cat let out a rather pitiful little mew.

"Oh. Okay. I believe you then, even if thousands wouldn't. Where'd you get it anyway?"

"He's a boy, not an 'it'. Well, actually, he's a cat, and we found him, likely hit by a car last night." Wellie reached out one finger and ran it down the cat's ear, and the pile of ratty fur, surprisingly, purred.

"Should we get him to Docky?"

"No. I don't think a vet'll do him much good."

"Hurt pretty bad, ay? Well then, I could send up a prayer or two, on his behalf, if you'd like."

"A prayer for a cat? You think that'll work?"

"Yeah. Don't see why not. I've seen plenty of cats that were nicer than a lot of humans I've known."

The Rev reached out a hand, and the 'sweet little pussycat' hissed at him, and the one undamaged paw, with a set of razor-sharp claws on it, slashed across his fingers.

"Of course I wouldn't be sure, in this case," and the Rev scowled at it, and sucked his bloody thumb.

They were all a bit nervous about how Mr. Rooney would react to this 'interloper' in his territory, but the second morning the cat was in residence the boys woke to find the two of them in the same basket, curled up together, sound asleep, so the anticipated 'issue' never actually became one.

When the cat finally did recover, it was obvious that his right eye was damaged beyond repair and the boys eventually did have to take him to the vet, to get the eye removed, to prevent infection, and to get the eyelid sewn shut.

His right leg healed too, but he now walked with an obvious, lopsided, gait.

Overall, it did not improve his already disreputable look.

"THAT's the church cat! Doesn't look like a holy cat to me. Looks more like a holy terror, or maybe a pirate, or at least a THUG!"

Thus 'the cat' received his first, and forever, name, and also his first, and forever, home.

Thug seemed to fit right in to 'the gang' on the front steps, and 'the three amigos' became four. Perhaps the others may have mistakenly thought Thug was actually a dog, or maybe they just didn't dare try to kick him out.

And the next year, when rats invaded the town, apparently an every-five-year phenomenon in the area, he more than paid for his room and board. Although even Hellie and Wellie cringed, and felt the need to leave the room, when Thug was noisily enjoying his ill-gotten plunder.

Sweet Revenge

Henry and his cousin Freddy had, almost from birth, been 'at war'. They were born only two days apart, and should have been friends, but they were always measured against each other, which does not necessarily produce warm and cuddly feelings, and Freddy always seemed to come out on top:

Freddy was toilet-trained earlier, learned to talk earlier, was smart, incredibly social, and well-behaved; "An Angel!" according to his mother.

Henry struggled learning to read and write, tended to be shy in public, and always seemed to be 'getting into trouble'. In fact, his escapades were already legendary in the family.

Freddy went to 'better schools', lived in 'better places', got way better jobs, in the 'big city', and altogether appeared to be a much higher quality family product. And Henry hated him for it. So when Henry was barely old enough to manage, he decided he was tired of hearing about the saintly Freddy, and he left home and set out on his own.

He traveled far and wide, sometimes hitch-hiking or catching 'free rides' on trains, working at odd jobs, on fishing boats, and farms, and in lumber camps. Picking up skills as he went, and eventually marrying and settling down, in 'the north' to farm.

Henry was finally happy; had finally gotten past being 'Freddy's loser cousin', when one day, out of the blue, Henry got a letter from Freddy.

Freddy had apparently decided he wanted to 'do a bit of traveling', to 'expand his horizons a tad', beyond his life in the big city, and was proposing to "come for a little jaunt into the wilderness" and "drop in for a spell. Just for a laugh!" on his cousin, to experience a bit of the "Wild winter up north!".

Henry replied, telling Freddy that he was 'welcome to come', which may have been a lie but, after all, Freddy was 'family'.

It had truly been a 'wild winter', in Henry's part of the world. Cold, even colder than usual, and Henry and his neighbors had been having lots of trouble lately, with wolves stealing their sheep.

(I suppose the wolves may not have realized that those sheep were not their own personal sheep, so they may not have been entirely at fault.)

There seemed to be one wolf in particular, a big black one, who was especially good at the job, and the farmers were determined to take him down. So they salvaged the body of a dead sheep, filled it with poison, and put it out on the edge of the field, in the area that seemed to be the wolf's preferred territory, and they waited.

And a couple of days later, the day before Freddy's arrival, when they checked back, the trap had worked: The big black wolf, even bigger than they had imagined, lay dead, frozen stiff, with a vicious, snarling grimace on its face, there in the snow…and Henry had an idea.

Henry's neighbors, who had heard quite a lot about Freddy, were delighted to participate. They loaded the icy, wicked-looking creature onto a sleigh, which was not an easy job, cuz he was really quite huge, and they dragged him back home to Henry's place and set up his rigid, menacing carcass, posed for maximum effect, in the gap beside the barn where the car was stored; right in the path Freddy would have to cross, to get to the house.

By the time they were done, all the neighbors, in fact most of the folk in the area, were in on the joke, and everyone thought it was pretty funny…except, apparently, God.

Cuz the night before the 'big scare', and Henry's sweet revenge, a warm Chinook wind descended, and, very similar to 'the wicked witch of the west', the wolf melted.

Just a Girl

Martha (Her brothers all called her 'Marty') had always wanted to be a boy. She had three big brothers, and it always seemed they were allowed to do WAY more than she was!

It wasn't the fact that they called her a girl, that irritated her—After all, she WAS a girl—It was that they called her 'just a girl'.

(Although, to be fair, Tom, who was only two years older, never called her 'just a girl'.)

"You're not allowed to do that."—Whatever it was; climb a tree, work on the car, help build a barn, go exploring in the neighbor's woods, pretend to be a superhero or a 'flying ace' and jump off a cliff.

(Not that Marty particularly wanted to jump off cliffs, or shoot things, or scrape her face every morning, like her two oldest brothers and her dad had to do.)

It was the principle of the thing! It seemed it was ALWAYS: "You can't do this" or "You can't do that!"

"But why not?"

"Well. Cuz you're just a girl!"

"It's not fair!" she would wail at them all, as her brothers got ready to go on a fishing trip in the middle of nowhere with their father, and they would shrug, and pat her on the head, and walk out the door, without her, and Marty would run off and hide in the barn loft, and write out her troubles, in an old scribbler, with 'JOURNAL' written on the front cover.

Her mother, who was just glad to finally have a girl to give a hand with the housework and the cooking, wasn't really much help, and eventually, in spite of being sick of hearing it, Marty too started thinking of herself as 'just a girl'.

But sometimes, when her two older boys were away on some forbidden escapade – or at least forbidden to her – Tom would let her help him work on the car (and he gave her driving lessons too), or he would take her into the woods with him, and show her how to track, and fish, and make a fire.

When the war broke out, and Marty watched her brothers – 'The Grey boys', as everyone had always called them, though they were now dressed in green – 'marching off to battle', in their new uniforms, with everyone cheering at the train station, Marty was determined that she too wanted to be part of this effort to 'serve her country'.

In fact, she made it all the way to the recruitment officer's desk, dressed in some of Tom's clothes, with her hair cut short—She'd done it herself in the barn loft, with the dog, and a couple of 'barn cats', and a chicken, in attendance—and Tom's old cap on.

But that's when the officer in charge actually took a look at her, then down at her name, and then back up at her again: "You're 'Marty'?" She nodded, and then he stood up, slammed his fist on his desk, and yelled in her face: "What the hell are YOU doing here? You're not a soldier! You're just a girl!"

Oh, it was not a good thing for him to say. Not good at all. Just like a red flag in front of a bull, those words!

It took two soldiers to carry her out, yelling, and spitting, and scratching, and to deposit her, none too gently, on the sidewalk, and tell her to 'NEVER come back'!

But the next day, just like the cat in the song, Marty came back.

"Not you again! Get out! I don't have time for this! I TOLD you—"

"You told me I can't be a soldier, right?"

"Damn right!"

"But there must be SOMETHING I can do? I just want to do my best!"

The officer sighed. He was not really a monster. He was just tired, and overworked, and sick of seeing bright-eyed boys, who should have just been at home, living their lives, sent off to, at best, terror, and, at worst, death, and he was not unsympathetic to her plea.

"Look. Maybe you could sign up to be a nurse?"

Marty closed her eyes: 'Great. The 'Three Bs': Bed baths, Bandages, and Bedpans', and she sighed.

A nurse was the last thing she had ever wanted to be. But if that was the only possibility?

"…or maybe an ambulance driver?"

"Yes! Yes, yes, yes!"

(Tom had taught her to drive years ago, way before she was legal, and even her father, who tended to just ignore her, had to admit she was pretty good at it.)

So Marty signed up to be an ambulance driver, and was sent overseas, to 'do her best'.

Every night, after her long shift transporting half-dead soldiers to and from the field hospitals, and even though she sometimes felt half-dead herself, she sat down and wrote out her day, and her thoughts, and her feelings, in an old scribbler, with 'JOURNAL' printed on the front cover.

Sometimes, every once in a while, she even copied out a bit, if she thought it was particularly good, and sent it home to the 'Saint Agatha Tattler'.

And sometimes, every once in a while, if there was enough space left once the advertisements were in, they actually published it.

Marty did meet that recruitment officer one time, years later, on the street.

"Well. Hello there! It's Marty, right?", and he held out his hand. "I've been keeping an eye on you, you know. Saw you just got some big, fancy, la-di-dah award for foreign journalism! Congratulations! Looks like maybe you're not 'just a girl', after all!"

Marty shook his hand, and looked him in the eye. "Thanks," she said. "But Sir, have you not heard?

"There's actually no such thing as 'just a girl'."

The Soldier

It was just a mild acid, used to clean the barrels at the molasses factory, and it looked like water, so Ed—they all called him 'Eddie'—didn't pay any attention to the spill on the floor. The one he was standing in.

He had been meaning to get new shoes; these old ones were getting pretty worn through at the side by his big toe, or maybe rubber boots, for work. His wife always said rubber boots would likely be best.

But rubber boots weren't very comfortable, and he could stand in these good old shoes, shaped to his feet by time, for hours, at work, usually with his left foot tucked up behind, and his right foot solidly on the floor, as he leaned against the machinery.

He didn't even notice his shoe, or his sock, getting wet.

Eddie had a bit of a hurt spot on that big toe, from an encounter with a fork, in the garden on the weekend, and his toe started to sting. But he was busy, and by the time his break came, and he had time to sit down and take his shoes off, he could smell the acid in his shoe, and on his sock, and his toe was red.

He didn't have anything else there though, so he just put his socks, and his old shoes, back on, and toughed it out to the end of the shift.

His wife said he should go see the doc, but Ed didn't have a lot of faith in doctors, and besides, the clinic was a ways away, and he would have to miss some work time, which the boss wouldn't like, for such an insignificant issue. So he just wrapped up his toe, and stuffed his foot back in his old shoe, and 'soldiered on'.

But after three or four days, there was no denying its significance. Eddie couldn't walk. The Doc said the infection had spread, and, eventually, Eddie's right foot had to be removed, and then a wooden one, crude but effective, made for him, to take its place and, a while later, a 'fancier' aluminum one, fabricated in the city.

And Eddie could walk again! With a bit of a limp, it was true, and sometimes, if he was tired, a cane. But Eddie always said it was "No big deal!"

When the war broke out, all the men his age in Saint Agatha were called to serve, and he went, proudly, to the recruitment station to sign up. But Ed's 'no big deal' seemed to be a big deal to them, and it appeared they didn't want him.

He cried that night; Ed, who 'never cried'! cuz he wasn't allowed to 'do his bit' for his country. They did tell him he could be useful 'keeping an eye out for trouble', as one of their 'eyes on the ground' at home, and they did give him a uniform, of sorts.

And he did do his best: patrolling the streets, checking on anything suspicious, helping where he could, but his heart wasn't really in it. He knew he wasn't 'a real soldier'.

When the war ended, and 'the soldier boys' came home to Saint Agatha—those who did make it home—lots of them were in pretty rough shape, and Bill did his bit for them too: Listening to their stories if they wanted to talk, down at the Legion, picking up groceries, taking them to appointments and such, when they needed him, and eventually, most of them forgot, like Ed did too sometimes, that Eddie hadn't actually ever been a 'real soldier'.

But sometimes, especially on Remembrance Day, someone would ask him where he got 'wounded', and they would point to his foot, or his cane, and he would start to explain: "Oh, I didn't get that in the war. I got it—" but by then his listeners would have lost interest and weren't really listening, or sometimes, had even walked away, cuz this was a day for 'Real Soldiers'.

He always felt bad, when they found out he was just some guy who hadn't 'done his bit' for the war and, sometimes, he felt angry: It wasn't his fault he hadn't 'gone over there'! He hadn't been allowed!

And eventually, when people asked, Ed stopped answering and just grunted at them, and turned and limped grumpily in the other direction.

It didn't improve as the years, and the birthdays, and the Remembrance Days, went by.

He was 98, and the molasses factory was long gone and forgotten. He was one of the oldest to attend Remembrance Day at the cenotaph that year, and to proudly wear his poppy on the lapel of his 'uniform', which fit him again, now that he seemed to be losing some weight.

He was using his cane most of the time now, because of his foot, and he was, in truth, a bit of a 'miserable old man'.

That day though, at the end of the ceremony, when everyone was wandering off home, some kid, a teenager actually, approached him, and asked him the inevitable question: "And where were you wounded?", and pointed to Ed's foot.

"I was wounded by acid," Ed snapped. Then his voice faltered, as the old anger, and the feeling of shame, returned, and he was barely able to whisper, "in the molasses factory." And he looked away, to get himself under control, and then turned back to the teen.

The boy nodded, as if he understood, and he shook Ed's hand. "Thanks", he said, before walking back to his friends, and Ed saw the teen pointing him out to the other kids, and them all looking at him with respect.

And Eddie felt like a new man! A soldier. A 'veteran' even! Someone who had done all they could to do 'their bit', for their country.

And he had told the truth! The absolute truth!

A few of the kids did wonder what secret mission 'The Molasses Factory' had been, in that elderly veteran's long ago, soldiering days.

But it sure must have been something pretty secret, if he could still only whisper the words and, even after all these years, obviously wasn't allowed to say exactly what 'The Molasses Factory' actually was!

Turkey Hunt

Henry Watson's cousin Freddy 'hung around'. He'd come for 'a little jaunt, up north' in the middle of the winter, and it was coming April, and he was still there. And Henry didn't even like him!

Although he wasn't as bad as Henry had expected; as Freddy had been when they were boys. In fact, Henry was starting to wonder if there was some other reason his cousin had come, like maybe he was running away from something 'down south', and, in spite of himself, Henry was a bit worried about his cousin.

Not that Freddy wasn't still a pain in the neck, and other parts of the anatomy. He was. Henry's wife called him: 'Lord Freddy', but not out loud, except to Henry. Freddy was always telling them how to do things 'properly', and making 'little suggestions' about this and that.

Henry's wife generally just smiled politely and ignored him, but it did grate on Henry's nerves, especially since Freddy usually didn't have a clue what he was talking about, even if he thought he did.

It was wild turkey season, and Henry and his friends were planning a hunt and there seemed to be no way to keep Freddy from being involved, though they certainly wished there was. For one thing, Freddy had never fired a gun. ("And he'll be a hazard to the public, with one in his hands!", was Stefan's comment ",...but the turkeys won't have to worry!")

Freddy had also been reading up on 'Proper Hunting Etiquette', so was informing them all how things should be arranged, and wondering if they could 'procure a few more hounds', to 'bolster the numbers'. ('The numbers' being 'One': Edon's sheepdog Jep.)

He was, loudly, voted down by Henry's friends, who were not particularly impressed with Freddy.

Freddy had never seen a wild turkey. It appeared he was picturing the chubby, rather dim, and reasonably benign birdies on the farms down south, or on his plate at Thanksgiving dinner, rather than the long-legged, savvy, and belligerent creatures, who attempted to 'rule the roost', even, sometimes, in downtown Saint Agatha, as well as out in the woods around Henry's farm.

All this being said, the sight of 'Lord Freddy', screaming, practically in hysterics, and pelting down the track, waving his gun in the air, with a huge, angry, tom turkey, close on his heels, in hot pursuit, made up for all the slights, and sneers, and put-downs Henry had suffered in his childhood, because of Freddy.

"So. Should we go rescue him?" Edon's lips twitched.

"Naw. You guys go ahead. I'll catch up with you once I know he's okay", and Henry headed back down the track toward home.

But when he got there, the picture was entirely different from what he had expected: Henry's wife, and two other ladies, one of them Henry's aunt, and the other, younger, but just as fierce-looking, were standing in the yard, and they—Not Henry's wife. She was well back, out of the way, with her hand over her mouth—appeared to be 'cleaning Freddy up'; whacking at him, to get the feathers off, and dabbing at the bloody pecks and scratches the turkey had inflicted.

Although 'whipping him into shape', might have been a more accurate description of the process.

"Come along now, Sweetheart! Come with Mummy and dear Marguerite, and we'll get you away from this, this, whatever you'd call it? 'Wilderness', I suppose!

I cannot IMAGINE whatever possessed you to come up here in the first place! And why your cousin," and his aunt flung Henry a venomous look, "wouldn't allow you to come back home, where you belong!" And she gave Freddy a rather vicious peck on the cheek, just below where the turkey had recently done something very similar.

The last sight Henry saw of his cousin was a final, rather pleading, glance back over Freddy's wife's shoulder, before the ladies shoveled him into their, very classy, car and drove him away.

And to tell you the truth, for the first time in his life, Henry actually felt kind of sorry, for his cousin Freddy.

The Woman Who Couldn't Sing

There is one major advantage to being a member of a church choir: They can't kick you out.

Well, I suppose they could, if they were desperate, but it's highly unlikely. So they're stuck with you, unless some act of God does the job; a bolt of lightning, perhaps, coming out of the sky in the middle of the service, and striking you dead. Also highly unlikely.

Lillian couldn't sing. Not everybody can, you know. Perhaps some brain/vocal chord connection the teensiest bit off? I'm sure there is some scientific explanation, and likely some site on the internet, which could tell you why. There might even be an app for that.

But anyway, she couldn't. Which didn't mean she didn't, cuz Lillian loved to sing, and she sang all the time. At home. Out walking. At the mall. Even at Canadian Tire. But she really shouldn't have. It was disturbing to the public.

When Lillian joined the choir at St. Aggies, she was happily responding to a plea from the choir director, straight from the pulpit, that they 'really needed' and 'really wanted' new choir members and that 'anyone was welcome'!

She didn't realize he hadn't actually meant her.

But the choir director was a kind man; a good man, and when Lillian showed up for choir practice that next Thursday evening, and he had her sing a scale for him, to see where she would best fit in the choir, he barely flinched at all, although his eye did twitch a bit, when she attempted high C.

The rest of the choir was another matter.

It wasn't that the other choir members were that great either, but, compared to Lillian! Well. You get the idea. A couple of them even visited the choir director privately, and suggested, strongly, that he should "get rid of Lillian."

(The choir director did not agree.)

Most of the choir were good people too though, and kind. It was true they cringed a bit, muttered now and then, and vented their feelings, at home, but they wouldn't for the world have intentionally hurt Lillian's feelings. So they closed their eyes, and bit their lips, and did their best to maintain their decorum, even on the high notes, and even if they did, at certain moments, as a group, begin to display identical pained expressions, as if they had all eaten the same bitter something they shouldn't have, all at the same time.

In short, they all just endured, and doggedly carried on.

Except for Lillian. Lillian blossomed and flourished. Her plain face, when she was singing at practice and on Sunday mornings, almost glowed with the joy of it, as if she were, right there before their eyes, turning into a heavenly being.

And the odd thing was that the singing, on Sundays, got better.

Every week, the choir improved. Every month they tried, and managed to conquer, more and more difficult music, to the point where they began getting requests, from other churches, from the mall, even from Canadian Tire at Christmastime, for them to come and sing.

And the choir director knew exactly why, and he smiled to himself at the knowledge: For the owners of those voices in front of him, before a bit weak and tentative, now put everything they had, their whole hearts, and every bit of volume they possessed, into their singing, all in a valiant effort to drown out dear Lillian.

The Stranger

It was Easter Sunday morning. The bells had been rung. The Easter Drama, with a most convincing Mary blasting up the aisle screaming: "Jesus is alive!", was a done thing.

The echoes of 'Hallelujahs!' still clung to the rafters, and the Rev was just starting his Easter sermon, when a young man, a stranger, in rough clothing, with a backpack slung over one shoulder, quietly entered the street entrance, at the back of the church.

He came to the edge of the doorway to the sanctuary, but no further. Like some timid woodland animal, a deer perhaps, more comfortable there in the shadows, where he could easily slip away, if need be.

The choir saw him, although he was too far away for them to see his features clearly, and they tried to encourage him, with smiles, or little nods which would not disturb the worshipping congregation; to let him know that he was welcome, to 'Come in, and sit down'.

Maybe he was someone's relative, come to find 'Auntie Ann', or he lived close by St. Aggies, but had never been in? Maybe he was some extremist, who hated churches, and had come to get some sort of revenge? Maybe he was just a lost young man, who needed direction? Or maybe he was Jesus, dropping in to see how things were going, on a sunny Easter Sunday morning.

The Rev saw him too, and thought of saying something, inviting him, from the pulpit, to come join the celebration, but he didn't want to embarrass the man, to make everyone turn and look at him, to center him out, when he, obviously, was shy, so the Rev just smiled toward the door, and carried on.

It was a good solid sermon, with lots to think about, and the young man stood and listened to every word, leaning on the edge of the doorway. Then, when the sermon ended and the music began, he left as quietly as he had come.

His anger dampened? His loneliness softened? His day improved? They never saw him again.

Sanctuary Sparrow

I don't know that they ever did figure out how that bird got into the church. Personally, I always thought it likely Thug had something to do with it, cuz the poor little fella—I mean the bird, not Thug. Nobody would ever think of calling Thug 'a poor little fella'.

Now where was I? Sorry to get off the track like that.

Oh, yeah! Cuz his flying didn't seem just right, the first little while he was there. Still, no matter the how of it, it was amazing the amount of rumpus – 'flutter', I suppose you could call it – one little bird could create.

Nobody fell asleep in church those days, that's for sure, and it was a real hazard wearing one of them big straw hats, with flowers and such on it, in case it reminded the little fella a bit too much of home, when your head was down 'n your eyes were closed, during one of the prayers.

It WAS terrible temptin' to just take a little peek, out one eye, every once in a while, just to check. I have my doubts if any of the prayers, those days, ever did make it too far up towards heaven, if concentration was required to go the distance, cuz as soon as you closed yer eyes, you took tuh wonderin' where that dang bird was.

The kids named him 'Tweety', or 'Chirpy', or somethin' like that. I can't just remember rightly. And he (or she); I think it was a boy, but I wouldn't be sure, was good entertainment for them, if the sermon got a bit long.

It made great fodder and inspiration for the Rev too.

"He sees the little sparrow fall" and "Birds of the air and fish of the sea" and all that. Although, thank goodness, we didn't have to worry too much about 'the fish of the sea', at that moment anyway.

I always thought of him as the 'Sanctuary Sparrow'. I'd bin readin' a book with that name at the time[1], and them words just sort of flitted into my head and got stuck there that first Sunday I saw him up above us, and they seemed fittin'.

---

[1] *The Sanctuary Sparrow* by Ellis Peters.

You'd wonder how it survived all those weeks, but I suppose a mite like that doesn't need much to eat and drink, and likely some crumbs left here and there, from the communion bread, or a cookie brought there by some mom to keep her baby quiet, and then forgotten in the pew, would be enough to keep such a tiny thing going.

I think maybe the Rev mighta left a glass of water, now and then, on the communion table too. Maybe by mistake (the Rev WAS a bit absent-minded), or maybe not.

It was likely warm enough. Better than being outside in the blizzards we had that winter, that's for sure, so no wonder he (or she) was reluctant to leave.

It didn't cause that much mess. It WAS only one small bird, after all, but you did have to watch where you sat down those days, and when some of the ladies in the congregation decided it wasn't particularly sanitary, and started to make a fuss, we all knew something had to be done!

So they set up a committee…which pretty well took care of that.

You couldn't say Hellie and Wellie didn't do their best to get that bird outta there, but you'd have to have an awful long broom, to reach way up so far, and that sparrow was no dummy, and they didn't want to call in an exterminator to get rid of the poor little thing, who, after all, only wanted sanctuary in the sanctuary.

So we just kinda got used to him, and pretended he wasn't there, which was easier sometimes than others, and, you know, when he (or she) disappeared one day in the spring, when the weather was getting a bit warmer—Likely through the door, or when Hellie or Wellie opened a window to air out the place—It felt kinda funny without him.

Somehow, St. Aggies seemed a bit less like 'The garden of Eden', without that bird there. Not that that big old building could ever be much like the garden of Eden no matter what, but you get what I mean.

And you couldn't help wondering, for weeks after, which of those birds, hopping around, cocky-like, on the window sill, during the singing of some hymn, or perched on a telephone wire, chirping like mad, when we all came out of church, might be our very own 'sanctuary sparrow', just sayin', "Howdy doo."

Pete's Burgers

Every Sunday morning, at exactly 11:30, the 'Pete's Burgers' truck set up shop in the St. Aggies parking lot.

St. Aggies got 'let out' at noon. That gave Pete a full half hour to organize himself and fire up the grill, so when the church doors opened, the churchgoers were ejected straight into the tantalizing aroma of frying beef, and onions, and hot dogs, and fresh brewed coffee.

In fact, when the weather was warm, and the church windows open, it definitely affected concentration on the sermon, and possibly even the speed of the last hymn.

Pete had considered calling his truck: 'The Holy Hot Dog Stand', and having round wieners, which he could put on a round burger bun, or maybe even a bagel, but he couldn't find anyone who would make round hot dogs.

He thought of gluing regular hot dogs in a circle, maybe with crazy glue (They did say it would 'glue anything'), but he wasn't sure if crazy glue was poisonous, and he figured killing off his customers might not be great for business.

Besides, the church ladies might not appreciate the play on words, and he DID set up at places other than the St. Aggies parking lot, during the week. So he ended up calling it: 'Pete's Burgers', cuz his name was Pete. Which was a bit boring, but there you go.

The organist at St. Aggies had rigged up a system so all the hymns were broadcast out through St. Aggies' old bell tower, which must have been pretty annoying to some of the neighbors who were planning on a late Sunday morning sleep-in, but, as the church ladies said: "They should have been in church anyway!"

So Pete would find himself humming along with: 'This little light of mine', or pelting out: 'Will your anchor hold!', in a noble baritone, while he got ready for the big, after-church, rush. And, you know, Pete sometimes almost felt like he was in church himself.

'Pete's Burgers' set up all over Saint Agatha, and Pete heard everything. Leaning on the edge of the counter at the side of his truck, Pete met, and chatted with, and listened to, pretty well everybody in town, at one time or the other, or at least everybody who liked burgers, and he seemed to be able to maintain the pace, and keep up with the orders, without effort, at the same time.

In fact, 'Pete's Burgers' passed out more than burgers and hot dogs, and sweet potato fries, over that flap. Pete passed out news, and advice too, and a listening ear, 'on the side' so to speak. Even the Rev, who hated the smell of onions, sometimes came out for a chat.

So, all in all, a trip to 'Pete's Burgers', on a Sunday afternoon after church, was worth every cent.

Ghosts and Tales

Every town has its stories; its history; its 'ghosts', if you will, and Saint Agatha was no exception. Tales handed down, sometimes in whispers, and sometimes with hoots of laughter. Some have never been true, but 'make good stories'. Others start out true, but change a bit every time they're opened to the air, until they're unrecognizable, or gradually just disappear into the 'mists of time'.

And some of them are too sad, or too terrible, or too scandalous to last long or ever be written down, while others, just as bad, hang around for generations, until they too are, blessedly, forgotten.

If you're 'just driving through' town, or even living there for only a short time, the locals generally keep their 'ghosts' to themselves, cuz you aren't really part of the place. But if you decide to settle down there; if you're 'a keeper', then, eventually, the stories came your way. Maybe in the line-up to pick up your order for Mr. Ho's Chinese food, or out fishing with your neighbor, or, for sure, down at the Legion.

Here are a few of those Saint Agatha tales, some of them 'straight from the horse's mouth'.

***

Bella

Her name was Isabella, but her owners just called her 'Bella', when they called her anything at all. Her mother was pregnant when she was scooped up, in the night, with others from her village, and hustled onto a slave ship, bound for America.

She was so sick the whole way, a combination of pregnancy, high seas, and confined spaces, that she almost died, along with about half of the others, who just got thrown into the sea, like garbage, off the side of the ship, when they did die.

But Isabella was still alive; "Not worth much", but still alive, when the boat finally got to its destination, and the human cargo was delivered, and the money for them received.

Bella's mother didn't last long after Bella was born, and her owners shrugged and commented that she was "never much good", but she, at least, was buried in dry ground.

When Bella grew to be a teenager, she was, fortunately or unfortunately, very pretty. At least her owner certainly thought so, and she was, regularly, barely able to fend off his advances. One night, when he attacked her in the kitchen, she grabbed a piece of firewood from the pile by the stove and hit him with it, and she knew he would never attack her, or anyone else, ever again.

The other slaves in the household knew Bella would be hung for 'her crime', if they didn't get her away quickly—and in fact, one of them was eventually hung 'in her place'—so they managed to get her out, across the border, to a new life, via the Underground Railroad.

It wasn't an easy life. Bella 'worked like a slave' – But she was not a slave, and that made all the difference—and she eventually married, and had a daughter, also named Isabella, who became a teacher. The first teacher, in the first school, in the new settlement, not yet a town, called Saint Agatha.

And that is likely the reason you'll hear her name, or at least some version of her name, regularly in Saint Agatha. Like a spirit; a good, strong spirit, passed down and kept alive, through the generations.

***

The Day the Lion Ate Grandma's Wig

Grandma always wore a wig. It was a brown wig, though I always thought Grandma woulda looked better as a blonde. I did see her without it a couple of times, but not often, and she did have a bit of hair underneath it, but not much.

It was a pretty good wig, not like those you see around Hallowe'en, and Momma told me Grandpa had bought it for Grandma, when they were courting, to show Grandma what a 'big spender' he was, before she married him.

Momma also told me that was likely the last red cent he ever spent on Grandma.

(Momma never did seem to like Grandpa much.)

I liked Grandpa, but even I could see he was a long way off from 'Big Spender'. Anyway, like I said, it was an expensive wig, 'n Grandma wore it all the time.

The day the 'Traveling Exotic Animal Circus' come to town was a big deal, and all us kids were crazy excited about it, though I can't say any of us were real sure what 'exotic' meant, but it sure sounded good!

We'd all bin readin' 'The Jungle Book' n' 'Tarzan', n' stuff like that, 'n we had visions of lions and tigers and bears (Oh My!) in our heads. 'N we begged; just begged and begged, Grandpa, to let us all go – Grandpa controlled the purse strings in our family – n' he finally gave in, mostly cuz everybody else in Saint Agatha was going, n' I guess he didn't want them all to think he was a skinflint. Even though he was, and everybody in town already knew it.

It was a poor excuse for a 'circus'. Even I thought that, 'n I wasn't very old then. The clowns were mean-lookin', n' the poor animals were in little bitty cages, where they could barely turn around, n' the lion was so old the 'Ringmaster' had to irritate him quite a bit before he would roar.

That lion did sorta remind me of Grandpa. Kinda irritable n' grumpy; Like he figured all the world was a bad place, which, I suppose, for him, the lion I mean, it was. And the whole place smelled.

Grandpa was grumpy too, that day, at havin' to pay "All that hard-earned money!" to get in. But then Grandpa was grumpy pretty often anyways, so we didn't pay much attention. N' I had hold of Momma's hand on one side, and Grandma's on the other, n' we were standin' in front of that lion's cage, just starin' at him, 'n he was starin' right back at us, likely wonderin' how we'd taste, for supper. Though I could see he was a bit low on teeth, so I wasn't much worried. 'N that's when Grandma sneezed.

When she sneezed, she sorta bent forward, like you do sometimes when you sneeze, and darned if that lion didn't grab the chance, 'n stuck his claws through the bars of that cage, and snagged Grandma's wig right off her head 'n lickety-split; quick as anything, he dragged it back into the cage, and he 'et it! Honest to God, I saw it myself.

I've always figured that wig musta bin a sore disappointment to that lion. Likely, it even gave him indigestion, or at least one big monster hairball!

Grandpa tried to get the circus man to pay for a new wig – though I have my doubts if any of that money woulda made its way back into Grandma's hands – but the circus man said it was Grandma's fault for sneezin' so close to a lion's cage in the first place, 'n there was a big kafuffle, and Grandpa said, "Nobody in HIS family would EVER darken the door of any 'Travelin' Exotic Animal Circus' ever again!"—Which I betcha didn't scare that circus man all that much—'n that everyone should 'BOYCOTT' circuses 'n that it was a " scruffy nuthin' circus, not worth payin' the $2.00 to see anyway!"

(Which was likely just an excuse fer not puttin' out any more of his 'hard-earned money', for anything else like that again, ever.)

After that, Grandma always wore a hat. Kind of a crocheted, rainbow-colored beanie, except she had a black one too, with a flower on it, for Sundays, 'n, once you got used to it, it actually looked a lot better on her than the wig. Kinda like she was a gypsy lady, 'n I really don't think she missed the wig that much.

Or coulda' bin the thought of another wig mighta just give her nightmares.

Likely Grandpa woulda refused to pay for another one anyhow, cuz he already had Grandma, so he didn't have to try to impress her with that 'big spender' stuff anymore *anyway.*

***

Mrs. Chadwell's Ghost

"Woman Killed in Car Crash!"

(Likely there was some man who said: "What was a woman doing driving a car anyway!?" before he knew the rights of it. But don't get me wrong now. Not all men would have said that, and, in general, I like men, in moderation, if they're kept in their place.)

It was all over the front pages of the two newspapers that existed in the province at the time. These days, it wouldn't have made such a 'news splash', it's so common. Maybe page two, or page three. But back then, when there were probably only two cars in the whole of Saint Agatha, it was major news, when the two of them ran into each other.

The family never really blamed the kid. He might have been partying a bit too much; might have had a 'bit too much' to drink, like lots do. We never knew for sure, and it didn't really matter. The woman was dead. It was done, and suing and all that nonsense was not such a big thing then. Still isn't, around here. Not like it is in big cities where the value of a life seems to get boiled down to a certain number of dollars.

It was news for quite a while in St. Agatha. Months at least. Maybe even came up in conversations for a couple of years but, eventually, everyone forgot the 'Woman Killed in Car Crash'.

Everyone but me. I never forgot.

Cuz that woman was my mother.

***

The Moose and the Volkswagen

["Did yuh never hear the story about the moose and the Volkswagen?"

"Aw, come on Joe! That old story. It's not even the truth!"

"Course it's the truth! I was in that Volkswagen myself!"

"Yeah, yeah. Sure you were. So tell him the story anyways, truth or not, if he's never heard it."]

"Well now. You all know what bull moose are like in fall rutting season. Plum crazy. Got love on their minds 'n nothing' else.—Kinda like young Dan here—'n they'll even tackle a tanker truck, if they think it might be a rival for their fair lady's affections."

["That's true you know! A moose took my brother's truck right off the road one time! Why he—".

"Hey! Who's tellin' this story anyway?"

"Oh, sorry Joe. You go ahead."]

["I'll tell you about my brother another time."]

"ANYWAYS! I was maybe 5 or 6, 'n my mom and dad were taking' me n' my little sister for a Sunday afternoon drive. My sister and I were squashed into that funny little spot behind the back seat that they used to have in them old Volkswagens. Maybe they still do have that, I don't know, and we were lookin' out the back, bouncing around on that rutty old back road.

"There were no worries about seat belts in them days. I guess they figured if your time had come, your time had come. Anyways, Mom and Dad were singin' 'Old Macdonald', to keep us entertained, n' all of a sudden the singin' quit, and there was a screech from our mom, and dad slammed on the brakes— n' we woulda went flyin', except me 'n my sister were wedged in so tight.

"And when we turned around, to look out the front window to see what was up, there was this big moose, 'n I mean BIG, with huge antlers like this! Standin' square in the middle of the road, right in front of our car.

He didn't look mean. He just looked sorta stunned.—Kinda like Dan here looks, when that pretty new school teacher's around."

["Hey! That's my good arm!

Not much of a punch anyway. I'll hardly have a bruise."]

"Now, where was I? Oh yeah. He didn't look mean. But he sure did look big, 'n he was eyein' up our little red Volkswagen, as if he couldn't rightly decide just exactly what to do with it?

"My sister and I slid slow, slow, down in the back, so just our eyes were just peekin' over the top of the back seat, and Dad, easy, easy, put the car in reverse, n' started backing down the road.

"My mom was just sittin' there, with her hands braced on her seat, not sayin' nuthin', just starin' out the window, straight into that moose's eyes. Maybe she was tryin' tuh hypnotize him 'er somethin', cuz I could see her lips movin', but nothin' was comin' out.

"Dad was backin' up pretty good, maybe a bit wobbly, but pretty fast, but the moose was havin' no trouble keepin' up. Even when Dad got faster, that moose didn't break a sweat—though I'm not real sure how yuh can tell that on a moose anyway—He still looked like he was just out for a leisurely afternoon stroll.

"But finally I think he got tired of us, in his way n' all, n' he started to speed up, closer n' closer, 'til he was so close we could see the breath comin' out his nose, in the cold air, 'n Dad slammed on the brakes, I guess cuz there was nothin' else he could think of to do, 'n that moose walked right over our car!

"He did seem to catch some at the top, 'n he slid a bit off the back bumper, but he just kept on a-walkin', on down the road. He was walkin' a bit funny, but then moose always walk a bit funny, 'n the last we saw of him, out the back window, was the tip o' them huge antlers, disappearin' over the hill."

["Good story."

"Yeah, Joe. Yuh told that pretty good."

"Yes, Sir. Gets better n' better every time he tells it!"]

St. Aggie's Ghost

Nobody talked much about St. Aggie's Ghost. I'm guessing because she was a bit of an embarrassment.

Everybody assumed she was a 'she', cuz she was dressed in a white flowey thing, but then you never know, and I'm not even sure if ghosts come in any particular gender anyway. She never spoke aloud either, just pointed and stuff, so you couldn't tell that way. And not everyone could see her, even if she was standing, floating actually, right in front of them.

Mostly it was little kids who saw her (they liked her), or sometimes some adults who were like little kids themselves; though I think the minister knew she was there too, cuz, every once in a while, he just stared off into space, and smiled.

I always thought it was likely cuz, once you got to be an adult, you had to be more careful what you said, so you wouldn't admit you saw her, even if you did. Which must have been discouraging, and maybe a bit lonesome, if you were a ghost.

Once you saw her though, you never forgot, so the adults never accused the kids of lying about seeing her, which was nice, and a change from the ordinary.

She never did any harm. Rang the bell in the tower every once in a while, even though there wasn't any bell up there anymore, or played a wrong note on the organ, which teed off Mrs. Chadwell, the organist, especially when it got stuck and just kept playin' the same note on and on, no matter what Mrs. Chadwell did, while the congregation tried to ignore it, which wasn't an easy thing.

I always thought likely she was Agatha; the original Agatha I mean, that the place was named after, just droppin' in for a visit, to catch up on the news, you know.

They did get an exorcist in one time, to see if he could get rid of her, cuz she was a distraction during the sermon at times. Big guy, with a loud voice and a long beard. Looked a bit like Moses, in our old bible at home. Only Moses looked nicer.

He stomped back and forth, and yelled—I mean the exorcist guy, not Moses—and wafted this terrible-smelling smoke all over the place, from a little gadget he had in his hand – We remembered him for ages after cuz the smell kinda lingered – and he swung his arms in the air a lot, and used up a lot of energy, but it didn't work anyway.

I think cuz he wasn't a real exorcist. I think he was just a real con artist.

It did seem to irritate our ghost a bit though, I know it woulda irritated me, if I was a ghost, and, for a while, the hymn books had the wrong numbers for the hymns, and the offering plate got dropped more than usual, and the coffee after church sometimes had salt instead of sugar in the bowl, n' the electric potato peeler the men used in the church kitchen when they did the potatoes for the roast beef dinner sometimes went crazy and flung potatoes all over the place, so it was like the baseball playoffs in there. But nothin' major.

I don't blame her for being upset, cuz, like I said, she never did any harm, and, sometimes, she livened the place up a bit. Maybe she was an angel anyway, not a ghost. How can a person tell?

I don't see much of her anymore myself, maybe because I'm older now, 'n, truth is, I'm kinda sorry.

Ghosts, or angels, aren't always a bad thing, you know.

***

The Vacuum Cleaner Salesman

We often wondered what Jim was like before the accident, —We assumed it was a car accident that rocked his brain, though we never asked too many questions—but afterwards, when we knew him, he sure wasn't 'just a regular guy'.

Some people would, and likely did, call him 'simple', but really it was more than thar; different from that. He was like a child; like 'a little brother' really, to us, I guess you could say, even though he was similar in age to us, around 24 or so, when we first met him.

I can't even remember that first time. I guess it was likely the same as all the other times: He just showed up, and we found him asleep on our couch, one snowy winter morning.

(Hardly anybody in Saint Agatha ever worried about locking their doors in those days, unless they were going to be away for a while. Maybe they still don't. So I suppose it could have been anyone who found a vacuum cleaner salesman, asleep on their couch, any morning, and Jim just happened to choose us.)

I can't ever remember him trying to sell us a vacuum; I don't think he actually ever did. I don't mean he didn't sell us one. We already had one; an old one, but it still worked. I mean I don't think he even tried. I think maybe he just kinda forgot that he was supposed to be trying to sell a vacuum to us, or to anyone else, for that matter.

He certainly wasn't one of those 'high pressure salesmen', that's for sure, and I've often wondered how he even survived at that job, or even survived at all. Maybe he had a whole bunch of people, with unlocked doors, and uninhabited couches, all along the Trans Canada Highway, right across the country. And cuz he was so sweet, and so 'innocent', like a slightly lost ten-year-old boy, we all just 'took him in', and fed him, and chatted and laughed with him, and thought of him as a 'little brother'…until we woke up one morning, and he was gone.

The Mission

No one really noticed the change. It was as if St. Aggies quietly picked up her skirts in the night, and, inch by inch, moved downtown, when, in reality, it was the downtown itself that moved: flowing very slowly past and around her skirts, until St. Aggies was the surprise gift in the middle of the pudding, instead of just one of the raisins, stuck at the edge.

The church itself, built of solid red stone and brick, looked about the same as it always had, except for a few chunks missing here and there, and it had adjusted to the new reality.

Part of St. Aggies was now 'The Mission', for the increasing number of souls who needed physical assistance, or protection from the deadly 'bad drugs' recently invading the town and killing them off, or, sometimes, for those just trying to find a place to 'be', as much as anything else.

Some of the St. Aggie's congregation had objected to this change, and had left the church, but most of the others felt it was a good thing, not a bad one, and they decided to 'go with the flow'.

The Rev, who particularly enjoyed meeting interesting 'characters', generally had a great time there, and he visited The Mission every morning, and sometimes in the afternoon too.

***

The Pastry Chef

Once a week, usually on a Friday evening, behind the Mission, a large car—the downtown people would likely have called it a 'posh' car—would quietly draw up to the back entrance, and a shadowy figure, with his cap pulled down over his eyes, would get out and knock on the exit door.

A pair of pale hands, from inside, would hand out a package, sometimes two, and, after the shadowy figure had passed over an envelope of cash, the car would silently drift away, leaving a lingering sweet smell in the air.

The hands belonged to Frank, the chef, in the kitchen at the St. Aggie's downtown Mission.

Frank had never planned on becoming the pastry chef at a homeless shelter. In fact, he had never planned on ever darkening the doorway of such a place. He had always planned to be a pastry chef though, from the moment his grandmother had handed him his first chewy molasses cookie, hot out of the oven.

And he had made it too.

Thousands of hours of work, although it never really felt like work to Frank, to get his Red Seal certifications, and finally reach the top of his profession.

But sometimes the top isn't that great a place: The fight to maintain his status and position, the long hours, the stress on his marriage and his family, and on his body. The pain of it all.

It started as just a little something to relieve the pain. His doctor had actually prescribed that first blessed relief.

But then it seemed to take a little more, and a little more, and a friend introduced him to something better; something that made him forget the pain entirely, and forget other things too, like driving that car—It wasn't even his car, cuz, by then, he didn't even own a car—and running down 'some old guy who shouldn't have been out that late at night anyway'!

But he did get to use some of his skills in the prison kitchen.

When he got out, he had no one who wanted him, nowhere to go, so he ended up, whether he had planned it or not, walking through that door, at the Mission, at St. Aggies…and their molasses cookies were disgusting!

He told them so too, and the volunteer cook there, who had already had a bad day, screamed: "So! If you think you can do better, you just damn well go ahead and do it!" and threw their chef's hat on the floor, and kicked it across the room, and stomped out the door, and Frank took over.

Until, one day, he met a guy who recognized him, and offered him a lot of money, for something only Frank knew how to supply. And so the surreptitious meetings, at the back door of the Mission, every Friday night, began.

The other staff at the Mission, and some of the clients, did find out, and, though they had no part in the scheme, they eventually knew all about it, and they snickered behind their hands, and supported it enthusiastically. Because the clandestine antics in the back alley behind the mission were not as you may have supposed.

All that shadowy business was totally for the benefit of Saint Agatha's 'Elite'; The 'big shots', with the money and the quiet cars, who proudly served the cheesecakes, and the eclairs, and the 'to die for!' tortes, to their friends, and business associates.

But they certainly would have "rather died!" than have those guests know that such exquisite, and very expensive, delicacies, had been produced by Frank, and his homeless kitchen helpers, down at The Mission!

The money made, every red cent of it, went to buy socks, and other essentials, for the people who visited the Mission every day, not for the cheesecake, but because they had no other place to go, and they all kept it quiet, cuz they certainly didn't want to lose 'their Frank', and he certainly didn't want to get lost again either.

And every Friday, at lunchtime, Frank, whose soups were spectacular as well, served them each a piece of cheesecake, or torte, or an eclair (although his chewy molasses cookies were actually their favorite), all made by the best pastry chef in Saint Agatha.

***

The Angry Man

I assume he hadn't always been angry. Denny, I mean. Likely he had been a regular little boy, at least for a while, until life caught up with him, and 'his cards' turned up a poor, even disastrous, hand. 'The Angry Man' name stuck, although no one would have dared call him that to his face, cuz the name was accurate. In fact, it was right on.

Mostly, he just smoldered, like some dormant volcano, but, every once in a while, he blew.

One particularly bad day, he walked into the bathroom at the Mission, and shut the door, and smashed the toilet to pieces, which, I suppose, was a lot better than smashing a person to pieces. At least a toilet is replaceable.

They didn't call the police. What would be the good of that? Putting him in jail? Demanding he pay for the damages? With what? He had nothing. Nothing but his anger. So in the end, they just asked 'The Angry Man' to please never do that again, because everyone needed those toilets, and he never did.

"Hey Rick! Where's Denny?" The Rev was looking around the room. "I haven't seen him in weeks."

"He moved on."

"What? You mean he died?"

"Naw. They gave him a ticket and put him on a bus. For Timmins, I think."

"Timmins? Does he know anyone there? Have family up there or something?"

"Nope. Not as far as I know."

Rick dug into his stew. He was hungry, and he couldn't speak for a few minutes, while he chewed. Then he looked up and found, with what appeared to be some surprise, that the Rev was still there, still interested.

"I mean, you know", he shrugged, "they got rid of him. A bit of a pain in the ass, Ol' Denny, I suppose. I didn't think he was that bad; Kinda liked him myself, but he was always complaining, always makin' trouble. I'm guessin' they finally had enough of him."

"This was", Rick thought for a moment, and counted on his fingers as he concentrated, "his twelfth home. He told me that: 'An even dozen'!" and Rick grinned, revealing his few remaining front teeth.

"Likely he's workin' on number thirteen by now. Lucky thirteen, ay?" and Rick grinned again, and grabbed a piece of bread, and swished it around the edge of his bowl, to soak up the last few drops of stew.

***

Molly and Sally

Molly didn't have much. She did have one thing though, that lots of other people didn't have: She had a friend, and her friend's name was Sally. Molly and Sally were inseparable. In fact, everyone always said their names together: 'Molly and Sally'; like 'Salt and Pepper', when they talked about them.

Molly and Sally had been together for 4 years, ever since the day Molly had found Sally, lost and crying, on a street corner, and brought her home, gave her some food, and a warm place to stay, and sometimes they even slept together, seeing as there was only one bed. Cuz, like I said, Molly didn't have much, but, now, she did have Sally.

It was a sad and desperate day, the day Molly got kicked out of her apartment. I don't know why she got kicked out. I suspect it was nothing Molly, or Sally, did or didn't do, cuz Molly was not a bad person.

Maybe it was a 'renoviction', or 'someone better came along'. I couldn't judge; I wasn't there. But it happened. So there was nowhere for Molly to stay now, as well as nowhere for Sally.

Molly got a place; a bed, at the Mission. It was only a bed, and food, and it was supposed to be only temporary, while the good people at the Mission tried to help Molly find another place. But Molly's friend wasn't allowed to stay there, so the authorities picked Sally up, and took her somewhere else.

Somewhere she could stay for a month but, because she was black, and so, less likely to be adopted, at the end of that month, if Molly hadn't come to get her, Sally would be 'put down'.

That was the policy at the Humane Society. That's just the way it was.

Sally's month was up that day and, that day, Molly was told it would be at least three months before they could find her a place of her own. So, that day, Molly's friend was 'put down'.

No more 'Molly and Sally'. No more "Salt and Pepper."

***

Martha Grey

Nobody paid much attention to Martha Grey. She was just so 'nondescript', I guess would be the right word. Just like her name, she blended into the background, and everyone quickly forgot her.

Even when she did something extraordinary, like the day she grabbed a kid off the street just before the rushing taxi ran him down, somebody else usually got the accolades, or the paper called her: 'random bystander', or 'unknown pedestrian', as if she was a bit of an embarrassment, if they called her anything at all.

Nobody had ever really paid a whole lot of attention to Martha Grey, and these days even less. Martha didn't mind. She sometimes felt like she was in a dream world she was just wandering through, and nobody could see her, but she could see them.

Martha was a 'bag lady', living on the street most of the time, although she did have a bedroom at a so-called 'Elders Rooming House', where she spent as little time as she possibly could.

It seemed to her there was always someone there telling her she 'should be in a home', or phoning some social worker about her, or forever nagging her what to do and not to do, and, to tell you the truth, the place reeked of mice and moldy bread, so she'd rather be out in the fresh air, unless it was really cold, or she was desperate for some other reason.

She knew she had a bit of dementia. She had been an ambulance driver, a long time ago, so she knew the signs, but Martha figured she'd carry on as long as she could. She had no relatives; no family left, although her friends on the street and at St. Aggie's Mission, some of them anyway, felt like 'family' to her.

Barely a soul ever suspected she 'wrote'. She smiled to herself at the thought; that she was 'an author'. Even funnier that she was the 'Heartaches' columnist for the local newspaper; the person who fixed everyone else's problems, or at least told them how to fix them themselves. (She did often wonder whether the things she told them to do actually worked, or not.)

They never knew that the 'Lavender Lace', of the weekly column in the Saint Agatha Tattler, was actually odd Martha Grey, in her outlandish layers of clothing, sitting on the sidewalk by the Goodwill, with her bags piled around her and her rusty old shopping cart, busily writing in her scribbler with half a pencil.

And every week, when she dropped off her article at the newspaper office, the editor would grab it, acknowledging her 'scratchings' with a nod, rush her out of his office, and publish her piece, if there was enough space left once the advertisements went in.

Sometimes, people walking by did wonder what words that shabby old lady could possibly be putting down on that paper.

"Likely crazy stuff!"

But really, who cared, and what difference did it make?

Martha had been all over the world, and she had 'seen it all', as they say, which may have been part of the reason for her fragile mental state, and she had always taken a pencil, and a scribbler with her, wherever she went. She called them her 'Journals', and she had a huge stack of them under her bed, in her cramped little room downtown.

Every time she had traveled, by plane, or train, or automobile, to the next town, or 'the big city', or even just on the bus to the local grocery store, she felt like a 'traveling reporter'; even a 'Freelance Foreign Correspondent', as she busily observed, and wrote down, things real or imagined, about her fellow travelers, or the people she saw.

She had especially liked the long plane trips, where she could just sit quietly and observe, and write, and nobody bothered her. She liked seeing the big cities too; the ones named in the news and on the television set, although she could only take so much of the uncaring push and shove of the city, before her head started to 'go funny', and she had to find some place to hide.

She never flew anywhere now, of course. Her old age pension barely covered her rent, and she usually ate downtown at the Mission, for company and to save money, and good old 'Lavender Lace', thank God for her, paid for 'necessities' like toilet paper and pencils.

It really was quite amazing how little a person could get by on, if they had to.

Hardly anybody knew about Martha's secret. The Rev knew, and a skinny old guy at the Mission, with no teeth, and a dreadful, bright red toque that clashed spectacularly with his 'carrot top' hair, which he wore summer and winter. He knew too. But they both felt the same: If Martha Grey wanted to keep her secret to herself, that was her business.

The toothless man in the bright red toque used to catch her eye though, and give her a thumbs up, every once in a while, when he felt her piece in the paper that week had been particularly good. But otherwise he said nothing, and just went on scrubbing the floors, as payment for his dinner.

***

The Big House

There are lots of different meanings for 'The Big House', at least in Canada. You can live in 'The Big House', if you're rich enough. You can go to ceremonies and community gatherings in 'The Big House', if you're a First Nation's person. You can even be incarcerated in 'The Big House', if your behavior warrants it.

The Wellington-Fitzhenrys, being in the first category, lived in 'The Big House', on Cranberry Hill Road. (There were no cranberries there, never had been, and not a sign of a hill, but that's all beside the point.)

Nobody seemed to know where all their money had come from, and nobody felt they should ask, except of course the tax people, and even the answers they got were a bit loose.

They did have a big chicken farm at the entrance to the lane up to 'The Big House', which generally caused people to avoid the place. (The smell, you know.)

The Wellington-Fitzhenrys always said, "Chickens are gold", so that likely explained it. Although, as Saint Agatha's locals often commented: "It would take a lot of chicken feed to build a house like that!"

They did spread their money nicely around town: 'THE WELLINGTON-FITZHENRY MEMORIAL LIBRARY'; The 'LOU-ANNE WELLINGTON-FITZHENRY DAYCARE AND ELEMENTARY SCHOOL'; even the local bowling alley ('THE JOSHUA WELLINGTON-FITZHENRY BOWLERAMA AND SNACK BAR'), were all named after them, which is a lot of letters, and took a lot of paint.

The first thing Docky knew about it all was a call he got, in the middle of the night. ('Docky' was a Doctor of Veterinary Medicine—as opposed to 'Doc', who attended to the needs of the human animals in Saint Agatha—and his special love was birds. He also did have particularly large, flat feet, like a duck, so 'Docky' seemed appropriate, although some of the older residents still called him 'the doc' when he was out on a call.)

This call was a 'cruelty to chickens' report, from the SPCA, via the local constabulary:

"Hey Docky, sorry to wake yuh. Chief Superintendent Jacob here. Can you get your act together and come up here to The Big House, quick as you can?"

When the doc got there, the ornate portals to the estate; two large shiny metal roosters facing off across the divide, were wide open, and he found dead chickens all over the place. All down the lane, and spilling out onto the highway (which had caused the first alert), around the farm buildings, and everywhere on the immaculately groomed lawns.

It was like a chicken war zone. It seemed the chickens had executed an escape, perhaps long-planned by some of the brighter lights in the flock, in the middle of the night, and, apparently, had died in action.

But Docky was puzzled. They certainly were dead, but what had killed them all? They didn't look hurt. They didn't even look unhappy, although only a vet, or perhaps an avid chicken-lover, could tell that.

They just looked dead. And nothing appeared amiss, other than an unfastened door at the side of the main chicken barn, swinging in the breeze and, yes, a trail of white powder, with chicken tracks running through it, across the pavement.

Docky didn't watch CSI fer nuthin'. He quietly took a sample of the white dust, and tipped it into an envelope from his pocket, just before the lights came on in The Big House, and Mr. Wellington-Fitzhenry, dressed in a dinner jacket hastily donned over silky black pajamas with colorful pictures of roosters on them, came rushing out the door.

It took the doc a few minutes to find Superintendent Jacob, but when he did, he whispered in the Super's ear, then slipped him the envelope.

And things took off from there.

It appeared the chickens were not the pure gold after all; It was, instead, the heroin, manufactured in a hidden back section of the barn which the chickens had, likely unintentionally, infiltrated.

By the time everything was sorted out, the sun was coming up, and a rooster crowed somewhere in a barn behind him, and, to Docky, it sounded like that crow had a plaintive, lonesome note to it, as he trudged to his car, and then drove home, for a cup of coffee, maybe two, before he started his day.

Halfway up the walkway to his house, he saw Mrs. Pickett, the most dedicated gossip in Saint Agatha, rushing up the street toward him, and he sucked in his breath, and prepared to meet the onslaught.

"Well, Docky!" She huffed and puffed to a stop in front of him, "You were up at The Big House last night." (It was a statement, not a question. He couldn't deny it.) "Who ever heard of such a thing? A three-headed chicken!"

A 'three-headed chicken'! What on earth was this woman talking about? Then he realized that Chief Superintendent Jacob, who did have a quirky sense of humor, must be giving out this silly excuse for all the commotion up at The Big House in the dead of the night.

Only Mrs. Pickett would have believed such a thing, and Chief Superintendent Jacob likely knew she would spread it around.

"Well, yes. You're right there, Mrs. Pickett. In fact, I can hardly believe it myself."

"I wouldn't mind seeing it, but I gather they've boxed it up and sent it away. To the Smithsonian, you suppose?"

"Yes. You're right. That certainly would be the place for it."

"Ah, well. But just think: A three-headed chicken! Likely caused by all those drugs they give chickens these days, I suppose?"

"Could be, Mrs. Pickett. Could be."

That day, the Wellington-Fitzhenrys made the switch from category one, to category three, of big houses, as 'The Big House' in the next county, opened its sturdy steel gates, and welcomed them in.

And by a couple of weeks later, all those signs, on the elementary school, and the library, and even the bowling alley, had quietly disappeared.

The Saint Agatha town council is still arguing about what should be written up there instead.

Likely something short.

The Fire

It was just past midnight, and Hellie and Wellie were lost in dreamland after a long day of hard labor. They had been working on replacing the side steps and railings at the church, and it was nasty, heavy, knuckle-scraping work—when a low, grumbling sound interfered with oblivion. The same sound in both their dreams.

At first, they just incorporated it into their imaginings, perhaps as thunder, or the hammering on the boards they had been hearing all day, and they both just turned over in their beds, and snuggled back down under the blankets, for their well-deserved rest.

But the sound persisted, and it started to drill into their heads, so sleep was no longer an option, and they both got up, and opened their bedroom doors, and peered blearily out into the hall to determine the origin of this irritating noise. And their identical mouths dropped, and their identical eyes opened in shock.

For the source of the sound was Mr. Rooney, their silent, soundless companion, who was yapping, growling, barking, howling, whatever he could think of, certainly no longer silent, and scrabbling and scratching at the bottom of their apartment door.

It was only then that they became aware of an orange-red glow in their living room window, and saw the tongues of flame, sweeping up the newly installed ramp, and framing the black hole of St. Aggie's open doorway, with fire.

It is really quite amazing how quickly news, especially bad news, can spread in a small town, and the fire engines arrived to the sight of the whole congregation, the whole neighborhood, if not much of the whole population of Saint Agatha, including many of the farm families from outside of town, surrounding the church, spraying it with garden hoses, and passing buckets of water up from the lake, to do what they could to douse the roaring inferno.

Most of the outside of St. Aggies was red brick and stone, thank goodness, so it was not the main structure that took the worst of the beating, but, between the fire and the water, the inside of the building, once they had finally extinguished the strangely stubborn flames enough to assess the damage, was a real mess.

It was because of this surprising intensity, and the open door, that the fire chief suspected the flames may have had 'a little help', and whispered this to the Rev, as they sat wearily in the boy's apartment, looking out at the smoldering wreck across the street, drinking coffee, and eating the sandwiches and cookies generously provided by the neighboring Salvation Army.

Mr. Rooney, once again voiceless, was licking his paw, where the fur had been singed off by the fire, and hungrily gobbling down his own chicken sandwiches, and peanut butter cookies, while Thug, who had been left behind in the apartment, yowling, when the door slammed in his face as the others ran out, was sulking in the corner, refusing to acknowledge their existence.

No one died in the flames, although Edon and Henry Watson were both treated for burns, and it took a couple of days to account for all the 'regulars' at the mission.

One odd thing, among the many, was a small something the Rev noticed the next day, when he was sitting in his office, still smelling of smoke.

That small something was his little gold cross. The gold cross, usually in the little wooden bowl in his desk, wasn't there, and it seemed not to be around at all, when he searched, even though the fire hadn't gotten very far into that part of the building.

But there were too many larger issues to deal with that day so, after a moment of sadness, the Rev forgot about it, and went back to dealing with life.

Mrs. Chadwell's Pig

Everybody wondered whatever possessed Mrs. Chadwell to go to that fair in the first place. It just seemed like such an unlikely thing. Mrs. Chadwell never 'gambled'; she considered gambling 'morally reprehensible!', and she hardly ever went to fairs either ('Dirty, noisy places!'), especially in a town that wasn't her own.

Her cousin did live there though, that's true, so maybe that was the reason, or perhaps Mrs. Chadwell was in the middle of a 'mid-life crisis' and her hormones were a bit out of whack, or she was on a one-time 'spree', or 'the sea air' was to blame.

It's unlikely she was drunk. Still, her cousin had been known to produce the odd batch of elderberry wine, so you never know.

Anyway, for whatever reason, Mrs. Chadwell did go to that fair, and did put down her dollar, to buy a ticket, to win a pig, when she—the pig I mean, not Mrs. Chadwell—was just a cute little handful of piglet.

And Mrs. Chadwell was just as surprised, and likely shocked too, as everyone else was, when she actually won the thing!

"It was for a good cause!" she always said afterwards, when anyone had enough gall to bring it up.

Which only goes to show you the perils of gambling.

But when she looked into those cute little beady black eyes, and saw those adorable floppy pink ears, and that 'sweet' little twirly tail, whipping back and forth, Mrs. Chadwell, for the first, and last, time in her life, 'fell in love'.

And that was the winsome picture, which remained in her head, for the rest of the pig's long and, as far as the local farmers were concerned anyway, 'unproductive' life.

(Likely, at some point, there must have been a 'Mr. Chadwell', to her 'Mrs.', but she never spoke of him, so there seemed to be 'no love lost', if there ever had been any, and there was certainly no trace of him, at the moment anyway, in Saint Agatha, and nobody had the nerve to ask any questions.)

Mrs. Chadwell obviously did not consider, or call, Queenie her "pet", (for 'Queenie', she had christened the pig. Not officially of course. Even the Rev refused to baptize a pig.) Mrs. Chadwell did not believe in 'pets' and she'd made no secret of the fact that she had, and still did, consider pets a "useless waste of time and money!"

And she always refused to call Queenie 'my hog', as she felt 'hog' was such a vulgar, uncivilized term.

'Watch pig' perhaps? It's true I would not want to attempt a break-in at Mrs. Chadwell's house and encounter Queenie, or Mrs. Chadwell herself, for that matter.

Or maybe 'Companion'? I have heard that pigs are supposed to be very intelligent, though I've never seen any evidence of it myself.

It did make you look twice, that's for sure, especially if you were a stranger from out of town, and passed by Mrs. Chadwell and Queenie, out for their Sunday afternoon 'walkies'. (Mrs. Chadwell being the one with the flowery hat.)

The rest of the week, Queenie lived the life of Riley, lolling around, rooting up the rose bushes, and eating, continuously, in Mrs. Chadwell's fenced-off back yard.

She got bigger and bigger – the pig I mean, not Mrs. Chadwell. Mrs. Chadwell stayed pretty much the same—and more and more cranky, except when Mrs. Chadwell played music for her, which did seem to have a mellowing affect, while Mrs. Chadwell appeared to retain that first loving mental image, of that 'sweet little piggy', in spite of all evidence to the contrary.

And every Sunday afternoon, as they waddled past the butcher shop (Well, actually, only the pig waddled), which was open from 2 to 4 on Sunday afternoons. This being the reason Mrs. Chadwell considered Mr. Tinnie a "Heathen!" —The butcher eyed her speculatively. (The pig, not Mrs. Chadwell), with a glitter in his eye, dreaming of all those pounds of bacon she could produce.

Not that *that* was *ever* likely to happen!

Boomerang

Chapter One

They called him 'Boomer'. His real name was 'Winchester Feldwood Trendham the Third', but how could anyone call a puppy THAT? 'Boomer' suited him. That one big 'whomp' of a bark, like the sound of a small cannon going off.

Boomer resembled a small cannon too; one of those squat, pot-bellied antiques you see around the walls of old forts: low to the ground, short legs holding them solidly in place, stubbornly hard to move.

Only Boomer was creamy white and chocolate, instead of dull iron black, and there were long, floppy ears, and a drippy pink tongue, and big, soulful brown eyes, and a whip of a tail; extras the cannon lacked.

Cannons are more symmetrical too; both sides exactly the same. Boomer was not. Which was the reason that, in spite of his long impressive name, no one really wanted him. One ear was just a tad higher than the other, one eye just a bit droopier, and he had one brown paw, when he should have had four white ones.

So he was sold at a surprisingly low price to a well-meaning uncle, and became a Christmas present for a five-year-old niece named Mindy Reed, who was part of a family of seven. One mother and six kids.

Well-meaning uncles should think before they buy.

Mrs. Reed, the mother of the family, burst into tears when Boomer popped his head out of the box that Christmas morning, and popped himself immediately into her children's hearts.

For their sakes, she tried for a while, almost a year in fact. She worked extra shifts at the all night Snack Shack to help pay for the shots at the vet, and the other extras a dog needs, and it WAS comforting to know that Boomer was there when she was not, that his warning 'whomp' would alert her children if anything was wrong; would tell an intruder that there would be something unexpected to deal with on the other side of that door.

Not that there was much chance of anyone trying to get in to steal things. It was obvious from the look of the place, that there wouldn't be much to steal.

Finally, when Boomer developed a persistent, itchy rash, which nothing seemed to cure, and his hair began to fall out in clumps, Mrs. Reed decided she just couldn't do it anymore. The money HAD to go to food, shoes, and school supplies. The vet could NOT get it all, and what if her children caught whatever was wrong with Boomer? No. She could not let it happen.

Tears tickled Boomer's ears, and he shook them away, as Mrs. Reed fastened his piece of rope around his neck. He romped around her, excited to go for a walk, his tail flinging back and forth, and his homemade aluminum nametags tinkling in tune to his dance.

She walked him a long way, further than he had ever been before, far into an unfamiliar part of the city. They walked until he was so tired his hind end could barely keep up with his front. Then she tied him to a lamppost, ran her fingers once down his long, silky ears, turned and walked away.

Boomer watched her go, until she was no longer even a speck in the distance. Then he gave a single, lonely 'whomp', laid down on the sidewalk, and closed his eyes.

Chapter Two

Boomer woke the next morning to the sensation of hands, softly touching. He opened his eyes to the sight of two old men, hunched down beside him, one with his hand lying quietly on Boomer's head, the other examining the dry patches of skin on Boomer's side and leg, where the hair had disappeared.

They were speaking in a language Boomer had never heard, but their caring came clearly through their hands, and he was not afraid. He rolled over onto his back, and they laughed and rubbed his belly, just the way he liked it. Then he followed them across the street and into a shop full to the brim with strange smells he had never before encountered.

The two men, brothers, had, between them, over a hundred years of knowledge and experience in the arts of healing. Even so, Boomer was a challenge to them. Almost every day he sported some different color of cream or salve or lotion, as they tried out their various ideas. Most of the concoctions smelled so disgusting that Boomer didn't even try to lick them off, and the few he did didn't seem to do him any harm.

The whole neighborhood got involved, and there were great arguments, and many sober discussions, about which herbs, and whose grandmother's recipes, and where the best ingredients should be purchased.

Boomer loved it. He spent almost as much time on his back, getting his belly scratched, as he did upright on his four flat feet, and his tail hardly ever stopped its rhythmic dance, as he waddled happily over to greet all his newfound friends, every time the chimes tinkled and the shop door opened.

By the time his skin had changed from cracking white flakes to a healthy pink, with a new layer of soft fuzz beginning to grow, Boomer had become a solid member of the community.

Every day, he did his rounds. Every morning, the brothers hitched him to a little wagon as he helped them deliver their medicines to those who were not able to easily come down to the shop, and the smiles that greeted him seemed to be an extra medicine in themselves.

Willy, a young man who lived in a room above the shop, and had a droopy eye, and a bit of a shuffling gait himself, so they made a matched pair, took Boomer for a walk every afternoon, after lunch, and while Willy mumbled to himself and ambled along, Boomer muttered to himself, and sniffed, and explored. Wherever Boomer wanted to go, that's where they went: Through bushes and flowerbeds, up and down staircases, in and out of back alleys. Anywhere a dog could wish.

The rest of the afternoon and evening was spent in social duties: The brothers had provided a sturdy stool for Boomer, so that, when some of their elderly customers came in, Boomer could climb on to the stool to do his visiting, thus avoiding the necessity of their bending down to reach him.

Sometimes, he 'babysat' while a mother checked her list and decided on her purchases, his solid, squat body making a very effective barrier to prevent inquisitive two-year-olds from touching untouchables, or escaping into the street.

And other times his 'whomp' warned the brothers that a stranger was in the shop, and they should abandon their supper and come tend to their affairs. It was one of these strangers who caused Boomer to growl for the first time in his life.

There was something about the young man. Even Boomer didn't understand what it was. The way he talked? The way he moved? The sneering way he looked around him, and at the two old men? But, whatever the reason,

Boomer knew he hated this man, and the hair stood up on his back, and the sound he had never made before came from deep in his chest.

That night, the shop went on fire. Boomer woke to the crash of something thrown through the big, plate glass front window, but, by the time his barks roused the brothers, the shop walls were walls of flame, and they only escaped by crawling on the floor, their smoke-filled eyes blinded, as Boomer led the way, and they hung on to his long ears.

When they finally reached the street, one of the brothers collapsed on the ground, his hand to his chest. "Willy!" he gasped, and they looked back at the mass of flames behind them, licking its way greedily up to Willy's second-floor window, with horror in their eyes.

"Where is Boomer?" asked the other, his arms around his brother's shaking shoulders. But Boomer was not to be found.

By the time the fire engines came screaming down the street, the front of the shop couldn't be seen. The door, with its tinkling chimes, the big front window, the proud display of mysterious healing herbs and medicines, had all blended into one crackling, glowing orange ball.

And when the shop roof collapsed in a blast of sparks that lit the sky, all anyone could do was stand and stare. Which is what they did, the brothers, their neighbors, the whole community with tears streaming down their faces.

"Whomp!"

The sound came from behind them, and it spun them all around, as if on cue, to stare, open-mouthed, at the sight before them: Willy, every inch of him black with soot, stood gaping at the fire. Boomer, in his matching suit of black soot, sat beside him, squinting up at his friends, his pink tongue lolling, and his tail beating a steady rhythm on the sidewalk.

"Went fer a walk," said Willy, "Me 'n Boomer," and the dozens of people, including the weary, smoke-grimed firefighters, burst out laughing.

Chapter Three

Perhaps it was the memory of the anxious look in Mrs. Reed's eyes, before she left him. It was the same look that Boomer saw when they sneaked him in to visit at the hospital and he caught the brothers glancing his way, as one lay, and one sat, in the sterile room.

It made him restless, that look. He shuffled over to the bed and stood on his hind legs, with his front paws braced against the bed railing, and the brothers stroked him, and ran their hands along his side, where there was no longer any sign of disease.

"Whomp!" He barked, and a nurse stuck her head in the door. She looked kindly on the scene, but rules were rules, and she told them the dog would have to wait outside. So Boomer was led out to the front of the building, and tied to a post, and the old man ran his fingers once down Boomer's ears, then turned and walked back inside.

Boomer stared at the doors until they slid shut with a final hydraulic hiss. Then he gave a snort and shook himself. It was getting dark. He sniffed the crisp evening air, and the restlessness came on him again. He felt like going for a walk.

He gave a tug to his leash, and then another. Then he shook his head again. The old man's loose knot jerked free, and Boomer went for a walk.

Chapter Four

If it hadn't been for the fact that Boomer really loved soccer, he might be walking still. But a couple of days later, when a soccer ball came sailing over a tall, chain-link fence, and landed right in front of his face, Boomer couldn't resist; he tucked his nose under the edge of the ball, and flipped it up into the air.

Then he ran to where it bounced down on the sidewalk, and bumped it along the ground with his solid forehead, just like he had done with the Reed children, zigzagging back and forth to keep the ball in line. When another flip landed it squarely in the space between two garbage cans, a great cheer went up behind him, and he turned to see 22 small faces grinning at him from the other side of the fence.

The noise brought their teacher running, but the look of concern on her face quickly melted when she saw the soccer player, his chin resting on the white ball, and his long ears hanging down either side, gazing soulfully up at her.

When she opened the gate and caught hold of Boomer's collar, to look for identification tags, all she found was a round metal disc, with a hole drilled in it, and 'BOOMER' written there. The teacher looked puzzled at the name.

"WHOMP!" boomed Boomer.

"Ah," she bowed toward him, and her eyes twinkled, "I understand."

"Can we keep him, Miss Minsky?" the children begged, "PLEASE!"

"No", she shook her head and peered down the street, "He must belong to somebody."

She patted Boomer's sleek coat, and looked into his eyes, glowing with health.

"He's been well looked after. Now! Who's going to phone the SPCA so we can find out where his family lives, and help him get home? I'm sure someone must miss him."

22 small hands vied for a resting place on Boomer's long back, as he followed her into the school, his tail wagging happily.

Chapter Five

To Miss Minsky's surprise, and the children's delight, no one had reported Boomer missing, and three weeks of advertisement in the 'Lost and Found' section of the Saint Agatha Tattler produced not a single response. Boomer, meanwhile, had taken on the task of playground monitor, and was capably earning his dog biscuits.

Punching and kicking quickly lost their appeal when a solid dog body kept stubbornly parking itself between you and the object of your worst intentions.

'Piggy-in-the-middle' became 'Doggy-in-the-middle', and the game's exercise rating increased considerably when the doggie in the middle actually caught the ball, and went tearing round the school clutching it in his mouth, with 22 panting, screaming children in hot pursuit.

Sometimes, he even tackled troubles of the heart: One lunchtime, he found Amanda, one of the tiniest of the grade twos, sitting in the corner of the school steps, her face buried in her arms, shaking with sobs. Boomer shoved his nose under her arm, and she raised her head. For a long moment, her tear-stained blue eyes looked into his mournful brown ones.

"It's not THAT bad, Boomer" she sniffled, with a twitch of a smile. "It's only that Annie won't play with me." She took a shuddering breath. "She says I'm not her best friend anymore," and a tear appeared at the corner of one blue eye, and made its way down one flushed cheek. "She says she doesn't like me anymore, cuz I'm yucky and boring."

Boomer snorted and shook his head, and his long ears flapped from one side to the other.

"You don't think it's true?"

"Whomp!"

They sat quiet for a moment, her little hand resting softly on the back of his neck.

"Maybe you're right!" shrugged Amanda. "Hey! You wanna play soccer, Boomer?"

"WHOMP!" barked Boomer enthusiastically, and Amanda ran to get the soccer ball, which may, or may not, have been Boomer's plan from the first.

During class time, Boomer listened thoughtfully, with his head tipped to one side, and his eyes traveling from the concentrated faces to the fingers pressed under the words on the page, as the children read to him. He showed not the slightest impatience over missed words or garbled sentences, and 'Boomer's reading center' became the kid's favorite center of them all.

Although Boomer obediently followed one or the other of the children home every weekend—the job of having him as 'houseguest' was diplomatically assigned alphabetically—It seemed that he wanted to stay at the school weeknights, and he could be surprisingly slippery when the bell rang and they tried to catch him at the end of the day.

So the class built him a doghouse, and set it up at the edge of the schoolyard. One of the children suggested they all dip their hands in paint, and put their hand prints on the outside, to keep Boomer from feeling lonely at night, so Miss Minsky got the paint, and they did it in rainbow colors.

When they had finished, Boomer pushed his nose inside to check out the place. The rest of him followed, and he turned around twice, and lay down contentedly, with his nose sticking out the door. Then Boomer sighed a deep doggy sigh, which sounded just like: 'Home!'

Chapter Six

Boomer had his own reasons for wanting to stay at school during the week. Fourteen of them. Monday's was Jodie Brown. Jodie was ten, and his most desperate wish, for most all of his ten years of life, had been to have a dog of his own.

Every birthday, it was the only thing on his birthday wish list, and every Christmas, the first and last request in his letter to Santa. But the 'NO PETS ALLOWED' sign on his apartment building lobby wall meant what it said and, after ten years, Jodie had pretty well given up. Until he ran into Boomer. Actually, they ran into each other.

Boomer, who had no intention of spending the long evenings behind the wire fence had, with a bit of inspiration, and a certain amount of digging, grunting, and squirming, discovered a Boomer-sized exit between the gate and the fence and, although every school day morning the kids found him innocently snoring in his doghouse, that didn't necessarily mean he spent a lot of time there.

That second Monday evening at school, a particularly irritating cat had sauntered by outside the fence, secure in the knowledge that solid metal stood between she and her nemesis. She stretched luxuriously before she sat down to tend to her toilette, just out of reach, on the edge of the sidewalk.

It must have been quite an unpleasant surprise when Boomer appeared, as if by magic, at her side, apparently bent on making a nice light snack of her. The cat did a 360-degree turn, practically in mid-air, and was gone, with a yowl and a flash of fur, and with Boomer flying after her, snapping at her tail.

Jodie, on his skateboard, came around the corner of the old penny candy store from one direction. The cat/Boomer combination came round from the other. And a grand, hissing, barking, yelling, fur-flying pile they made.

By the time it all got sorted out, the cat had gone where all smart cats go, and Jodie was flat on his back, with Boomer sitting on top of him, licking his ears.

Jodie finally made it to his feet and tucked his skateboard under his arm. With a last rub down Boomer's neck, and a last longing look at the dog gazing lopsidedly up at him, he turned and limped toward home. When Boomer came trotting along beside him, Jody simply didn't have the heart to shoo him away.

Surely letting him walk there for just a few minutes would do no harm, and it felt so good.

"That's a nice dog you've got there," a lady smiled down at them, as Boomer sat patiently, with Jodie's hand on his collar, waiting for the 'WALK' signal. "What kind is he?"

"He's a Basset Hound," beamed Jodie. "His name is Boomer."

"Ah. Boomer," nodded the lady. "You must be very proud of him."

Jodie's eyes grew wide as he realized she thought Boomer was HIS dog.

"Yes," he gulped. "Yes, I am."

"He loves you too. I can tell," and she walked off, with a little wave, as the light changed.

But Jodie just stood there, like a statue of a boy with a dog at his side, as the people, and the lights, shifted around them.

Boomer walked Jodie all the way home that evening, but just across the street from Jodie's apartment building, he turned and loped away in the direction they had come. Jodie watched sadly as the low form blended into the busy sidewalk traffic.

When Boomer appeared again the next week, and the next, Jodie realized, with awe, that every Monday evening, he finally had a dog of his own.

"Why don't you bring Boomer home to play sometime, dear?" suggested Jodie's mom one Monday evening, as Jodie sat on the front steps, fastening his roller blades.

The family had heard nothing but: 'Boomer and I did this' and 'Boomer and I did that' for weeks, and they were pleased and fascinated that Jodie had found such a wonderful new friend. But they had never met the boy, and it did seem to be time to get to know him better. They didn't even know his last name, or whether 'Boomer' was short for 'Bobby', or maybe 'Benjamin'.

"I don't think so, Mom. He's not allowed."

"Not allowed?" Jodie's mother frowned, "Why would he not be allowed to come over to play?"

"He's not allowed to come in this building," Jodie answered over his shoulder, as he swung down the steps and out the door.

Jodie's mom stared after him, then she turned and looked around her, as if seeing the old familiar apartment building in a whole new light.

Chapter Seven

Tuesday's reason was 'a different kettle of fish', as she would have said herself. Martha Grey was what some people would call, 'a bag lady', and what others would call, 'a poor old soul'. Martha called herself 'an entrepreneur'.

Martha was Boomer's inspiration: His first evening in the schoolyard, she had come trudging by and flopped down with her back propped against the schoolyard fence, to eat the bagels she had been given at the Salvation Army.

Halfway into the second one, something wet nudged her neck, and she turned to look into a pair of big, brown, bun-begging eyes.

"So! You're a bagel man, I see!", and she grinned a toothless grin, "Raisin or herb?"

Boomer chose raisin.

"What yuh doin' in this here big cage? You do somethin' bad? Rob a bank? Hi-jack a mail man? Hey! You're not a cat-burglar are yuh?"

Boomer barked, and the sound echoed off the buildings around them.

"Ah. Disturbing the peace! I done time for that myself. Always thought it was silly. A person should be able to sing if they want! I bet the Beetles never got arrested for disturbing the peace!" She looked down at Boomer's attentive face. 'Nor Lassie either'!

"Now, let's see if we can spring you from this filthy joint! I only said that cuz that's what they say in the movies. It really doesn't look too bad, you know 'n you don't exactly look like you're starvin' I kinda like your cell. Rainbow, ay? Maybe the boys in The Big House should take a look at this place and get some tips."

As she talked on, Martha Grey walked slowly around the perimeter of the school fence, pushing on one spot, pulling on another, checking for gaps. Boomer kept pace on the other side. Finally, she stopped beside the gate.

"Looks like this is it, Pal!", and she stuck her foot through the small hole at the bottom of the gate, where it swung shut, to connect to the fence.

Boomer sat down and looked, puzzled, at her foot wiggling there in front of him.

"Well?" demanded Martha Grey.

Boomer whined.

"Come on then! Are you a dog or a mouse?" and she scraped her foot in the dirt, "If you're a dog, DIG!"

Boomer dug.

They had a lovely stroll down the avenue that evening, stopping now and then to check out a likely trashcan, or admire the aroma wafting forth from one of the local eateries. By the time they ended up back at the schoolyard, the bagels were exhausted, and so were they. Martha Grey scratched Boomer behind his ears, kissed him lightly on the top of his head, and gave him a helpful shove back through the hole in the fence.

"A delightful evening, Sir! Shall we do it again next week?"

"Whomp!" replied Boomer.

"Keep it down now!" shushed Martha, "We don't want to let everyone in on a good thing! Till Tuesday then!"

And she limped off into the night.

Chapter Eight

Wednesday was Boomer's night to eat out. Carlo, of 'CARLO'S RIBS Best ribs in town!' saved him the rib ends, sometimes with barbecue sauce, sometimes with honey-garlic.

Sang-lee, at the doughnut shop next door, provided dessert, flipping day-old doughnut holes into the air for him to catch, sometimes two or three at a time, while an appreciative audience of customers cheered him on.

Then a quick stop for a drink at the fountain in the park, and it was off to the game.

Boomer's soccer team didn't start off being called 'The Losers'. They earned the privilege. They had lost every game they had ever played, and they were on the verge of being banned from the league entirely.

Who knows why Boomer picked them, out of fields and fields of more promising prospects, for his allegiance. Perhaps it was the quiet over on their part of the sidelines. He certainly didn't have to worry about being trampled by over-enthusiastic fans. He was it; the only fan they had.

The first night he went to the game, the coach didn't even show up, and the players stumbled through, like a huddle of lost sheep. Boomer watched the ball whiz past him repeatedly, until, as if he just couldn't stand it one more time, he leaped up and charged onto the field. Boomer scooped the rolling soccer ball into the air with his nose and ran, as fast as his stubby legs would carry him, over the turf, toward the goalposts.

One of the Losers just happened to be in the right place at the right time and, with more reflex action than planning, kicked out as the ball landed. To his own, as well as everyone else's astonishment, the ball whizzed past the other team goalie's head, and into the upper corner of the net.

It was the start of something great. Five weeks later the Losers won their first game, and even their opposing team cheered as they sprinted triumphantly, with Boomer bouncing high on their shoulders, twice around the field.

By the end of the season, the Losers had turned themselves into The Winners, and the threat of being thrown out of the league had become merely a ghost of a bad memory.

"They can't throw US out!" boasted the team captain, his proud, if somewhat sweaty and dust-covered, face beaming into the TV camera. "We'll ALWAYS come back! We're—"

"Boomer!" yelled the team goalie. "Give that ball back!" And he streaked past in the background, with Boomer, desperately galloping, just out of reach, down the field.

"Yeah!" laughed the captain. "We're like boomerangs! In fact, that's gonna be our new name! The Losers are GONE! The BOOMERANGS are comin' flyin' home!"

He grabbed the trophy, held it high above his head, and ran after Boomer and the goalie, with the rest of the team, cheering wildly, streaming along behind him.

Chapter Nine

On Thursday evenings, Boomer watched ducks. Henry van de Mere watched ducks too. They watched them together.

The first time Boomer plunked himself down by the park bench at Henry's feet, the man didn't seem to notice, didn't even blink, just sat staring at the ducks. The second week, he moved his foot to give Boomer a bit more room.

By week six, they had progressed to the point where Henry van de Mere put his hand on Boomer's head, if only for a moment, when Boomer placed his paw politely on Henry's knee.

From suppertime to dusk, every Thursday, they watched ducks. Henry van de Mere may well have watched ducks, all alone, the rest of the day, maybe every day, but on Thursday evenings, he had company.

Then, one gray Thursday evening, Henry van de Mere began to speak:

"I didn't mean to kill her, Boomer," he said quietly, his accent softening the harsh words. "How was I to know that the things they say are true? I've smoked since I was a boy, a pack a day. Sometimes two. My Anna-Marie always said I should go outside; that our home smelled like smoke. I said it was MY home. I could smoke where I wished."

"But it was my Anna-Marie who started to cough," his voice was a hoarse whisper now, hanging in the damp evening air. "It was my Anna-Marie who made the warnings on all those cigarette packages come true, when it should have been ME!"

Boomer felt the pain in the words, and edged closer, as if he could cushion the man's shaking, and absorb some of his hot tears, while the ducks swam placidly on the mirror of water in front of them, nibbling the weeds at the edge of the pond.

Chapter Ten

It was a warm Monday evening, with the promise of spring just teasing the air, when Jodie Brown came whizzing to meet Boomer. He hopped off his skateboard and grabbed Boomer's solid body in his arms. He hung on so long, and so tight, that Boomer finally tried to squirm out of the embrace.

"Sorry Boomer!" Jodie apologized breathlessly, "I'm just so excited! We're MOVING! Into a house, a REAL house! A whole one! All our own! Do you know what that means?" he whispered into Boomer's ear, as if saying it aloud might make the dream disappear.

Boomer shook his head at the feel of the tickling breath.

"Real houses don't have 'No Pets Allowed' signs! I can have a dog of my own!"

Then, feeling he may have hurt Boomer's feelings, he quickly added, "I mean on Tuesdays and Wednesdays and Thursdays and Fridays and Saturdays and Sundays. On Mondays, I will have TWO dogs of my own!"

And he danced around Boomer until they were both quite dizzy, and had to lie on the ground to collect their senses.

"I hope you can find it okay," said Jodie, suddenly serious, "Do you think you'll be able to find me, Boomer?"

But Boomer had no intention of ruining a perfectly good spring evening with sober discussion. He snatched Jodie's baseball cap in his teeth and took off, and Jodie scrambled to his feet and ran, yelling, after him.

On moving day, Boomer was nowhere to be seen, and Jodie was in despair. But at the last moment, just as the Browns were pulling out of the driveway, he padded into sight. Jodie yelled, "Boomer! There's Boomer! I have to say

'Goodbye'!" And he scrambled over the seat and out the door for a quick, fierce hug, then a dash back to the car, before any tears could start.

Jodie's mom strained to see around the cartons and bags, to finally catch a glimpse of this elusive friend who had meant so much to her son that past year. But all she could see was a squat, brown and white dog, with sad eyes, sitting, watching them go.

"Bye, Boomer!" yelled Jodie, out of the crack of the partially opened car window, and the dog barked, "Whomp!" and his tail thumped the grass.

Suddenly, Jodie's mom realized what she was seeing.

"THAT'S Boomer? Boomer is a DOG! Not a boy?"

"Well yeah, Mom," sniffed Jodie. "Don't you think he's awful short and hairy for a boy?"

And the car shook with laughter, as the family drove away toward Jodie's new home.

Chapter Eleven

It was almost the end of the school year, with the whole world looking rosy and inviting, and innocent and sweet. But it's true that looks can be deceiving.

Boomer was lying outside his doghouse door, sleepily soaking up the early summer sunshine, when Amanda, who had grown up a bit over the year, but not much, came skipping out through the school door.

School was still in, and Amanda was by herself. She was dressed in a frilly pink dress, with a white sweater, and her golden hair was in two carefully done braids, with matching bows.

"I am taking the bus to Daddy's new house," she informed Boomer importantly as she bent down to scratch his ear. "I have a bus ticket," and she dug it out of her Pooh Bear purse, and showed it to him, "and I am taking the bus by myself because I am old enough now! My daddy says I must act like a grown-up."

She stood up proudly, and straightened her dress.

"I will see you on Monday, my dear. DO have a lovely weekend!" And she gave him a final pat, and walked, in her best 'grown-up' walk, out through the schoolyard gate, and shut it carefully behind her.

Boomer watched lazily as she made her way to the bus stop across the street, sat down primly on the bench, and arranged her various accessories carefully about her. The sun beamed down on him, and he shut his eyes, blissfully enjoying the day.

When a car pulled up outside the fence, he barely noticed. Cars came and went. It was part of the rhythm of the town. But when he heard a man's voice, he opened his eyes and sat up.

"Hello there!" The man called, to the little girl sitting on the bench.

"You mean me?" Boomer heard Amanda ask.

"Yes dear, of course I mean you!" answered the jolly voice. "You shouldn't be there all by yourself, you know!"

"I'm waiting for the bus, to go to Daddy's house," called Amanda.

"Well now, I know THAT!" laughed the man, "Your daddy sent me to pick you up so you wouldn't have to sit in the sun and get your pretty nose sunburnt. Come get in the car and I'll take you there."

Boomer started to growl, as the little girl stood and began gathering her things, and the man opened the car door.

"Quick as you can now, dear! Your daddy's waiting. He has a surprise for you!".

But as he reached out and grabbed the frilly dress, to pull Amanda into the car, the man also got a surprise, perhaps as much of a surprise as a certain arrogant cat had had in the very same spot, as Boomer appeared, snarling, at his side, and sank his teeth into the man's arm and hung on.

Amanda, in the meantime, had realized, just a bit too late, what the story Miss Minsky had been reading: 'Never Talk to Strangers', had been all about, and she began to scream.

The man decided enough was enough and, with a curse, and a vicious shake of his bleeding arm, he flung Boomer and Amanda away from him, turned the car with a spray of gravel, and was gone.

Amanda lay, unconscious, on the ground, her dress torn and bloodstained, and her face scraped from the fall. Boomer stood over her, with her arm in his bloody mouth, trying desperately to pull her back toward the safety of the schoolyard.

Unfortunately, when Miss Minsky came running—Boomer's barks had been heard inside the school—the picture did not look good.

"Boomer!" The teacher cried in disbelief. "You get away from her!" And she grabbed Amanda from him, and pushed him aside with her foot. "Someone call the police!" she screamed, "and the S.P.C.A.! Oh, Boomer! How COULD you?" and she backed fearfully away from him, with Amanda clutched in her arms.

Boomer sat and looked, puzzled, up at her. Humans sure were strange at times! Suddenly, the wind from the north, in the form of a shrieking, shopping bag-swinging Martha Grey, came swooping down upon them.

"What do you think you're doing, you stupid woman?" she howled. "I saw the whole thing! That silly little twit almost got herself taken off by a creep of a man in a car. Boomer's the only reason she's still here at all! And you're running off at the mouth and thinking HE attacked her! How could you THINK such a thing? You! You! NINNY!".

"Boomer!" wailed Amanda, abruptly waking in Miss Minsky's arms. "Oh please, Boomer! Make him let me go!" and she threw her arms around Miss Minsky's neck and buried her face in her collar.

"See?" glared Martha Grey.

The realization of her injustice hit Amanda's teacher so hard that she began to shake. She handed the little girl over to others, in case she should drop her, and turned to Boomer, to put right her wrong.

But Boomer wasn't there. Boomer, who knew very well when he wasn't wanted, had quietly gone while the going was good.

Since it was Thursday, he had headed for the park, and the ducks, and Henry van de Mere, none of whom were likely to yell at him or to mind if he was a bit early. The ducks didn't care whether he came or not. Henry van de Mere did.

No one would have recognized this Henry van de Mere as the same pitiful figure who, for months on end, had sat staring at the ducks. The change had been gradual but complete. This Henry van de Mere was a whole man, grown back from a dead twig of nothingness. He watched while Boomer came trotting across the grass to their bench by the pond, and he cupped his hands under Boomer's chin, and smiled into Boomer's eyes.

"You dear old dog," he said, "I have something to give to you and I also have something to tell you. Would you wish presents first, or news first?"

"Whomp!"

"Ah. Presents first. That is what I thought," and he chuckled at Boomer's reaction when he produced a huge rawhide dog bone, with a wide red ribbon tied around it, from a bag on the bench beside him.

"Now. I have two things I wish to tell you. The first, and I do not care whether you understand or not, I must tell you anyway, is that you have saved my life, my Boomer. You have brought me back from the dead, and I thank you, more than I can ever thank you, for that."

"The other thing I must tell you (He smoothed an unruly tuft of fur behind Boomer's ear) is that I am going away. I am going to start a new life, in a new place, so this moment is to be goodbye", and he impatiently stabbed away a tear, with a white handkerchief, before it got beyond the corner of his eye.

"Now, I must go. For I want to remember you, and the ducks, and our place here, with gladness, not sadness. Goodbye, my friend."

He stood abruptly, and walked swiftly out of Boomer's life.

For a while, Boomer sat and watched the ducks alone. Then, with a resigned snort, he began chewing on his gift. A bone was a bone, after all, and tomorrow was another day. With any luck at all, it would be, at the very least, interesting.

Chapter Twelve

Boomer had been roaming the streets for four days when his luck ran out. He was only trying to reach a tender tidbit of Kentucky Fried someone had discarded after a hasty lunch. But the garbage can was high, and Boomer was not. The precarious balancing act on the edge of the container went woefully wrong, and Boomer slid in, headfirst, with his legs still hanging outside, over the edge.

Boomer made his opinion of the situation loud and clear and, bouncing off the inside of the metal can, it sounded like a whole pack of angry beasts, rather than just one disgusted Basset Hound. The racket prompted a hasty call to the dogcatcher and in a depressingly short time, Boomer found himself incarcerated, and speeding swiftly on the way to the pound.

"Whomp!" commented Boomer mournfully, with his head pressed against the wire of the van door, and "Whomp!" again, just to make his feelings perfectly clear.

There was a commotion on the sidewalk, and a man burst out of the crowds and into the middle of the noon-hour traffic. Horns blasted and tires squealed, but the man didn't seem to notice.

"Boomer!" he roared, "Boomer! Where yuh goin'?"

He pelted down the middle of the street in the wake of the dogcatcher's van. Finally, two blocks later, at a stop sign, he caught up and thrust his head through the startled driver's open window.

"Boomer!" he panted. "You got my Boomer!"

"Your what?" squeaked the driver, as he tried to lean back, out of reach of the accusing, curiously lop-sided face.

"My BOOMER! You should let him go!"

"WHOMP!" agreed Boomer, from the back.

"Oh!" stammered the driver, "Your DOG! That dog is your dog?"

"Yep," smirked Willy proudly. "My Boomer."

"Well now, why didn't you say so?" laughed the relieved driver. "Did he run away?"

"Boomer runs good," grinned Willy.

"Well, you'd better not let him run away again, and you'd better get some proper dog tags for him, in case he does."

"Yep!" nodded Willy enthusiastically. "Now you open the door."

When the man unlocked the gate, Boomer, who was no lightweight, flung himself into Willy's arms, and Willy, staggering under the load, and ducking to avoid Boomer's wet tongue, made it safely back to the sidewalk.

"Bye, you!" he called to the driver.

The man returned the wave, and nosed his vehicle back into traffic, smiling and shaking his head.

It seemed just like old times as Willy lumbered down the sidewalk, with Boomer dawdling along beside him, exploring here and there, sniffing this and that. The meandering seemed aimless, but eventually they did arrive at Willy's goal; a tall, white building, with trees in the yard, and a big garden. Willy's new home.

It was not your regular home, and Willie's new family was not your regular family. The sign at the gate read: 'HILLTOP HAVEN', if Boomer could have read it, and 'the family' was a large one. Thirteen people lived in that rambling white house, and an odd assortment they were too. Even more so than in your usual family. But they felt like a family, and they acted like a family, and when they saw Willy's Boomer, they welcomed him with open arms and hearts, as if they had been impatiently waiting, just for him.

It may not have been your regular home, nor your regular family, but it suited Willy, and Boomer decided it suited him too.

Chapter Thirteen

It didn't take long for Boomer to find his place in the family. Within the week, dodging wheelchairs, and fetching and carrying, became second nature to him, and when he flopped down at the end of Willy's bed at night, and Willy turned off the light, the duet of snores they produced were the music of a rest, well earned.

The rambling walks resumed, as if they had never been interrupted, and this Willy's bit of town became as familiar as that of the Willy before.

It was on one of these rambles that Boomer encountered just a whiff of an old enemy. He and Willy were wending their way through the piled up trash of a particularly interesting back lane when, across the mouth of the alley, flashed the figure of a young man.

Just as he crossed their line of vision, the sunlight caught his silhouette, and his sneering look was frozen there for a second in time. That second was enough. Boomer tensed, gave Willy one "Whomp!" of a warning, and lunged forward, dragging a bewildered, stumbling, Willy along with him.

Willy didn't even think of letting go of the leash, and by the time the two of them reached the street, the flashing figure was long gone. Boomer's sharp eyes, and his keen nose, checked out the whole area, but all he ended up with was a snout full of dust, and he sneezed in disgust, and sat down on Willy's foot.

"Bad man?" asked Willy, as he squinted in the direction he decided the young man had gone.

"Whomp!"

After that, their walks seemed to change: No longer drifting, relaxed wanderings, they took on the feel of a hunt, with Boomer leading the way, and Willy, his faithful sidekick, trailing along behind.

It took almost three weeks for Boomer to track down his quarry. Even then, the man looked harmless enough, sitting, drinking his early morning coffee, in a corner cafe, just staring out the window. But when you followed his stare, you realized that his attention was focused on an elderly man, setting up his vegetable stand, outside 'Mr. Ho's Chinese Restaurant and Grocery', across the street.

And when you saw the look of hate in the eyes of that silent observer, all thought of his harmlessness vanished.

Every morning, that whole week, Boomer and Willy sat at the bus stop across the street from that cafe and watched the watcher. Every morning, he sat in the same place, and watched the same old man, bustling in and out, carefully stacking vegetables, ready for his customer's viewing.

Only twice in all those days did the young man shift his focus to them. The first time was merely a passing glance, barely recognizing their presence, before his eyes, and his thoughts, shifted back to the old man and his shop. The next time, however, the look lingered, as if Willy's slack stare was a bit of a puzzle; a small irritation, but no more than that.

Boomer was a patient dog, and Willy was perfectly content to be with him, whatever the reason. So every day, like two rocks, they were just there, and, eventually, the man began to notice, to take a quick peek their way, and then turn his face back into the shadows, as if he had some idea of their thoughts. His focus on the man at the grocery began to waver, and the look in his eyes changed to impatience, then to anger, with perhaps a bit of fear there behind it.

It certainly wasn't obvious what he had to fear from a dog such a Boomer and a man such as Willy, and the source of his anger wasn't clear either, but one morning, he abruptly stood up from his place, grabbed his coffee cup from the table, and threw it furiously against the window. Then he bolted out of the cafe, shoving the startled waitress viciously against the wall, to get by.

As he rushed past Willy and Boomer, the look he flung in their direction would have flattened two less stolid souls. They followed him with their eyes as he turned the corner and disappeared.

"Bad man gone," sighed Willy contentedly, and he sat back on the bench and closed his eyes to enjoy the feel of the soft breeze on his face.

Boomer barked once, then settled down at his feet, to do the same.

And the old man finished arranging his last head of bok choy, stood back to survey the results, nodded his satisfaction, and passed, humming, back into his shop.

Chapter Fourteen

But Willy and Boomer were wrong. The 'bad man' was not gone. He was not the type to hang on to fear. Only hatred stuck to him, and his hatred asserted itself when he was barely out of their sight. Boomer's parting bark had seemed familiar, a sound out of a memory from some time past, associated with the smells of smoke and terror; smells which excited the man. So he turned back and, standing, hidden, he watched them as they sat relaxing in the sun. And so, the hunters became the hunted.

Their trek back home that afternoon was pleasant, leisurely. They were not aware of being followed, instead giving all their attention to the sights in front of them, the sounds of the town, and the fresh air on their faces. Hilltop Haven looked good to them after the long day, and supper was waiting, so they gave no thought to what, or who, might be at their backs.

The man whistled a little tune to himself. He had revived the forgotten memory, and he would make sure that this pathetic excuse for a dog would not defeat his purpose again.

It was close to midnight before the lights had all gradually gone out in Willy and Boomer's home, and the house appeared asleep. One small light, outside, hidden from view behind the gardener's shack, flickered on. It illuminated a concentrated face, and hands busy with the tools and materials needed to make fire, plenty of fire; all the fire even this young man could wish.

Boomer was restless that night, and his tossing and turning woke Willy from a sound sleep. When Willy got up and wandered to the window, Boomer followed close on his heels, and propped his paws on the sill, to join Willy in gazing at the moon. But the moon lost its interest when a shadowy figure appeared from behind the shed and sprinted across the yard into the blackness below.

A low growl started in Boomer's chest and spread outward to make the hair on his back stand on end. Willy quietly opened the window and leaned out to get a better view. There was an odd smell in the air, and suddenly a flash of fire lit the scene beneath them. Willy turned and tore out of the room, and down the stairs.

"The Bad Man!" he yelled, bursting through the door into the kitchen, where the cook sat, planning the week's meals. "The Bad Man will put us on fire!"

It may not have been the clearest of messages, but the main points came through, and the cook took one look at Willy's face and ran for the phone. Boomer, meanwhile, took the more direct route into trouble. He scrambled over the sill and out the window, and with one indignant 'WHOMP'! he landed on the man crouching below.

It knocked the wind out of both of them, but the man was up first. The sight of Boomer, like a vengeful, hairy, demon, coming at him out of the flames, sent him lurching backward over the grass and onto the gravel driveway, where he promptly fell over Boomer's soccer ball.

Boomer was almost on him when he clamored to his feet and fled into the street, with Boomer snarling and snapping at his heels. The squeal of brakes, and the sickening double thud of bodies on metal brought the race to an abrupt end.

The man was lucky, in a way. His couple of broken bones would heal, even if it was in a prison hospital. The dog was not so lucky. He dragged himself away from the noise and the lights, to lay in the cool, dewy grass. The restlessness he had not felt for so long came on him, stronger than he had ever felt it, stronger even than his pain. Yes, he decided, he would go for a long, long walk.

Willy found him there, in the bushes, and the big man neither saw the flashing lights, nor heard the sirens. All he saw was Boomer, lying so still, and all he heard was the silence, where there should have been Boomer's booming bark.

A kind hand touched his shoulder, as he knelt there by his friend. It was only a policeman, come to give some comfort, but Willy shoved the hand away, and ran, stumbling, into the darkness, and he did not return that night.

Chapter Fifteen

Next morning, the front page of the Saint Agatha Tattler ignored the political state of the nation, and relegated royalty to page two. Page one featured a picture of a dog; just a plain Basset Hound, not even a perfect one, and the headlines read:

BOOMER GIVES ALL TO BUST SERIAL ARSONIST

The last line of the article was a plea for Boomer's owner to come claim his body at the police morgue.

It was a surprise when, instead of Willy, a girl of about eight, from way across town, nervously clutching her mother's hand, showed up to claim Boomer as her own. But when an eleven-year-old boy, a stooped old man pushing an identical old man in a wheelchair, a 'bag lady', an erect gentleman in an immaculate business suit, 22 school kids, with teacher included, and an entire soccer team, followed close on her heels, the surprise turned to astonishment.

"Boomer belonged to ALL of you?" asked the puzzled police officer.

"Yes!" answered the crowd.

"No!" shouted Willy, pushing through the door, at the end of the line. "MY Boomer!"

"Willy!" cried the two old men, and Willy gaped at them, and then rushed over to envelop them in the circle of his big arms.

"It appears Boomer owned us all," the distinguished man in the business suit spoke softly, "and together we must find a suitable resting place for him."

"I think Boomer should have a park!" declared little Amanda.

"Boomer Park," Willy repeated dreamily, as if he could see it in his mind's eye.

"It needs to be round," said Mindy Reed solemnly, "so you can go for a long walk, but always still come home."

"And pets should be allowed there," added Jodie Brown.

"How about it has a soccer field?" suggested the captain of the Boomerangs. "Boomer sure loved soccer."

"And beds of herbs, for the body, and flowers, for the soul," the old man in the wheelchair whispered.

"And a pond with ducks," the man in the suit added quietly. "With plenty of seats for men, and dogs, to sit and look at them, and get their lives in order again."

Martha Grey peeked at him from under her battered felt hat, with mischief in her eyes, "And I suppose nosy old bag ladies could sit there too, and maybe even sing if they wanted!"

Amanda looked up at the man and smiled. "And you could pay for it, couldn't you?"

"Amanda!" scolded Miss Minsky.

But Henry van de Mere looked down at the little girl and a grin slowly spread across his solemn face. He knelt down until he was directly in front of her, and their eyes could meet.

"Yes," he nodded, "I could, and I believe perhaps I will."

"Hey, Rev!" (It was Chief Superintendent Jacob) "I wanted to give you this," and he placed something small in the Rev's hand.

It was the little gold cross, which had 'disappeared' after the fire at the church.

The Rev smiled, and closed his hand protectively around it: "You know, I thought I would never see this again. Where did you find it?"

"We were searching the apartment of that guy who tried to set fire to Boomer's group home, and there it was, in the middle of a pile of other little things, on his bookshelf. Sometimes people, weird people, in my opinion, keep little 'souvenirs' of their crimes."

"Thanks. I've been missing it."

"I thought you might be, and you're welcome."

***

It was a varied group who met at 'Boomer Park', a couple of months later, beside the newly planted bed of roses, lavender, and oregano.

All ages and stages, and not all humans either; there was a fair smattering of other species there as well, and they were all surprisingly well-behaved, as the Rev spoke the words, and they, together, scattered Boomer's ashes around the roses, and patted them down.

And God sat in heaven, looking down at the gathering round the pile of earth, and placed a hand gently on the head of Winchester Feldwood Trendham the Third, sitting there, watching too.

"Good dog," God said.

"Hey Boomer!" chirped a troop of small angels, peeking their heads through the mist. "You wanna play soccer?"

"WHOMP!" boomed Boomer joyously, as he tore off after them.

And the little group on earth looked up to the sky, and they smiled.

The common folk may have thought that sound merely a stray roll of thunder but Boomer's friends knew better.

***

Everything you say,
everything you do,
everything in life,
comes back to you.
Like a boomerang.
Like a boomerang.
Like a boom, boom, boom, boom, Boomerang!

Charlotte Diamond[2]

---

[2] 'Boomerang!' by Charlotte Diamond.

Martha Grey

It was a blustery winter day, a few months later, when Martha Grey, the local 'bag lady', disappeared. She wasn't at the Mission, or the park, or sitting in her usual spot on the sidewalk by the Goodwill, all that day, or the next, so the Rev went to her rooming house, to make sure she was okay. But she wasn't there either, and no one, ever, did figure out what happened to her.

What was at the rooming house, on top of the pile of junk on the floor outside her door, ready to go out with the rest of the garbage the landlady was clearing away, was a pile of scribblers. 'JOURNAL', was written on each one, and the landlady gladly let the Rev take them away.

The Rev read Martha Grey's journals into the night, and the next morning, he went to the Mission and invited the man in the red toque to join him at Tim's for coffee.

When they got there and sat down, the waitress at the coffee shop frowned at the scruffy man – Their policy, posted on the front door, stated that homeless people were not welcome – but she served them their coffees anyway, and left them alone, while the Rev handed his friend the old scribbler.

'JOURNAL' was written on the front cover.

"Read this."

The man in the red toque raised his eyebrows, reached for the scribbler, and began to flip through the pages. The more he read, the more thoughtful, and the more excited, he became. Finally, he closed the last page, and ran his hand gently over the tattered back cover, as if this was something precious.

"Martha's?"

The Rev nodded.

"Are there more?"

The Rev spread his hands apart to indicate a pile, at least two feet high.

"Can I keep this one for a bit?"

"As long as you like. Nobody else wants them. They were on their way out to the garbage."

The man in the red toque looked shocked.

"I'll keep the rest in my office at the church. You know where to find them, and me," and the man in the red toque nodded, finished his last slurp of coffee, and pushed himself to his feet.

The two men shook hands, and he smiled his toothless smile at the Rev:

"We'll do right by her, Rev. No one will forget her this time."

And he shuffled off toward the *Tattler* office, just up the street.

Excerpts from Martha ('Marty') Grey's Journals Toronto

The Beggar

A pile of filthy rags, sitting, lying really, in the corner. Apparently alive, although only a second look proved it. It was the eyes. The eyes were alive; terrifyingly alive, like fire. Everyone walking by, trying their very best not to look into those eyes, confirmed it.

Cuz if you looked into those eyes, you might unwittingly, unwillingly, be compelled to give the man, if that was indeed what he was, your hard-earned, hard fought for, hard won, two bits. Maybe even four bits.

He did not sit, like the common beggar, in the middle of the busy sidewalk, compelling the people to walk around him, or to step, disgusted, across him, or to leap gaily over him, as some were wont to do. He had a certain dignity; the dignity of those who have gone so low that there is nowhere more low to go.

The corner was it. And he was there. What there was of him; there did seem to be a decided lack of ordinary parts, where ordinary parts should have been, there among the rags. But he appeared to be past caring. Perhaps even past knowing. Only his eyes knew.

His eyes knew everything; saw everything. Right into the souls of the rushing crowds; certainly right into their pockets.

Perhaps he wasn't real. Perhaps he was only a guilty mind's personification of all our mother's words: "Share, Annie!" "Share, Joe!" "You MUST learn to SHARE!"

He didn't look real, you know. He just looked like a pile of filthy rags with eyes, there in the corner.

Halifax Airport

The Perfect Man

The perfect businessman
The perfect suit
The perfect tie
A shade, perhaps two, off the suit
Accenting the perfect shirt
The perfect hair, recently cut
but not TOO recently
Nothing too, too
Understated
The understated, perfect, man
Standing aloof
Aware of his perfection
His presence
His space
Unwilling to come too close
to the common souls around him
Unwilling to sit
in case the common air
should enter his space
and touch him
Willing to stand, impatient, uncomfortable
until
bowing to distasteful necessity
Perching, measured distance from the others
at the very edge of the common seat
Measuring time

A man of business
Quickly, clearly, marking his distinction
His importance
Taking out his Day-Timer
His business pen
His pocket calculator
His cell phone
And transferring his busyness
from the smaller to the larger
Expanding his busyness
Inflating his worth
in case no one has noticed
Insulating himself with his importance
Irritating man
But then, another man,
Not perfect
Not important
Obviously not a man of business
But happy
With a wife
Carrying a laughing little one
Passes by
The perfect man
Unguarded, a look of longing loneliness
A fleeting glance
Before he pulls his eyes away
Makes him real
No longer quite so aloof
so important
so cold
so insulated
so perfect
Human after all
Perhaps even a little sad
Waiting until the Special Others
Leave to board the plane

Rising
Gathering himself together
With tidy efficiency
Inserting himself in the space
before the Common Folk descend
Alone, by choice
Or not
On the tarmac
The perfect man
On business
Enters the plane.

New York

His Place

He was just an old man without a voice. Not a dirty old man, nor a particularly clean old man. Just an old man who sat at a table, in the back, out of the way, at the little restaurant that served, with speed and efficiency, the speedy and efficient people of the city, who strode by on their way to their important places, to do their important things.

He knew he was not important. Everyone knew it; could see it. He had no important places to go, no important things to do. He was just an old man, without a voice, there at his table, out of the way. Still, sometimes, he made a difference.

He had a wary look about him, as he sat there with his plastic grocery bag, stuffed with who-knows-what. A worldly, observant look, as if, maybe, he was there for a reason. An odd, possessive, protective look, as if that small bit of the street was HIS bit, this dining room was HIS dining room. As if these people, who really didn't see him at all, were his personal guests, if not his family.

Everyone who came through the door received his full attention. Not an impolite attention, but he saw each one, was fully aware of each one, while they were not in the least aware of him. If he did not approve of them, or of their behavior, his wary eye stayed on them while they ordered, while they ate, until they left, and he was free to relax again.

Sometimes, one of the odd people who live in the city would rush into the little restaurant. Not one of the nice, harmless people. One of the wild-eyed, scary ones, and the old man would become tight like a fist drawing into itself. But he knew his limitations.

He knew he was an old man, without even a voice to scream at the intruder. He could only watch with black eyes, as the angry, irrational words bit and stung the innocents there, their only guilt their uncaring.

When the restaurant manager chased away the wild one and 'law and order' was restored, the old man looked around at the people. He straightened his coat, smoothed his hair, pushed his bag more neatly under his seat, as if to distance himself, as if concerned that these people, in this place, might associate HIM with THAT one.

He stood and gazed furtively out the window, checking both ways, trying to see around the corners. Wondering, perhaps, whether the front door should be locked, to block another invasion. But the door was not his to lock. He could only go back to his chair and keep watch.

It was odd. He had no coffee cup in front of him, no pretending prop to show that he deserved his spot there in the back, and the restaurant was not a cozy family place, which might easily tolerate a local 'character', lending 'local color' to the scene. It was an efficient rush of a place, one of hundreds, all the same, which did not tolerate uselessness.

But still, they tolerated the old man. And when the security men came to question the manager about the invader, it was the old man who rushed to meet them; the old man who grunted and pointed frantically, who dragged the young, strong ones with the uniforms out the door, and waved, and nodded, and almost howled, in his frustrating efforts to try to tell them where the angry, scary one had gone, the one who had DARED to come, uninvited, into the restaurant. HIS restaurant!

And when they were gone, the old man walked proudly back to his table. Not proud because the others were proud of him. They didn't even look at him, once his entertainment value was spent and he didn't care either. Proud because he knew he had done all he could, his bit. Just because this was his place.

Afghanistan

Ela's Cup

Ela was a poet. She saw her life inside her head, in flowing words and colors that filled her tired, dirty world with joy. Even the tattered streets, where old papers shuffled endlessly in the wind, became a kingdom of flitting beings, lighter than air, in Ela's mind.

Ela had nothing. We would say she had nothing. Even those others who had nothing felt rich, and sad, when they thought of Ela.

But Ela didn't notice. In her mind, she had a world no others had, peopled with delightful beings no others saw, with things so wonderful, so amazing, and solid and true, that there was nothing else to wish for.

Ela did have one possession; one thing that she could touch with her hands, not just her mind. It was a perfect china cup. It had somehow survived the feet, the guns, the blasting, howling horrors, and when the soldiers had gone, it remained, perfect and untouched, until Ela touched it one day as she felt her blind way along, through the tangle of corruption she called home.

It was a beautiful cup. "Robin's egg blue", a connoisseur of cups, from another world, would have said, "with a spray of rosebuds hugging the rim." It shimmered like a pearl in the sunlight, after Ela washed it in the river and dried it on her rags. Although she couldn't see it, she knew exactly its perfection, and she glowed with wonder that it was hers.

Every day Ela took the cup down to the river and drank from it, and the filthy water seemed to clear when it touched the lovely thing, and Ela never got sick, and when there was something to eat, seldom as that was, and poor as the fare, it became a banquet to Ela, when eaten from her wondrous cup.

Then she would, again, make the trek to the river and carefully wash it clean, and carefully tuck it away among her rags. Just the feel of it there made her happy, and poetry rang, and tumbled, and sang in her mind, more than ever before.

The only thing that would have made her sad, that could have made her blind eyes cry, was if something had happened to the cup. But nothing ever did. Amid the many tumbles Ela took, the rough shoves and bumps she got, through other's haste, the cup remained secure, as if it rode on a royal cushion, instead of on a bed of rags. Even the thieves; the cruel ones who cared for nothing but themselves, left the cup alone, when they could have so easily, in a flick of an eye, snatched it away, and been gone. For the cup was valuable.

But no one stole it. It was as if they didn't even see it, or Ela either, in her blissful struggle to survive, there on the streets.

Perhaps Ela loved the cup too much. It lifted her spirit high above the squalor and the rubble of the streets; flew it away, and her mind followed. To the green forests, and the clear skies, and the clean, sparkling waters she had dreamed, and knew MUST be there, somewhere.

And suddenly her feet too wanted to follow; HAD to follow, as if she were no longer in control of them. So she walked, further than she had ever walked, through the heat and the clamor, and the stink of the day, across streets where she passed, miraculously unscathed; through the quiet dangers of the night, until the dawn, and the edges of the city.

And paradise was there, stretching before her. She knew it was. She could feel it. The signs were there: Fresh air on her face. The chatter of birds she had never heard before. The sweet smell of flowers. Flowers!

Other signs; signs with words, warning that paradise was filled with hidden danger, for others who could have read the words, meant nothing to Ela.

All she knew was that her heart danced, and poetry flowed like a bubbling, chuckling stream, through her mind. She could even hear the stream, and she moved toward it, feeling for her cup, ready to fill it with the laughing water.

Perhaps she even heard the click, as her bare foot touched the buried, evil thing, but surely nothing more. The blast that ripped paradise apart blotted out all else.

And Ela's cup flew up, and up, and smashed itself against the sky, but there was no one left to cry.

Calgary to Toronto

Across the Aisle

"Good morning, folks. This is your captain speaking. Just to let you know that we will be landing in Toronto in 20 minutes."

The smooth voice awoke us, assured us, and the two people, across from each other, on the aisle, startled out of their daydreams, and sat up. A napkin, precariously perched on her knee, slid to the aisle floor, and the two of them, at the same time, reached for it, their heads colliding.

"Oh! So sorry!" The young man apologized and handed back the napkin.

He was ordinary looking, but his voice, and the laughter in his eyes, made him a bit more. She too was ordinary looking. But she looked nice. They both looked nice. She smiled, and accepted the napkin, and they drew timidly back into their seats, into their separate shells, on opposite sides of the aisle.

"A bit crisp out there today, ay?" The man, as if reluctant to stay put in the shelter of his shell, offered a tentative comment, seemingly into the air.

(The weather, in Canada, was always a safe topic, with endless possibilities.)

And she picked up the thread.

"Yes. But I don't mind. I like the cold."

"Me too!" He nodded vigorously, as if this was a wondrous thing, and he laughed again.

And the conversation, at first cautious and awkward, seemingly dull, but not to them, proceeded, developed, and flowed on. It appeared they were from the same city, or at least pretty close, and it seemed they both liked Thai food and had matching tastes in music.

She even loved hockey, which apparently delighted him.

The lady, on the aisle, two rows back, watched them idly, and eavesdropped unashamedly, just for something to do. She looked at her watch and she wondered.

She had seen that look before, or at least one similar; had felt that developing warmth herself, even if it had been a long time ago. But 20 minutes? Was 20 minutes long enough for two people to fall in love? Actually, 15 minutes now.

10 minutes.

The passengers around them were becoming restless, as the wheels on the jet moaned into place, but the couple; yes, they were beginning to seem like a 'couple', didn't appear to notice.

"Seat belts fastened, please! Seats backs in the upright positions, and tray tables stowed."

5 minutes.

"Where do you—?" the girl breathed out the words shyly, but perhaps a bit desperately, then broke off, and they abruptly, reluctantly, stopped talking, as an efficient stewardess came between them, checking for compliance, leaning in to see that their bags were 'properly stowed under the seats in front of them'.

3 minutes.

The girl's friend, on the other side of her, bent forward, and peered at the man. She seemed, perhaps, a bit irritated, even a bit jealous maybe, with the lack of attention she had received, and she touched the young woman's arm, made a comment, and pointed out the window, and the thread was broken.

The pressure of the landing pushed them back into their seats; back into their shells, as the plane's wheels hit the ground. They didn't look back at each other. Instead, busily gathering parcels, and putting on jackets, and then standing, heads bent uncomfortably, until a space appeared in the flock of impatient 'frequent flyers', and they each slid into their spot, and were gone.

The lady, two seats back, watching as they went their very separate ways, felt vaguely, unaccountably, sad. Then she sighed, and shrugged.

"Was 20 minutes long enough to fall in love?"
Apparently not. At least not today.

Montreal to Edmonton

Just a Boy

There were two of them. A matched pair. Conscious, but trying not to appear conscious, of the picture they made: Crewcuts, smoothly shaved faces, serious eyes. Their uniforms pristine. Their dress uniform jackets, folded with exaggerated care, laid across their knees. Their, obviously new, brushed, buffed, uniform hats, surrendered, after a glance to check the helper for trustworthiness, to be stowed in the overhead bin.

Boys, to her middle-aged eyes. Perhaps 19 or 20, the age of her own daughters. Just boys, although they would certainly have resented the thought. And only a matched pair at first glance.

The one by the window, a bit older, was calm, apparently unimpressed and unaffected by the bustle going on about him. 'Cool', as her children would have said. Not quite bored, but close. Possibly demonstrating his 'coolness' to the other. Trying, perhaps, to model the behavior he felt the uniform should imply, but not quite succeeding. Not quite making the impression he wished on the younger.

The other was not 'cool'. He was trying. Trying to match the actions and behaviors. But not desperately trying. He was young, but not that young. His bright-eyed excitement, bubbling under the surface, made her wonder whether he might be a new recruit, whether this might even be his first flight on an airplane.

When the flight attendant came by to give a whiff of the delights which could potentially be purchase for lunch, he smiled at her and shook his head, then rooted in his pack and pulled out a bag of homemade snacks.

'Packed by his mom', popped into the woman's mind, and a feeling of loss, pain, and fear; a picture of his mother, desperately waving, until the plane was just a black dot that finally, totally, disappeared into the clouds.

When he refused purchase of earphones for the in-flight movie—the other young man, more worldly, had brought his own—She realized that money might be an issue and paid for two pairs, and the flight attendant, noticing and, likely, going against company policy, offered the boys both their lunches, "On the house!"

It was a long flight but conversation was minimal. Her few words of French and his few words of English exhausted themselves quickly, and when she understood that he had left his home at 4 AM to make this flight, and he yawned hugely, she smiled at him and left him to doze peacefully by her side for the rest of the flight.

But her thoughts were not peaceful. What was in the future for him? Fear? Pain? Forces that would warp his personality and his values? Would he come back to his mother forever changed? Hardened? His bubbling innocence lost? Or would he come back at all?

When the plane landed, she wanted, needed, to say something, to let him know she would be thinking of him.

She said it badly; almost choked it out. "God bless you!" she said, "Stay safe!", and she shook his hand.

It embarrassed him, I think. Embarrassed them both. But she thought it was important. Important in case he needed to remember, in some awful desert place, where he was hated, and lonely, and in fear for his life, that he was not alone.

The next day, on the front page of the paper, a boy, with a crewcut, and a smoothly shaved face, and serious eyes. The paper said he, and his vehicle had been blown up by a hidden grenade.

Just 20.

Just a boy.

Toronto to Ottawa

The Terrorist

He was a young man—but perhaps not that young. It was hard to tell—in the line-up to clear security, before being permitted on the plane.

Dark, curling hair, uncombed, a bit long; padded blue ski jacket, with a vibrant striped, homemade scarf, thrown haphazardly around his neck, and patterned rubber boots, one with the pant leg of his jeans partially stuffed in the top, as if he had dressed in a hurry, not paying much attention to how he looked, or not caring.

His brown, almost black, eyes were curiously blank, almost glazed-looking, with dark smudges under them, and he barely spoke to the officials, when they questioned him about his meager belongings: Just an old backpack, and the monkey.

A big monkey, as long as his forearm, knitted or perhaps crocheted, held tightly at his side. He, reluctantly, allowed it to be scanned, and then grabbed it off the conveyor belt, and tucked it carefully, safely, back under his arm, and he stumbled a bit, as he, and his monkey, made their way up the steps and boarded the aircraft.

He was tall – the man, not the monkey – and people moved aside to make way, as he ducked his head and wove down the narrow aisle of the Dash 8 to his seat, clutching the monkey protectively to his chest.

More than one passenger glanced at him a second time as he passed. The frowning face seemed ominous, the blank eyes disturbing, perhaps even threatening. What was with the monkey? A good place to hide something?

An undetectable weapon, or worse?

When he got to his seat, he folded his coat and stowed it, and his pack, with minimal fuss, in the overhead storage bin, and he collapsed down into his seat, staring straight ahead, with the monkey on his lap.

The flight attendant moved down the plane, checking for seatbelts and answering questions. When she got to the man, she stopped, and turned to him.

"Nice monkey," she said, and she smiled.

Then the sun came out: The young man, so grim and foreboding just a moment before; the very picture of a possible militant bomber, at least in his fellow passenger's minds, laughed a glorious, infectious laugh, and nodded.

"Thanks. Yeah, I like him. His name is Milton. My sister made him for me," and he smothered a sudden, shuddering yawn, and rubbed his hands over his eyes. "Oh! Excuse me! I just came off four-in-a-row 18 hour shifts at the hospital, and I'm so tired I can hardly see straight."

"Time for a nap then?" she raised her eyebrows, and nodded at him.

"Umm. Time for a nap. Nighty-nite," and he beamed up at her again, tucked the monkey around behind his neck, sighed a great sigh, and went to sleep.

And the rest of the plane, as if one entity, also let out a big breath, one they hadn't even realized they were holding, shook their heads at their own foolish thoughts and fears, and relaxed back into their seats to 'enjoy the rest of the flight'.

Massachusetts

The Cowboy

It was a small place, tiny really, with maybe a dozen 'tables for two', but it was packed. She suspected it was always packed, cuz these were the best bagels she had ever tasted, and they were 'made fresh'. So fresh they were still warm in your hand when you got them. Baked in the tiny, open kitchen, right in front of the customers.

There must have been at least 20 kinds; different flavors, fillings, even different colors. The bakers were obviously a family. Dad, Mom, a son, maybe 10 years old, and a pretty girl who looked about 16, with long, curly black hair, and gentle, glowing eyes.

Their accents were strong, perhaps Jamaican, but quite understandable, and the most obvious thing about them was their smiles, their friendliness, their obvious joy being able to do what they were doing, together, in this new country. The customers responded to their joy, and the place was filled with laughing faces and friendly chitchat.

She ate slowly, with enjoyment, dragging out the experience as long as she could and she sighed happily, and stared out the window, at the early morning sunshine, and the birds, as she settled back in her chair. She barely noticed the sound of the little bell, as the door opened to let in yet another customer; the bell rang pretty steadily in that busy place, but there seemed to be a slight change in the atmosphere, and she turned to see why.

A young man not all that young, maybe 25, had walked in the door. He was obviously a 'cowboy', or at least trying to look like one. Tall, muscular, with a white 'cowboy hat', and tooled leather 'cowboy boots'.

He was not overly large, but his presence seemed to fill the small space, and his eyes ran over the other customers, and he nodded at some, and called his hallos, as if he was a regular, making sure there were no unfamiliar 'riffraff' there, as if this place, maybe even this town, was his, rather than theirs.

He looked friendly, but perhaps not 'harmless', to the lady at the window, and, for some reason, she realized she didn't like him. When he turned toward the counter, toward the mother at the till, he tipped his hat, and wished her a "Good mornin', Anna!" perhaps a bit louder than the usual, and he flashed a wide, toothy grin, then nodded to the father, "and you, Joe", and the mother smiled brightly back at him, and the father nodded.

"Good morning to you too, Mr. Coates."

All the right words, and the right actions; normal and benign, but still the lady at the window watched, and noticed a certain tightness in the faces, which had not been there before. The girl had disappeared, perhaps behind a back cabinet, or maybe she had gone out for some reason, and the cowboy leaned closer, his elbows on the counter.

"So! Where's Camilla?"

"Oh, she's gone out for a minute, Mr. Coates."

"Ah. That's too bad."

At this point, an elderly woman came in the door and the cowboy transferred his attentions to her, his boyish grin again in place. He clapped his hands against his cheeks. "Well! Look what the sun just brought in! Suzie! Suzie! Suzie! My favorite lady!"

She laughed coyly. "Oh, You!" and punched him playfully on the arm, while he bowed, and gave her his spot in the line.

The other customers watched the antics, and smiled at the 'nice young man', and went back to their bagels and coffee.

When Suzie had gone, the cowboy returned to the counter and placed his order, and continued a steady chatter with the family behind the counter, but he kept looking around, back into the kitchen. His voice, and his face, were friendly, but the lady at the window saw something else, in his eyes.

'Predatory' was the word that came into her mind.

"So how's it going with your immigration papers, sweetheart?" he asked the mom.

An innocent question; a friendly enquiry, but, again, his voice a bit too loud and carrying, in the small space.

"Oh!" The woman answered cheerfully, "Good I think. I have my test next week."

"Great! You bin studying lots, I hope!"

"Oh yes, Mr. Coates, as much as I can."

"Well, good luck! You'll soon be an 'American Citizen' then! Just as long as nothin' interferes! Say 'Hi'! to Camilla for me, won't yuh, and tell her I'll be seeing her around sometime, soon!" and he flashed his toothy grin at them all again, grabbed his order, and strolled out of the room, the heels of his shiny cowboy boots clacking on the tile floor.

"You know*"*, the lady at the window thought to herself, "I could get tired of those teeth, and that voice, pretty quickly."

The bell on the door had tinkled as the cowboy left, and the teenager; obviously this was 'Camilla', peeked out from behind the last big rack of trays at the back of the store, and then moved to the front of the counter, to serve the customers there.

Her eyes seemed less bright, perhaps even a bit haunted, and the family subdued, their smiles forced, not free and friendly like before, and they talked low, among themselves, as if their circle, previously open, was closed now. The woman at the window frowned and gazed back out of the glass.

She could just see the last of the dust, where the cowboy's big truck had scudded in the gravel, as it tore up the road.

Maybe she was just getting a bit paranoid? Maybe there hadn't been an animal presence, and a threat given and understood, there, among the bagels?

Likely, she was totally wrong; Likely, she was just a paranoid, middle-aged lady, sitting there at the window.

But she didn't think so.

Montreal to Vancouver

The Diplomat

His name was Thomas. A handsome young man who stood out among the self-isolated beings on the sky-bus. He was with a woman, considerably older than he. Most likely a relative. They had the same hair; a mop of strawberry blond, and the same eyes.

But no one really noticed her. It was Thomas who sparkled among the stones.

At first, he seemed shy. Reluctant to meet a gaze, quickly looking away when his eyes inadvertently met another's. But it was a long trip from Montreal to Vancouver, and Thomas was incapable of reigning in his glow for five hours.

It was a very short time before his immediate neighbors were aware of him, liking him, responding to him, to his smile and his chatter, in spite of their determination to remain aloof. The flight attendants were pushovers to his charm, vying for his custom, for a glimpse of his shining eyes; the sound of his bubbling laugh. By Timmons, they were putty in his hands.

By Edmonton, the four rows of serious souls closest to his seat were with him, the fact that he spoke barely a word of their language irrelevant.

By Vancouver, most of the plane was aware of him. Aware that he had, somehow, drawn this tin can full of strangers together into a warmer, more human, band.

When the plane landed, and he and the woman stood to go, he touched those, now friends, closest to him. They smiled, and knew they would not quickly forget this young man.

This diplomat.

Only ten months old.

***

Hippies

Even I remember the first day the hippies came to Saint Agatha. You couldn't really miss it: Big old rusty van, with flowers and peace signs and stuff painted all over it, n' when the side door slid open, n' then just fell off right into the dirt, and they all just laughed! Well, the amount of hippies that kept comin' out of that van, it was amazing! Just like them Cadbury cows, in the commercial, that just keep comin' out of the barn. Them hippies musta bin packed in there like sardines!

You could tell they were hippies: the long hair, even on the boys, and the draggy skirts—only the girls wore the skirts, as far as I could tell—and the beads n' homemade dangly earrings.

N' once they all did, finally, get out of there, 'n onto the the parking lot at St. Aggies, they started haulin' out a bunch of other stuff too. Guitars, and camping gear, n' bags of clothes and things. Honest to goodness, I have no idea how they fit it all in there, though there was a rusty old rack thing on the top.

They did smell a bit funny too. Not bad really, not like they never washed or anything. Just kinda funny and, truth be told, I had my doubts about them funny cigarettes. They did offer me one, one time, but I told them I thought I'd just stick with my Du Maurier, at least for now.

Mrs. Chadwell took one look at them and decided they were 'weird', which, to be honest, they were, but then Mrs. Chadwell thinks pretty well everyone is 'weird', even though she's the one walkin' a 300 pound pig down the sidewalk every Sunday afternoon.

Mrs. Winters wrote a letter to the mayor about them.

(Likely, the mayor still has a whole giant turnip bag full of letters from Mrs. Winters, just waitin' for a big enough weenie-roast bonfire.)

Some people hated them. I never could figure out why. But, yuh know, I didn't mind them, the hippies, I mean, and just as well, cuz there got to be quite a few of them after a while, all camped out on that woodsy bit of land across from the soccer field. Kinda like gypsies, I suppose, though I must admit I've never met any gypsies and I'd guess all that bad talk about them, or at least most of it, is a pile of baloney anyway, and likely only cuz they're 'different'.

Everybody's 'different', and as far as the hippies go, I couldn't see that they did anything too terrible. It was mostly like they were just a bunch of big kids, just let out of school, 'FREE'! for summer vacation and, as far as I was concerned anyway, most of that 'live off the land' stuff was a good idea.

I'm not sure about the 'free love' thing, but I was too old to worry about that anyway.

I think some of them were likely 'draft dodgers', from the States, which, considering what happened (I watch 'M.A.S.H' too!), I can sort of understand. Though we won't talk anymore about that right now, cuz lots of people still get pretty het up about it, and I got quite a few friends down there, 'n I don't wanta start nuthin'.

They were around for two or three summers; the hippies, I mean, though generally they left for somewheres warmer in the winter, and some of them didn't ever come back. Just stopped being hippies, I suppose. My guess is they grew up, which is a bit sad really, but it happens to the best of us, and maybe some of them even snuck back in there and joined 'the establishment'.

A few of them did stay in Saint Agatha. You could tell them cuz their kids had names like 'Wolf', and 'Meadow', and 'Rainbow', and quite a few of them raised goats, but even they just gradually 'blended in' with the rest of us, and 'The Hippies' just sort of disappeared and got forgotten.

Though I must admit, when I'm downtown and see one of my friends, every once in a while I do get the urge to flash them a peace sign.

And sometimes, if I'm out for a walk, and I see something really spectacular, like a big eagle, or maybe one of those monster salmon in the river, I have been known to whisper: "Cool man!", but just to myself.

Good Day Indeed

Mrs. Winters was having a bad day, right from the moment she woke up: She had forgotten to set her alarm and missed *The Social* on TV.

(Jim, her husband, 'SHOULD have woken her'! before he snuck off to work.)

She couldn't find the dog, to yell at him for spilling water by his bowl.

(The dog; not a stupid dog, was hiding under the bed.)

There appeared to be "Not a grain of coffee in this house!"

(It was in the cupboard, where Mrs. Winters had put it.)

She burned the toast: "Who turned up the dial?"

(She did.)

And to top it all off, when she grabbed the two big garbage bags she wanted to take with her, and slammed the front door behind her, her coat got caught in the crack and she didn't notice before she locked the door, so she had to unlock it, then pull her coat out (It was "FILTHY!"), and then lock the door all over again!

A bad day!

But then, every day was a bad day, for Mrs. Winters.

Mrs. Winters wasn't paying much attention to her driving, as she pulled out of her driveway. She did miss the paperboy, but not by much, and she frowned at a young woman, limping along the sidewalk. *I wonder what's wrong with that one?* Mrs. Winters thought, not that she actually cared, as she poked along, holding up traffic, planning her shopping, and checking for the latest on 'Tic Tack' on her cell phone, slowing her car down to a stop quite a ways short of the yield sign at the end of the street.

Just as she was about to speed up again, her side door opened and the young woman she had seen hopped into the car, and Mrs. Winters, eyes bulging, mouth open, but nothing coming out, slammed on the brakes.

The man in the truck behind her started honking his horn, and shaking his fist at her (Perhaps he was having a bad day too?), so Mrs. Winters had no choice but to drive on.

"Oh, thank you so much for stopping!" The young woman had collapsed back into the seat. "The buses are on strike again, and I live miles from the college, and I keep wrecking my knee trying to walk there and back for classes every day! I don't know how to thank you enough! You're so kind!"

(Mrs. Winters was NOT kind. She was just not saying anything, yet, because she was so flabbergasted by the 'GALL' of 'this creature'!)

But she finally got her breath back: "Well! You can just get out—"

"Yes, right here would be lovely! Again, thank you so much! Your good deed for the day!" and the woman smiled, and was gone, leaving Mrs. Winters 'all-a-sputter'.

Mrs. Winters did not believe in good deeds:

'Every man for himself'!

'No good deed goes unpunished'!

'God helps those who help themselves'!

(She had dozens of 'wise words', and spurted them regularly, to prove her point.)

Poor Mrs. Winters' nerves were shot. She felt she needed, and deserved, a coffee, so she swung into the nearest Tims, and pulled up to the drive – through window.

"Coffee!" she growled.

"What size, Ma'am?" The boy at the window looked a bit jittery.

("Oh No!" 'Just great! A newbie'!) Mrs. Winters gave him one of her best dirty looks, but he didn't notice.

"Big."

"How big?"

(She closed her eyes, and shook her head, as if he should have known.)

"Biggest you've got, of course! When I say 'big', I mean BIG!"

"Yes Ma'am. Anything else, Ma'am?"

"Give me a couple of those new double stuffed doughnuts you've been advertising, and they better be fresh! and stop calling me 'Ma'am'!"

"Yes Ma'am. Cream and sugar, Ma'am?"

Mrs. Winters snatched the coffee from his hand, pulled a bill from her purse, and shoved it in his face.

('These darn new bills! Always sticking together'!)

As she drove away, juggling her hot cup, she heard something, and glanced back over her shoulder. The boy at the drive through window was waving the bill at her and calling out: "Thanks a lot, Ma'am! You're great! Have a good day!"

"What one earth?" (Mrs. Winters particularly hated it when people told her to 'Have a good day'!) She'd only given him an extra two cents! Dumb kid! Must be on drugs!

By the time Mrs. Winters got to the grocery store, she had finished her doughnuts and coffee, and her nerves had settled, but when she went to pay for her groceries, and opened her wallet, the twenty she had expected to find turned out to be the five she had not expected to find, and she realized she had given 'that stupid kid' a fifteen dollar, and two cent, tip.

She snarled at the lady behind the register, and pulled out her credit card, and the cashier took one look at her, did the world's fastest bagging job, and turned, thankfully, to her next customer, as they both peeked across at Mrs. Winters, storming out the door.

Mrs. Winters was in a rush (as well as in a snit). She was running late for her hairdresser appointment, and she sped up to get through the intersection before the last of the yellow light turned red.

There were people at the crosswalk, waiting for the cars to stop. Two teenage girls ("Should be in school, this time of the day!"), and a middle-aged man, standing close behind them.

The girls looked nervous, but Mrs. Winters didn't pay any attention. She was busy checking her watch and, just as they stepped off the sidewalk, she decided she didn't have time for this, and she slid her car in between the girls and the man behind them.

The man glared at her, and she glared right back, as he stepped back onto the sidewalk and the girls hurried away.

Mrs. Winters made it in time for her hairdressing appointment. In fact, she was five minutes early, and she was just climbing out of her car, when the two teenagers from the crosswalk rushed up to her.

"We wanted to thank you! Thank you SO much!"

"For what?" Mrs. Winters snapped.

"You know! You saw that creepy man following us! We couldn't get rid of him, and when you cut him off with your car, we got the chance to run! It was amazing! You're so nice! We'll never forget you!" and they both hugged the stunned Mrs. Winter, and then dashed off, waving goodbye.

Mrs. Winters glowered after them, then sniffed, and checked the time.

"Late, of course! Dang teenagers!"

On her way home, as Mrs. Winters was driving past St. Aggies, she thought, not for the first time, *what a wreck the place was looking*!: Those bricks at the corner coming loose, and the door always open, that bunch of stupid animals sitting on the front steps, and all those lazy vagrants hanging around the back! It lowered the tone of the whole neighborhood!

What were those people doing there anyway? Why didn't they just go home, or at least somewhere else, out of sight! The whole place should be torn down anyway! With that lovely big parking lot, it would make a great place for a strip mall. Yes! She'd write to the mayor about that!

As she puttered by the parking lot, with the traffic piling up behind her, she noticed a dumpster by the fence, and remembered the two big black garbage bags on the back seat, she had meant to take to the dump.

(Mrs. Winters was tired of her husband wearing the same old clothes: His 'favorite pants', the sweater his grandmother had knit him, his bowling team sweatshirt. She was ashamed of how he looked, and she had finally had enough of it, and bagged them all up, along with a few other things from his closet, to go to the dump; to get rid of them, once and for all!).

She slammed on her brakes, and the driver in the truck behind her (The same truck as the morning), slammed on his brakes too, again, and honked his horn, and shook his fist at her, again, as she backed up, and pulled in to the lot, and up to the dumpster. She leaned over, opened the back door, and shoved the two big garbage bags out onto the ground.

She hadn't even noticed the thin man sitting on the pavement, leaning against the side of the bin, but, as she pulled away, she saw him in her rear view mirror, rooting in the bags, and then starting to wave and run after her. He was yelling something, and she sped up.

But the man was faster that you'd think he would be by the look of him, and he made it to her car, when she had to stop at the red light, before she could pull out on to Main Street. He knocked at her window, and she nervously opened it a crack.

The man was panting: "I wanted to thank you, lady! Those clothes are just my size. You have no idea what this means to me! You're a real nice person!", and he yelled: "Have a good day!", as the light changed, and Mrs. Winters was, finally, able to make her escape.

By the time Mrs. Winters got home, she was practically bursting with indignation, and she saw her neighbor Emily, out in her garden on the other side of the fence. The same neighbor she frequently tongue-lashed about dandelions 'sneaking' over the line; the 'terrible music, playing at all hours'! (Emily taught violin lessons after school); and the leaves falling "from YOUR tree, onto MY side of the fence!".

(Mrs. Winters had forced this neighbor to cut down almost half this beautiful maple tree; The half whose branches had dared to peek over 'HER!' railing.)

Emily, a quiet woman, who had thus suffered the wrath of Mrs. Winters on numerous occasions, stood in the hot sun, and listened to the whole sorry story of Mrs. Winter's whole frustrating day, until Mrs. Winters got it all out, and stomped off.

Mrs. Winter's neighbor watched her go. She put down her hoe, and took off her gardening gloves, shook the dirt out of them, and put them in her pocket. She walked into her house, and carefully shut the door, then climbed the stairs to the bathroom—the bathroom at the side of the house opposite to Mrs. Winters' house—and quietly closed the window.

Then Emily sat down on the side of the tub, and she laughed, and she laughed.

She needn't have worried; Mrs. Winters couldn't hear her anyway. Cuz Mrs. Winters was in her bedroom, on hands and knees down beside the bed, with a broom, still looking for the dog.

But the dog, not a stupid dog, wasn't there.

Steps

There were a lot of steps and Emily was feeling old that day. Sometimes, she didn't feel as old as she was, but today she did.

Emily was a 'homebody'. She didn't often venture out of Saint Agatha, but this fall gathering; this 'before the snow flew', conference, was important to her. She wanted to be there. She was interested.

Interested enough to make the long climb up this mountain? Yeah, sure, and she smiled at the thought of her grandmother: "One step at a time", her grandmother used to say. So Emily started the long climb, 'one step at a time', up the auditorium stairs.

"Why did they make so many steps?" She sighed to herself, with each step. "But I suppose there's no other way to get to the top of the mountain."

Someone else was climbing the mountain too, beside her. She could hear the small grunts, with each step. The two of them were like a pair of odd instruments, percussion I suppose, playing together: 'Sigh', 'grunt'; 'Sigh', 'grunt', and she glanced down.

It was a little girl, 5 or 6 maybe, First Nation's, by the look of her, with her long black hair tucked down into the back of her little coat. Straining too, with each step, and for some reason Emily felt a bit lighter, with this small soul, struggling too, beside her. So for a while, they just continued, up the mountain, together.

"Sure a lot of steps," Emily commented to her small companion, as the rest of the crowd pushed past them, unnoticing, to get to their seats.

She and the little girl, a tiny island, in the way, with the river rushing round them.

The little girl looked up at her solemnly: "37," she said, "So far."

They both looked up, at the top of the stairs, then back down, to the bottom. The start of the journey.

"Halfway or so", Emily said, "wouldn't you say?" and the girl nodded, as they resumed their efforts. "My name's Emily," Emily said, as they both stopped to catch their breath.

"You don't look like an 'Emily'. You look like a 'Grannie'."

Emily had always hated being called 'Grannie'. She wouldn't let any of her grandchildren call her that on 'Zoom', but she didn't seem to mind this time.

"Well, you can call me 'Grannie', if you want, even though I'm not your Grannie."

"No. I know that, but you are *a* Grannie, aren't you?"

Emily thought of her grandchildren, at two ends of the country, with Emily in the middle, and she sighed again, though, this time, it wasn't the steps that caused it.

"Yes. I guess I am."

She noticed the little one flagging behind, straining and shrugging her shoulders, under her coat.

"What's the matter?"

"It's my hair. My mom put it under my coat, to keep it from flying around, but it pulls when I do a step. Can you help me get it out?"

"Sure," and Emily tucked her hands under the hair at the little girl's neck, and gently pulled it up and out, over the back of her coat. It was long, and black, and shiny, and it fell almost to the little one's waist.

"Thanks, Grannie."

"You're welcome. What is your name anyway?"

"Rose, and my family name is 'Starchild'."

"Nice to meet you, Rose," and they stood in the middle of the flowing stream of humanity, and gravely shook hands.

It was then that it struck Emily that this was not right: "Where is your mom anyway?"

"She had to go to the bathroom and I thought I'd come up the stairs by myself and surprise her."

Emily had a sudden vision of the time, at a large county exhibition, her daughter disappeared. She was there, and then she was just gone, and the uncontrollable fear; she supposed it was 'primal fear'. The feeling all parents had likely felt, now and then, from the 'dawn of time'. A feeling of rising panic, almost terror, until, half an hour later, they had finally found her, unworried, watching the 'nice cows'.

"'Stop and stay,' Janey! Next time you get lost, just 'Stop and Stay'!, just like we told you."

"But I wasn't lost!" Janey had looked up at them innocently. "YOU were lost."

"We'll just 'stop and stay', Rose. That's what we should do."

(Emily could almost *feel* the other mother's fear; could almost *see* her rushing frantically here and there, among the thousands of strangers, trying to find the one small one who was not a stranger.)

"And your mom will find us. Would you like to hold my hand?"

"Yeah, sure. Would you like to hold my hand?"

"Yeah, sure."

Their hands felt warm and secure together, and they moved to the side. 'Bystanders'. Such an appropriate term, Emily thought. Just 'standing by', watching the flow of the river.

"They're kind of like fish, aren't they?" The little one waved her hand back and forth, to show what she meant.

"Exactly what I was thinking."

Emily grabbed a red-coated usher, from the passing crowd, and whispered something in his ear, and he turned and pushed his way, against the current, back down the stairs.

A few minutes later, the public address system squealed into life: "We have a lost little girl, Rose Starchild, waiting for her mother, in the middle of stairway number 8."

"That's my name!"

"Yes. I believe it is. That's pretty cool, ay?"

"Yeah. But I'm not lost. I'm with you."

A few minutes later a woman with long black hair, the same as Rose's, and tears in her eyes, rushed up the stairs, and Emily, almost reluctantly, let go of the small hand, and placed it in her mother's hand, as Rose's mother pulled her daughter into an embrace, and thanked Emily, over and over, for her care.

When they were gone, Emily smiled, and looked around her: What a lovely day it was, and what a lovely child; a 'Starchild'. She looked at her hand and she realized that this was the first time she had held a child's hand in a long time, and the first time, ever, she had held a First Nations' person's hand.

It was nice. She must try and find a way to do it again!

The Sack

Everybody in Saint Agatha just called it 'The Sack', which was more than a bit confusing, if you were not from the area.

"Take her to The Sack. They'll fix her up."

"Why don't you call up the Sack, and see what they say?"

"Have you been to the Sack lately? She's a whole different color inside!"

'The Sack' was actually the 'Saint Agatha Health Center-S.A.H.C'; The 'Sack', if you tried to pronounce it.

At first, it was a bit of a joke, but as time went by, the name just got to be part of the language in Saint Agatha, and people thought it a bit odd, when someone didn't understand.

"Ground Floor. Going Up. Staff Will Please Use Back Exit."

The Bicycle Man

He was a funny little guy, the Bicycle Man. It was his job to look after the bicycles, at the back entrance to the hospital, for the staff who came and went, at all hours of the day and night. It wasn't much of a job, and I suspect he wasn't paid much for doing it, if he was paid anything at all.

Anybody could have done it. There wasn't much skill required; no hidden talents or techniques, to sitting, usually on a rickety old wooden chair, by the stone wall, next to the garbage cans, watching the bicycles.

His name was Fred. Fred 'wasn't quite right'. His body was not quite right, and his head didn't seem to be quite right either, but his heart was in the right place, and no one could say he didn't do his best at his job, such as it was.

When the hospital staff came out of that place, usually exhausted after a too-long shift, often looking grim and worn and older than their years, Fred was there for them. Ready with their bike, all polished up and set to go, to get them home safely, in the black night, or the busy afternoon traffic, back to their 'caves', where they could wind down and rejuvenate.

Fred always had the right bike ready to hand over to them at the door, as if he had been standing there, holding it, just waiting for them personally, the whole time. They never could figure out how he knew it would be them walking out that door at that moment, and he always gave the bike a pat, as he handed it over, as if he was saying goodbye to it, wishing it well and 'safe journey' on the way home.

Fred didn't say much, to the people anyway. He talked to the bikes though, as he checked on their condition, when each of the riders handed theirs over. Muttering over them, commiserating if they were muddy, as he wiped them down with an old towel; smiling proudly as he stood back and looked at his handiwork, after he had tightened a spoke, or added a bit of air to a tire that seemed a tad flat.

Scowling after someone who seemed rough with their bike; almost throwing it at him, when they were late for their shift, as they rushed inside, already looking tight, already wondering what lay inside, on the other side of that door, for them that day.

But even if Fred didn't say much to them, the staff said a lot to him. They told him their troubles, when they came out and finally breathed the fresh air, even if it was in an alley; the air that didn't smell like hospital.

Sometimes, after a bad shift, it was like they exploded on him; as if they couldn't hold it in a minute longer, and they had to get rid of it, before they could be normal again, and Fred was the first one there, ready and willing to take it away, and get rid of it for them, just outside the door, holding their bicycle.

He didn't have to say much. Sometimes, he didn't even understand everything they were telling him. But he didn't need to. All they needed was someone to listen, and nod, as if they were understood, and to send them on their way, feeling a bit better.

Sometimes, they brought Fred a doughnut, or something from the cafeteria. Sometimes even a whole meal, especially on Fridays, which was pierogies day in 'The Caf'. Fred did love perogies, with lots of onions, and chez whiz on top.

He knew all their stories: Dr. Janes, whose mother was in the hospital, and who might, or might not, make it out; Jack, who worked in x-ray, and hated his job; Little Tina Tan, the new nurse who worked in Pediatrics, and always smiled, not matter how tired she was, and told him about her two babies, twins, waiting for her at home.

He worried about Nurse Tan. She seemed so child-like, so vulnerable, heading off into the dark streets on her bicycle, and he used to walk with her to the end of the alley, and keep an eye on her, and an eye out for any possible dangers, until she disappeared into the gloom.

Recently, she had a brand new bike; a really good one her husband had given her for her birthday, and she and Fred discussed it, and he treated it like gold.

Fred did talk to Lucky, the security guy, close to retirement age, who came out and sat with him, for a smoke, on his break.

Lucky lived alone too, and they were both interested in hockey, and they would laugh and discuss the most recent game; how good, or bad, 'The Habs' were doing, until it was time for Lucky to get back to work.

'The Sack' was downtown, in a bit of an iffy part of downtown; a bit of a dangerous place. Even with security, there were some 'bad dudes'—Fred always used to think of them as that—sometimes hanging around.

They didn't usually bother Fred, but he knew they sometimes had their eye on the bikes, as a possible commodity to sell for other things, and he guarded them, with his life really, when one of these was around. Nobody was going to steal 'his bikes', if he could help it!

But one night, he couldn't help it. Two of the 'bad dudes' were waiting, there across the street, at the end of the alley, when Tina came off her evening shift and peddled away. When Fred, watching over her as she sped off up the street, saw them come out and grab her, he ran, yelling, like a madman; like an avenging angel, and tackled them both, and saved Nurse Tan, and her new bike, from this indignity; this onslaught.

The two men, after a brief struggle, decided the bike, and the girl, weren't worth the trouble, and they ran away.

But Fred didn't run away.

Fred was broken, and all of the doctors, and all of the nurses, and all of the hospital staff, who rushed to try to help him, couldn't put Fred together again.

And Fred would likely have been amazed, even shocked, at how much they missed him, and how many tears were shed; At how much they had actually loved 'Their Bicycle Man'.

"Main Floor. Clinic and Doctors' Offices. Please Watch Your Step."

The Purple Chair

Evan

All the chairs in the doctor's office waiting room, on the main floor of the Saint Agatha hospital, were a uniform, boring, charcoal gray, except for one. One was purple. Evan always tried to commandeer the purple chair, whenever he had to come see the doctor, for one of his regular scrapes or sniffles visits. Purple was Evan's favorite color.

Evan generally colored mostly purple pictures with his crayons, when he got to sit on the purple chair. It seemed only proper.

"There's a real black man over there, Mom!"

(Evan had looked up from his coloring book, kneeling on the floor by his chair, and was gazing, amazed, with his crayon still clutched in his hand.)

"Hush, dear!"

"But Mom! I never saw a real black man before. Well, except on TV but that's not real."

(Evan had just turned four and a half, and once he'd learned to talk, he'd hardly ever stopped. Only when he was eating, and only then because his mother refused to let him eat and talk at the same time in case he choked, and when he was asleep.)

"How come that guy sitting next to him is giving him such a dirty look? That's not very nice, is it Mom?"

(Evan's mother glanced up from her magazine, at the two men across the waiting room. 'The look', she had to agree, was definitely unfriendly, but she put her finger to her lips, handed Evan another crayon, and resumed reading her article: "Five DELICIOUS ways to prepare cabbage".)

"Do black people have kids, Mom?"

She tried to ignore him, but he just repeated the question, only louder.

"Of course they have kids, dear."

"Are the kids black too?"

"Well, yes," she raised her eyebrows and shrugged. "Maybe different shades, I suppose, just like you and your brother look different."

Evan appeared satisfied, and blessed silence reigned, for about ten seconds.

"So, how come there's no other black people around here, Mom?" Then his eyes widened: "Are they all dead, Mom? They're not ALL buried in the black people's cemetery outside town, that you showed me, are they? Did they all die at once? What did they die of?"

She put her hand gently on Evan's shoulder, to stop the flow: "No, dear. They're not all dead."

"Whew! That's good! Then how come no black people live here? How come I never see any around?"

"Maybe because they don't want to live in this neighborhood."

"But why not? There's a park, and an ice cream place, and the kids could go to my school! Why wouldn't they want to? They could even live on our street, in Mrs. Tanner's old house that's for sale! Can I go ask that man if he lives here, and if he has kids, and if he would like to come live on our street?"

"No, Evan." She reached for his arm, and steered him back on to the purple chair, before he escaped. "They likely wouldn't want to live in this part of town, love."

"But why not?"

There was a long silence as Evan's mother gazed down into his puzzled eyes. Then she pressed her lips together and sighed, and she decided she might as well be honest.

"Probably because we don't treat black people very well around here."

"But why? Aren't they good?"

"Well, yes, I suppose they're just as good as anybody else."

"So, can I go and sit by him, Mom? He looks lonely. That would be a nice thing to do, don't you think?"

She smiled down at her son, and put her magazine back in the rack on the wall.

(Who cared about 'Five DELICIOUS ways to prepare cabbage' anyway? She hated cabbage!)

"Yes Evan, I think that would be a very nice thing to do. Just give me a second, and I'll go with you."

"You're not really black, you know."

"I'm not?"

"Nope." Evan dug into his pocket, produced a crayon, and held it up beside the man's cheek. "I think yer more like 'Chocolate Brown'!"

***

140

Cindy

Cindy lowered herself gingerly into the purple chair. It appeared to be the most solid of the lot in the doctor's waiting room, and it had arms, and besides, she liked purple.

She wasn't that heavy but, even after almost nine months, she still had difficulty judging her changing size, which had led to some embarrassing moments when she had had to be unceremoniously hauled, like a bulging sack of potatoes, out of chairs or cars, by friends or, sometimes, even passing strangers.

Jason was not much help. He had not wanted her to get pregnant in the first place; Being a 'free spirit', he did not want to be 'tied down'. But as her mother used to say: "These things happen", and Jason was not pleased, or helpful.

Mostly, Cindy was just tired. She was still working, as a Personal Support Worker and, since 'free spirits' don't make a lot of money, she was working for as long as she could. And, sometimes, she had headaches.

She tried not to take anything for these, in case it might hurt the baby, but the headaches seemed to be getting worse, and she thought she'd better get it checked out. So here she was, in the purple chair, at the doctor's office.

"Oh dear!" (Her stomach muscles tightened in that weird way.) "Another of those darn Braxton-Hicks contraction things!" and she braced herself on the arms of her seat. But then she felt a burning, blinding flash of pain, as if her head was exploding, and she reared up out of the chair, and that's the last thing she knew.

A young man with thick glasses; a medical equipment dealer new to the job, sitting across the waiting room, caught her a split second before she hit the floor. It was good he was there, and good that the 'hospital' part of the building was so close.

It was almost a day before Cindy became aware of the noises around her. The sound of quiet voices; the muffled 'ding' of a call bell; traffic outside on the street, and she opened her eyes. Her vision was odd, as if she couldn't see past her own nose on one side, as if the room ended there.

But she knew it didn't. She knew there must be a door, and when she turned her head, she could see the door, and the nurses at the desk outside, and a clear plastic container, like an open box, on wheels, there beside her bed.

Something moved in the box. Something whimpered, and then started to cry. *My God!* she thought, *It sounds like a baby*!

And then she knew. It was her baby. A girl! (She had a pink hat on). Cindy reached out to touch her, to calm her. But her hand, her arm, didn't seem to want to do it. Like a dead thing, it just lay there, on the bed, beside her.

The stroke, and the baby, had come at the same time. A tiny leak, in a tiny blood vessel, in her brain; the cause of the headaches. The start of labor was 'the last straw', and the blood vessel had burst.

She called the baby 'Grace', because they were both still alive, and she and Grace went home, in a wheelchair, two weeks later, on the 'Handibus'.

Jason appeared to have evaporated. 'Poof'!, as if he had never been there at all, which was pretty close to the truth, the day she had gone to the hospital.

He had never even seen Grace, and Cindy was so overwhelmed, and so busy, that she was kind of glad she didn't have to deal with him. One baby was enough.

So it was just she and Gracie.

Her leg, weak but not useless, improved, and her balance returned, until the wheelchair was just a memory. But her left arm did not improve and people around St. Aggies got used to seeing the young woman, with the edges of a baby blanket clamped in her teeth, and her right hand tucked underneath, holding her baby close, lifting her here and there, as if this was just a normal, everyday thing.

And, more and more often, they seemed to be accompanied, proudly, it appeared, by a young man, with thick glasses, who, according to Mrs. Pickett (who knew everything in town), was a medical equipment salesman.

***

The Farmer

The man strode through the clinic door, lowered himself carefully into the purple chair, and picked up a magazine. He looked perfectly fine, and Jackie, the lone receptionist that day, was busy, so she didn't actually pay much attention to him.

There was a 'rash of chicken pox' going around (Jackie always called it that, though the joke was wearing thin), and allergy season was well underway, so the place was full of sniffling, snorting, puffy-looking people.

And, to top it all off, there had been a 'wild party' last night, on one of the back logging roads, and three young men, and two young women, had been bounced out of the back of a pickup truck, when they were 'joy-riding', and it wasn't joy they were feeling this morning, when their angry parents dragged them in for 'the Doc to take a look at them'.

When things finally seemed to settle down a bit, the receptionist remembered the quiet man in the purple chair.

"So sorry to keep you waiting, Sir."

The man was holding up his magazine, with two hands, straight in front of his face. *Must have trouble with his eyes*, Jackie thought, and she had to say her words again, before he noticed, and lowered the magazine.

"What seems to be the problem?" The receptionist was filling out forms, as she spoke.

"Aw, Nuthin' much. Bit of a sore neck. The wife made me come."

"Ah." Jackie sighed to herself: "Could he not have just taken an aspirin, and put a cold pack on it, and gone to bed for a while?" But he looked like a farmer, and it was haying time, and farmers don't go to bed much in haying time, so he probably didn't have time for that.

She wondered that he had had time enough to even drive himself all the way into town to see the doctor, for such a minor issue, but maybe his haying was done.

"Well now, Sir. It is lunchtime, and the doctor has been working all morning. We usually close for lunch, but, if you don't mind, you can sit there and he'll be able to see you in about a half an hour or so?"

"Sure. No problem. I'm not goin' anywhere. It's good to sit down for a spell, even if it is in this purple chair. I'm not killed on purple. Reminds me of an ugly old velvet hat my great aunt Elizabeth used to wear. Wore it right to her grave, and, to be honest, I wasn't too killed on her either, when she was alive.

Sorry to blather on. You go ahead, and I'll hold the fort", and he gave her a friendly wave, and picked up his magazine again.

It was actually almost an hour before Doc, and the receptionist got back from lunch, and the place was filling up again. Fact is, Jackie had entirely forgotten about the man in the purple chair, and, when she did notice him, she was shocked that he was still sitting there.

Well, at least he was a 'patient patient', and she smiled to herself at the thought.

"The doctor will see you now Sir, and again, sorry for the wait."

The man just shrugged, and eased himself out of the chair, and followed her back along the corridor to the last examination room.

It was less than five minutes later when the doc, white-faced—his face was usually red, or at least pink—sprinted toward the receptionist, and ordered her to call an ambulance.

"And make it quick, Jackie!" He called, as he grabbed something from the corner cupboard, and dashed back up the hall.

The two of them watched as the ambulance crew rushed the stretcher, with the young farmer, in a neck brace, lying on top of it, into the waiting ambulance, and it roared away, on the way to the big hospital, in the city.

"What on earth was all that about?" gasped the wide-eyed receptionist.

"Well," the doc shook his head and blew out a big breath, and turned to her: "He said they were putting bales of hay on the escalator, four days ago, to get them up into the loft, and a bale fell off the top, and landed on his head.

That man's been walking around—and not just walking around! Working!—for four days. Four days! With a broken neck. Right at the top of his spine too! He should be dead!"

"But you know what he said, when I told him he had a broken neck?"

"No. What did he say?"

"He said: 'Well, at least we got the hay in.'"

"Second Floor. Medical. Please Turn Left. Have a Nice Day."

Nobody

It was a dark and stormy night. Honest it was. And the dimmed hospital lights didn't help much, and neither did the distance buzz of the alarm bells, or the quiet mutter of voices; an irritating hum she couldn't understand anyway, but at least it proved she wasn't alone.

Sleep hadn't come at all that night. Sometimes that happened. "The blessed oblivion", as her sister used to call it. (Her sister had been a bit on the over-dramatic side).

There was one of those glow-in-the-dark clocks, by her bed. Times it was a blessing, and times a curse. Sometimes, she didn't really want to know it was only 10 minutes later than the last time she'd looked.

"Good mornin'! Good mornin'! Up with the birdies, I see! Here's your hearing aids, love! You want help putting them in? There, that's better. Though you may be sorry if I keep nattering on. Just let me know if you want me to take them back out, or you can just roll your eyes at me, and I'll put a bit of that tape there over me mouth. Works a treat in church!

"Will you look at that rain! I brought my bathing suit with me for the walk home. It's one of them frilly pink jobs. I gave up my bikini. Started gettin' complaints from the public. Was a bathing suit model one time. You'd never credit it, would you? For that second hand store downtown. Til it started scaring the customers away.

"Just kidding dear. How about I put this fancy cushion on your chair, for when they get you up. You know what they say: 'Look after your tush and the rest will look after itself!' My name's Lillian, by the way. Yeah, almost the same as your name, only a bit longer, and with different letters—I saw that look! See! I knew you could roll your eyes!—But my friends all call me "Lil', so you can too.

"Doctor Marsh is on today. You lucky thing, you! Looks a bit like Elvis. You know what I mean? Only a bit older. I come over all faint when he talks. A handsome man does improve the scenery, don't you think?"

The muttering voices were getting closer, and words spanned the space as the door swung open:

"And this is Mrs. Dawson. Not much to say about her. No real response since she fell and hit her head, and we're not expecting much. Just keep her comfortable. Get her up in the chair for the day. Better for her lungs. Who are you?"

"Oh, nobody dear. Just the housekeeping lady. I'll stay out of your way and deal with the bathroom while you do your thing."

"Ah. Now, on to Mr. Bradley, in 207. A most interesting case!"…and the door clicked shut behind them.

"See what I mean? Isn't he about the handsomest thing you ever saw! Could do with a haircut though. My, you do look like the queen on her throne now, there in that chair! Only without the jewels. I'll bring them in and drape they around you later. I think your tiara is out for cleaning.

"That little nurse looks pregnant, ay? Did you notice? Better her than me. Do you remember that? My husband used to have to roll me out of bed, towards the end, and all I wanted to eat was grapefruit and ice cream. Haven't been able to look a grapefruit in the face since. No problem with ice cream though, as you can see.

"What's your favorite kind? I like maple walnut. No? How about orange pineapple? Rocky road? Black Cherry? Ah hah! Black Cherry! I can see that! I'll leave a note for your daughter! That's her there in the picture, I presume. Pretty. Takes after her mother I can see! And your grandkids. Like stair steps. They grow up so fast, ay?

"I got grandkids. One's a holy terror, but cute. I figure he's going to be an explorer. Got stuck in the kitchen cupboard the other day, and they practically had to use a shoehorn to get him out!

"Did you want me to turn on the boob tube? There's hockey on, and 'As the world turns'.

"Speakin' of which, do you think that red-haired fella will ever settle down and ask that blondie girl to marry him?—Though I have my doubts if that hair's natural—It's not like she hasn't been hintin' long enough!

"Hey! The sun's out! Look! There's bunnies on the grass down there. I'll just turn your chair a bit, so you can see them better. I had a rabbit as a pet when I was a kid. We used to dress him up in doll clothes, and cart him around in a doll carriage. We called him 'Beauty'. Funny name for a boy rabbit, but he didn't seem to mind.

"Did you have a pet, when you were a kid? I bet you did! A cat? A dog? Ah, a dog! Oh! Look at that! There's a robin chasin' a little baby squirrel. The squirrel's got his tail up out of reach, and is just a-bootin' it. Lookin' over his shoulder as if he can't quite believe this is happening to him!

"Now, wasn't that about the funniest thing you ever saw? Up with your feet now, Love! Time to clean under your hooves! Must be breakfast pretty soon. I see them out there milkin' the cow.

"I'll be back again tomorrow! No rest for the wicked, you know. Bright 'n early too. None o' this lolly-gagging 'n sleepin' in till noon around here! You keep an eye on the place while I'm gone, will yuh? Us girls have to stick together, you know! And don't forget, I'm 'Lil' to you! Bye-bye now, love!"

The door to the room slid shut, with a dry hydraulic hiss.

And the lady in the chair smiled.

"Top Floor. Long Term Care. Going Down."

I Had a Dream

I had a friend. His name was Jerry, and he lived in the Manor on 23rd Street, before they moved him to the Sack. I used to go to see him every Saturday.

His roommate's name was Louie. Louie was a bit odd. But then, I'm a bit odd myself, so who am I to talk?

Louie used to pee in a pop bottle (with a screw-on lid) once every two weeks. I don't really know how he did it, and I don't want to know. In fact, I don't even want to think about it. He kept the bottle at the back of the big drawer in his bedside table. Jerry told me. It was a ginger ale bottle.

Then, at the end of two weeks, he would dilute it with water, and water the plants in their room. Louie and Jerry had the most amazing plants. The place was like a paradise, or a jungle, according to how you feel about plants, and no one knew why, except for Jerry, and Louie, and me, and none of us were telling.

I don't drink ginger ale anymore.

I don't know if Jerry had lived in a nursing home all his life, but, when you're born with a body like his, it seemed to be inevitable, and I only ever knew him living in a nursing home, so that's where I picture him, in my mind.

I assumed his body was due to Cerebral Palsy, I never actually asked, even though I've known lots of people with Cerebral Palsy who do okay, in this crazy old world where 'perfect' is 'good', and 'less than perfect' is not. I expect it's a hard life though, but they manage, if they have enough support.

Jerry's head, his brain, the thing that really matters, was just fine. In fact, it was great. It was his body that was the pits. When I knew him, he spent all his days, 24 hours a day, day in and day out, in bed. Likely, he would not have been able to sit up, even in one of those really skookum wheelchairs, and the cost, I suspect, would have too much for his family. If he even had any family, which, if he did, they never showed their faces in his world, at least when I was around.

Jerry could talk politics, and world issues, and even philosophy, with the best of them, and he could hear and see; his eyes and ears were okay, so television and radio gave him his link to the rest of the planet, cuz computers, and the internet and all that were not really part of everyone's lives at that time.

I think Jerry would have been a great man, maybe even a mover and shaker, if he had had the chance.

On icy days in the winter, Jerry and Louie used to watch the Saint Agatha version of 'Demolition Derby', as the cars slid down the mountain road that went right by the place, and ended up in a pile at the bottom, but most days, in the summer, he just lay in his bed, with the head raised as high as he could sustain it, watching Saint Agatha go by, through the window there at the end of his bed.

He could just see the park, over to one side, and the soccer grounds. Not close enough to really follow the games, but close enough that he could imagine them, if the team colors were different enough.

And every once in a while, Jerry had a dream.

He dreamed of dancing, in an open field of clover. He could even smell the clover, in his dream. His feet so light they barely touched the ground, as he leaped, and twirled in the air, and, every time, in his mind, he wondered why he hadn't done this before; why he hadn't known that he could dance.

It was a ridiculous dream, of course, as our dreams often are, but like our 'flying dreams', if we're lucky enough to have them, it took Jerry out of his reality, into a place of joy, and he never wanted to wake up, and tried his best to stay there. But that never works.

Sometimes the joy of the dance sustained him for quite a while, and he would be happy; look happy – even though I never, ever, heard him laugh – for the rest of the day.

Eventually, Jerry's body decided enough was enough, and it was cancer that finally took him away. It wasn't a long fight. I'm guessing he didn't have a lot of fight left in him, or maybe he just didn't feel much like fighting anymore.

I didn't know he had died, cuz it wasn't on a Saturday, but the night of the day he died, I had a dream, and when I went to tell him about it, they told me.

I dreamed I saw Jerry, dancing, with the sun shining down on him, and the birds singing, in a big field of clover. You could even smell it!

And Jerry was laughing.

***

Family

Things were buzzing at the Beauty Emporium, and it had nothing to do with hair. Rumors had been flying around town for weeks, ever since Jim and Lennie had 'disappeared'.

(The rest of the staff at the Emporium had kept their mouths firmly shut, in spite of questions, and hints, and even bribes.)

The rumors were true, and everybody seemed to have an opinion.

Mrs. Winters, the most miserable person in Saint Agatha, thought the whole idea was 'disgraceful', and she wrote a letter to the mayor about it.

(The Rev had been working on Mrs. Winters' attitude for quite a while, but even he had to admit it was an uphill battle, possibly even a lost cause.)

She even threatened to 'Take her business elsewhere'!, though it was unlikely she would actually do that, cuz the staff at the Beauty Emporium were very good at their jobs, and the customers of the new shop across town tended to all walk out the door looking exactly the same, even if they were different genders.

Jim and Lennie had been watching The National on TV one night; a report about the plight of the children in one of the many poor countries of the world, and they decided it was time they did something about it.

It wasn't a snap decision; they had been talking about it for some time. But now they were off, on the other side of the world, making it happen, and today they were due to come home.

When Jim and Lennie walked into the Beauty Emporium, each carrying a small bundle in their arms, there was, for a moment, shocked silence. But only for a moment, and then pandemonium erupted!

"TWO of them! You got two of them? I thought you were only getting one!"

"Let me see them!"

"They must be scared stiff, the poor little things! Everybody settle down!"

The 'poor little things' were, by this time, wide awake, and peering out from among their blankets. They did not appear to be 'scared stiff' at all. In fact, they appeared to feel quite secure and comfortable in their new parents' arms, and the littlest one, with her hand firmly entwined in Jim's beard, even smiled. She only had 3 teeth, but it was definitely a smile.

"We were only planning on adopting one," Jim explained, "but these two are sisters, and it seemed an awful thing to separate them, so we ended up with two!"

They were twin sisters, not identical; one was smaller than the other, but close. Ada and Nala, and, as the days went on, it appeared they had not only been adopted by their two fathers, but also, automatically and immediately, by their 5 'aunties' two 'grandmas', and one 'grandpa', at Bill's Gas Bar and Beauty Emporium.

As they grew from toddlers: underfoot, fussed over, and cuddled, to preschoolers: teased, loved, and taught, their new 'family' was really only worried about one thing:

"How would things go for them, when they started school?"

And, that first day, when they all watched, peeking through the windows, as Ada and Nala, hand in hand, walked down the street, with their new backpacks, and their bit-too-big puffy jackets, and disappeared around the corner, their family was feeling just like every other family feels the first day of school and, it must be admitted, the haircuts and perms, and even the engine and muffler jobs that day, may not have been quite up to snuff.

But they needn't have worried. The kids worked it out themselves, no problem, that first recess, under the big chestnut tree, in the corner of the schoolyard:

"My mom says you have no mother. But how could you be born, if you had no mother?"

"Of course we had a mother. She just died."

"Oh. Do you have a father?"

"Yeah. We have two fathers."

"Oh. Are they married?"

"Yeah."

"Oh, okay. That's alright then. You wanta play tag?"

"Sure."

Oliver—The Musical (Act One)

Michael Jacob Gregory Findlay—his father insisted he be called his entire, unwieldy name, but otherwise paid very little attention to him—was not a bad child. In fact, he was quite an engaging little imp, who never really did anything 'bad', or at least intentionally bad, or at least anything not originally motivated by good intentions.

The Rev had a particular soft spot in his heart for the boy, having gotten in many worse scrapes, for similar reasons, when he was the same age.

"Will someone PLEASE control that child!"

Mrs. Chadwell, the St. Aggie's organist, had little patience with unruly children and, having never dealt with any of her own, felt that children should be 'properly trained up', like small dogs perhaps, and was a dedicated member of the 'Children should be seen and not heard' club.

Most of the rest of the congregation had a sneaking sympathy for little Michael Jacob Gregory Findlay, and tolerated more from him than they might have from many of the other kids in the pews.

Often, when Michael Jacob Gregory Findlay got home from school, the door was locked (The key was under a flower pot) and he would let himself in, to find a scrap of paper, usually taped to a glass of water with some sort of flower in it; a daisy, or maybe a dandelion, and a message: "Gone out. See you later, Sweetie. Get yourself something to eat. Home soon. Love you, Mom.".

(The neighbors considered Michael Jacob Gregory Findlay's mother a 'flighty little thing', and kept an eye on the boy, even if his father considered this 'None of their damn business'!)

After his supper; often whatever was left over from breakfast, Michael Jacob Gregory Findlay would tidy up the place a bit, pick a few weeds in the garden, humming all the while, do his homework, and put himself to bed. Basically, Michael Jacob Gregory Findlay was raising himself.

When his mom eventually did show up, sometimes quite late, she always slipped into his room, kissed his cheek, and tucked him in. Sometimes, if he were still awake, they would sing together. Maybe kid's songs. Sometimes show tunes, or whatever else came to mind and, in the morning, she was always there to make him breakfast. Baloney sandwiches? Chicken salad? Cheesecake? Whatever he wanted, before he left for school.

Generally his dad had already 'gone to the office', to do whatever he did there, and since he frequently, practically always, 'worked late', his son sometimes almost forgot he even had a dad.

Regularly, Michael Jacob Gregory Findlay dropped in to visit the Rev, and Mrs. Rev (as he called her), and sometimes stayed for supper. Mrs. Rev taught piano, and, seeing how interested he was, she started to teach him too.

The Revs didn't have any kids; Couldn't have any kids, according to the 'medical authorities', so they sometimes 'borrowed' Michael Jacob Gregory Findlay, with his mother's permission, when they were heading out on some sort of an 'adventure' that involved children, and which they thought he might enjoy. He always did.

Michael Jacob Gregory Findlay told them he would like to be a 'singer', or 'an actor!', or 'a trucker', when he finally grew up and, even though he was still small for his age, he was growing up fast.

Fast enough to be 12, and a willing and enthusiastic babysitter, for 'the Revlett', when the Rev and Mrs. Rev proved the medical authorities wrong.

Brute

Brute was a pushover. Everybody in town knew it.

So if you were planning on robbing 'Bill's Gas Bar and Beauty Emporium', where Brute was supposed to be a watchdog, you'd have to be from out of town, to be scared.

(But I mean, what were you going to steal anyway? Gas? And how do you steal gas? In a bucket? Or a bunch of scissors, from the Emporium?)

I don't know what kind of a dog he was. Maybe a cross between a dog and a donkey, and a hard-looking dog, with a lot of extra skin, and a scruffy-looking, cross-eyed donkey.

The only thing scary about Brute was his name, and the only beautiful thing about him was his personality.

Brute was the sweetest thing ever. The two little girls he was supposed to guard used to ride him down the street, like a big, hairy 'steed', holding his ears like reins, and him slinging spit from the sides of that loose-lipped, silly looking grin—Brute was a bit of a drooler—as they galloped by.

It nearly killed him, the day they started school. He howled, locked in the back porch of the Emporium, that whole day. You could hear him all over town, and I bet the customers at the Emporium got quite an earful.

But once they let him out, and he realized that Ada and Nala would be coming home again every day, he was all right, and I think he actually started to enjoy his work 'guarding' the Gas Bar and Emporium, as well as half the rest of Saint Agatha.

Cuz there's no way they could have kept him home all the time, short of locking him in the porch every day, which would have been hard on the clients, as well as everyone else in the neighborhood. So Brute roamed the town, generally, at some point in the day, meeting up with Mr. Rooney, and Thug, and 'the rest of the guys', on the front steps of St. Aggies, but never failing to appear at the entry door of the school by 3:20, every weekday, to greet the kids, and receive his due of hugs and pats, usually lying on his back, with his legs in the air and that silly grin on his face, and then walking his charges home –

well, actually, the girls usually rode, until they got too big for him – but during the day, you might see Brute anywhere, at any time, around Saint Agatha.

Except on Sundays of course, when he could be found, just before noon, hanging hopefully around "Pete's Burgers", waiting for 'his girls' to get out of Sunday School.

Mrs. Henley and the Aggravations

'The Rev' and Mrs. Rev, had just produced a new baby—which was a bit of a surprise to them both, as they had been told by numerous medical authorities, after multiple personal and often embarrassing investigations, that this would not be a possibility for them,—and the Rev was looking rumpled and bemused; The usual new parent look; A mixture of joy and no sleep, when the Chairman of the St. Aggies church board approached him after church one morning.

The Chairman of the Board was an 'assertive' man, bordering on 'aggressive', the 'Big Boss' of several large companies in the area, and the Rev, in his weakened state, was no match for him.

Standing in front of the desk, with his hands behind his back, and his chest pushed out (*Like a pigeon*, the Rev thought, irreverently), he announced that 'The Board', as a whole, had decided that it was high time St. Aggies had a 'Youth Group'.

There were apparently 'youths' available (even if this was not obviious in the pews on Sunday mornings), and the other churches in town had 'Youth Groups', so St. Aggies should have one too!

"And we've decided you should lead it, Rev! Good experience for you, now that you're a dad! I'll make sure my boy Jack comes! Nothing like a bunch of teenagers to keep you on your toes!"

He could see that the thought did not thrill the Rev, although maybe all those exclamation marks were just giving him a headache, after such a long night. In fact, the Rev looked terrified by the whole idea, but the Chairman of the Board plowed on:

"You can do it, Rev! It'll be fun. Just have snacks and stuff. That'll bring 'em in!"

And it did. A large group of teens, at least 20, showed up the next Sunday evening for 'Youth Group', but the Rev didn't have a clue what to do with them.

Oh, he had read plenty of books on the subject, frantically, all week, but he had had very little to do with teenagers in his life, and frankly, they scared him to death.

The first meeting was a disaster. When he walked in, that first night, the teens were slumped across their chairs, most of them looking bored and irritable.

The Rev took a deep breath, and chirped cheerfully: "Well! Hello everyone!" He received a few mutters in return. "So!" He clapped his hands together. "Lovely to see you all here! Lots of good brains!" and he laughed, nervously, apparently to himself, as there was no response.

(The imp in his head wondered if maybe they were all deaf.)

"How about we come up with some ideas for this group! You go first!"

(Complete silence reigned.)

"Ok then. How about we sit in a circle?" (The Rev had read lots about circles. Circles were good!)

They shrugged, and eyed him skeptically, as they dragged their chairs into some semblance of a circular shape, and sat on them glumly, staring at the floor.

"First of all, I think we should have a name!" The Rev's voice was beginning to sound a bit strained—"How about we all think of one, then vote on it?"

The kids groaned, rolled their eyes, and shifted in their chairs, but otherwise, there was no verbal reply.

And things went downhill from there.

Finally he gave up, and sent them home early, and drove himself, slumped down behind the steering wheel, looking more than a bit like a beaten dog, back to 'the manse'.

The Rev talked it all over with Mrs. Rev, and the wee 'Revlett', when he got home, and Mrs. Rev listened, commiserated, and kissed him gently on the top of his head. On the little bald spot he didn't know was there, and which she secretly thought was kind of cute.

Then she gathered up their small, howling, 'Revlett', promised it she would feed it, and carried it wearily up the stairs to bed.

By the next Sunday evening, the Rev had given himself a good talking to, and felt a new man; ready for anything.

If the Board wanted him to start a 'Youth Group' then, come hell or high water, he would do it! He would show them all! What was he afraid of anyway? They were just a bunch of punk kids and, by George, they would all have 'fun' together, even if it killed him!

He marched off 'to war', having had his two favorite things: Shepherd's pie, and apple pandowdy (Both on the same night!) for supper. His wife watched him go, and shook her head, and wondered if the carbohydrate high would last him long enough.

That second meeting was not good. Possibly even worse than the first. The Rev did his best. But every time he suggested something, the teens either ignored him, or laughed at him.

"Music?"

"No."

"Games?"

"No way!"

"Fundraising?"

"No."

"Discussions?"

"Are you kidding?"

It was just so discouraging.

He had always thought he was a good person; a good 'Rev', but he just could not seem to be able to bridge the gap. The 'Generation Gap', he supposed it was. Obviously, teenagers were just not 'his thing'. Especially these teenagers.

Sullen, uncooperative, uncommunicative, at least with him. They seemed to have endless things to say to each other, sometimes in whispers, with snickers in between the words.

Of course, he knew they weren't 'bad kids', or at least not all of them. Jeremy, a quiet boy, just looked shy, and Bethany seemed to be reasonably nice. He had his suspicions about a couple of the others though, who, unfortunately, appeared to be the natural leaders in the group.

Overall, the whole thing was a long way from 'Fun'! But then, he hadn't expected to have much fun with them anyway.

By week three, the Rev was to the point of pulling his hair out—and his hair was none too plentiful in the first place—and the group had dwindled down to eight. In other words, down to the kids whose parents 'made them come', and when the Rev brought up the idea of 'a Project'; 'Something for us all to do together', they moaned, and sighed, ('Projects' were familiar, from school, and generally meant 'work'.), and they would not agree.

They all agreed on one thing though: That this 'Youth Group' was a 'stupid idea', and they refused to have any part in making it work, and, in his head, the Rev agreed. Maybe this was a 'stupid idea'; at least for him, to try to lead such a thing, with this bunch of whiney, self-centered, pain-in-the-neck kids!

"I know what!" Jack piped up, "I 'vote'", and he made quotation marks around the word, in the air, "that we get a new leader!" He gave the Rev a challenging look, as the rest of the kids snickered.

But the Rev, finally, had had enough: "Yeah well, too bad," he snapped. "You're stuck with me."

And the teens, and the Rev, in a circle, sat back and crossed their arms, and glared at each other.

"Listen! I know you don't like me, and at the moment, I'm not particularly fond of you all either. In fact you are, at the moment, my greatest source of aggravation! I find you a rude, self-absorbed, bunch of know-it-alls, who care for nobody but yourselves and, after tonight, I'm done with you! But tonight, we are going to visit Mrs. Henley."

(The visit to Mrs. Henley was the Rev's idea. He had decided it was past time these pampered teens saw a bit of 'real life', in person, not just on TV or the internet.)

"And we ARE going to sing Christmas carols to her. Whether you like it or not! So put on your coats, and get in the van, NOW!"

And they did.

It was a subdued and rebellious group he drove that couple of miles into the country, and finally parked in the weeds at the side of the road, just beside the start of a long dirt lane, and by the time they got there the sun, what there had been of it that day, had gone down, and it had been 'sleeting' for days, and still was, so the trek down the mucky lane was grim.

It wasn't any use trying to take a vehicle down there, even the Rev's big old van, which could get through almost anything. And really, calling it a 'lane' was just being nice. It was actually more of a 'track': Narrow and winding, with hidden potholes that were more like 'sink-holes', lurking around every corner, with the whole way lined by two rows of ancient spruces, shutting out the moonlight, and creaking in the wind.

In fact, the whole thing felt more like Hallowe'en than Christmas, and it seemed a long time before the group reached Mrs. Henley's dilapidated old farmhouse, and knocked on the peeling front door, hanging precariously on one hinge, and providing very little hindrance to any cold drafts waiting to slide through.

Mrs. Henley had been 'queer as the crows', according to the locals, most of her life, which may only have meant that she didn't think the same way, or do things the same way, as they did. At some point, 'Mrs.' Henley must have been married, but no husband had been seen for a long time.

(The kids in the neighborhood joked that she'd likely killed him off, and pushed his bloody corpse through a secret hole in the floor, into the cellar, but it's likely they'd been watching too many crime shows on TV.)

She opened the door and peered out at them, then she recognized the Rev, and stepped back while the teenagers navigated the broken stone steps, into the room.

"Watch out for that hole in the floor!"

(The teens' eyes widened, and they edged back against the wall.)

"And steer clear of Bonny. She's in a bit of a mood tonight!"

'Bonny' was a cow, standing in the middle of the kitchen. Not a small cow either. Not a dainty little Jersey, for instance. She was a big, old, black and white Holstein, with protruding hipbones, a hairless tail, long sharp horns, and a nasty look in her eye. No one but Mrs. Henley would have ever thought her 'bonny'.

A beautiful, multicolored quilt was slung across the cow's back, and tied in place with two pieces of twine, one around her neck, and the other under her tail.

For once, the kids couldn't think of a thing to snicker about. They just kept glancing around, at the bare cupboards, and the broken floorboards, and the layers of tattered clothing Mrs. Henley wore to keep herself warm; the signs of poverty and neglect.

"Nice quilt!" Jack finally blurted out.

"Yes," Mrs. Henley nodded, and patted the quilt proudly. "The church ladies gave it to me for Christmas, and I put it on Bonnie here, to keep her snug and dry." (She glanced up at the ceiling, to a small hole in the roof, dripping, and pulled her rocker a bit further to one side, before she sat down.)

The said Bonny turned her head, and shot them all a wild-eyed, malevolent look. Bethany, one of the girls in the group, gasped, and her own eyes grew bigger. Bethany's mother was the president of 'The St. Aggies Church Ladies' group, and one of the best quilters in town, and Bethany had just recognized some of her mother's handiwork, on Bonny's back.

She pressed her lips tightly together. There might actually be some things a person should NOT tell their mother, and this was clearly one of them.

Mrs. Henley pushed herself up from her chair, and hobbled off into the next room. When she came back, she had a tin in her hand. She offered them each a cookie, obviously old, and likely made in her less-than-clean kitchen, and the kids began to refuse the 'treat'.

But one look from the Rev convinced them to change their minds, and they meekly accepted, and ate, their cookies, and smacked their lips, and one of them even said, a bit weakly, that these were 'the best molasses cookies he had ever tasted'. (Which may have been true, from a certain point of view, since he had never actually eaten a molasses cookie before.)

They sang their Christmas carols to her, while Mrs. Henley sat in her creaky old rocking chair and gazed off into the distance, gently smiling. The Rev also smiled, as he watched the teens; 'his teens', who for the first time ever in his eyes, did remind him, slightly, of angels.

After singing, the kids shouted: "Merry Christmas!", waved goodbye, and got out of there as fast as they could. They were uncharacteristically quiet as they slogged their way back through the half-frozen mud, toward the Rev's old red van. But about halfway up the lane, they heard a yell behind them.

It was Mrs. Henley, with her old sweater clutched over her head to curb the winter wind, and a pair of ancient rubber boots, much too big for her feet—perhaps they had belonged to Mr. Henley—running after them. She was out of breath by the time she reached them, and she bent over, with her hands on her knees for a minute, before she could speak.

Then she straightened, reached beneath her apron, and produced the rusty old cookie tin, and handed it to them.

"This is the last of these cookies you all liked so much, dears. You take 'em. You're growing kids, and good kids too I'd say, and I can always tell. Merry Christmas!" and she gave each of them a shy hug, turned on her heels, and limped back down the lane, until she disappeared from sight in the wintry evening darkness.

As they scrambled into the van, nobody said a word. It seemed none of them could think of anything to say.

Then Bethany burst out: "Why does she live in such a horrible place? She should be in an old folk's home or something!"

"Don't think it hasn't been suggested"—The Rev lifted himself into the driver's seat, and began to buckle up his seat belt—"Likely at least a couple of dozen times. But she doesn't want to live in an 'Old Folk's Home'. She wants to live here, in her own home."

"So why doesn't someone help her fix it up?" This from Jack, and then they all chimed in: "It was COLD in there! And did you look at that door? You could see right through it!"

"And she barely has enough to eat!"

"And what if she falls through that hole in the floor?"

The Rev shrugged, and started backing up the van.

As he dropped each of the unusually quiet teens at their homes, they seemed wrapped in their own thoughts, and they didn't actually notice the hint of satisfaction, even pride, in his eyes, as the Rev said goodnight and watched them walk up their nicely-paved driveways, and in through their comfortably solid front doors.

The next day, after school, the group presented themselves at the church office, delegation-like, and handed the Rev a piece of paper; a 'DECLARATION' apparently. (The word was written in capital letters at the top of the page), then they marched back out the door.

The Declaration read:

"We have three demands:

Number one: We wish 'the Rev' to stay on, as our 'Fearless Leader'.

Number two: The 'Youth Group' (which is a stupid name, by the way) is to be called 'THE AGGRAVATIONS',

Number three: We have decided we ARE interested in 'a Project', and Mrs. Henley is it."

And it was signed by them all.

The Rev sat back in his chair; an elderly office chair, well past it's prime, which immediately, possibly for the thousandth time, almost tipped him over backward, and he closed his eyes, and rubbed his hands up into his hair, over the bald spot he knew perfectly well was there.

Jack, who, obviously, had been waiting with the others, outside the office door, stuck his head back in.

"So! See yuh Sunday night then, Rev?"

Their eyes met, and the Rev took a deep breath:
"Yeah. Okay. See yuh Sunday night."

The Writer

['A sneer flashed across his craggy features, and then was gone, before the others noticed'.]

"Jeremy! Breakfast!"

['The shriek burst into the air, as it had dozens—' (No! He scribbled blackly across the word – 'Hundreds'. No! 'Countless'!), 'times before'.] (Umm, that works!)]

['It hovered in the sky, and then disappeared down the tunnel of time.'] (Hey! That's good: 'Tunnel of time'. I wonder if that has two n's or one?)

"Yeah, Mom! I'm coming!"

***

"Can you take out the garbage—"

['The proofs of an endless existence of waste'.]

"before you're off to school?"

['His mother looked haggard. Worn down by the crap'. (No, I don't think I can say that!) 'by the dregs of a lifetime of left-overs, thrown in the bin'.]

"Sure, Mom."

"And good luck on your test, dear!"

['He trudged down the dreary path, as he had done so many times before, and contemplated his sad fate. A life in the salt mines undoubtedly awaited'.]

***

['The room was quiet. Even the mice were tiptoeing; flattened against the walls, like tiny gray spies, as they edged past, behind the teacher' (No 'the warden'). 'Only the deep sighs of the hapless' (Yeah! 'Hapless' I like that!) prisoners, broke the silence, and these were largely ignored, especially by the evil one at the desk.

"Clandestine hands (Hmm. 'Clandestine hands'? I'm not sure if hands can be 'clandestine'? Oh well) passed a stick (No, 'a wad') of gum around, much-chewed by many mouths (Yucch!), but still elastic."]

"All right, class!"

["The blare of the prison bell had broken the silence, raised the dead, and the warden held out her wrinkled paw."]

"Time to stop writing, and hand in your papers! Jeremy! That means you too!"

***

['Another pirate! Over the side into the endless, rolling sea, and another, and yet another! Disappearing into the cold, whirling abyss. Grabbed, and gleefully strangled, by the creatures of the depths. Never to be seen again!']

"Jeremy! Are you still down there? What's taking you so long to put in the laundry?"

***

"Don't forget to brush your teeth, dear, before you go to bed."

"I won't, Mom."

['No! Not again! Run! Run! It's the deadly, germ-killing toothpaste! Grab Auntie Maude, and Grandpa, and don't forget little Germy! We'll hide in that cavity. They'll never find us there'!

'We'll just hope against hope. Pray even, if there is a God of germs, that they don't swish! Not with that green stuff'!

'Hang on everyone! He's swishing! Here it comes! Grab him! Oh, no! There goes Grandpa'!]

***

[She took one long look at him, and her smile hung in the air between them until he grabbed it and pasted it, briefly, across his own face, before it escaped (No, 'flew away') on the wind.

'She looked like an angel, only without the wings, as she stood, mesmerized by his handsome visage'. (I think maybe that's French. I better hunt it up).

'She liked short men. "The salt of the earth," she said. Tall men disgusted her'!]

"Jeremy! Turn off your light, and go to sleep. Tomorrow's a school day, you know!"

"All right, Dad!"

['And the soft darkness enveloped them, together, and transported them into blissful eternity'.]

"I'm turning it off right now!"

(Hey! 'Blissful eternity'. That's good. I'll have to write that down. Where's my flashlight anyway?)

***

"So what do you think our son will be when he grows up?"

"He's only twelve! He's got a lot of growing up to do yet!"

"Yeah, I know. But what do you think? A doctor? Or a lawyer? Maybe he'll have his own shop, or become an engineer, or a writer?"

"Jeremy? A writer! I don't think so! He hasn't an ounce of imagination in him!"

The Best Christmas Concert Ever

Edon played a flute. It kept him from feeling so lonely, living all by himself, so far from any other human beings, especially in the winter. He usually played it to his sheep, when he was out in the fields and, sometimes, if it was cold, in the barn.

The sheep didn't seem to mind, though they didn't appear to be particularly musically-inclined, but Jep, his old sheepdog, seemed to like it. He had inherited Jep, the day he bought the little piece of land with a wreck of a cabin on it, when the owner moved 'down south', to live with his daughter. Jep was old then. He was older now, and Edon dreaded the inevitable day the dog would be gone, and he would be truly alone.

It was cold in Saint Agatha, and the winters were long. People latched on to anything that would break the monotony, and stave off 'cabin fever', so the school Christmas concert was a big deal; a big event, in Saint Agatha.

It was always held in the basement at St. Aggies, cuz the school was too small to hold the crowd.

This year there was a new teacher at the school. Emma was her name. The kids called her 'Miss Emma'.

It was her first year of teaching, and she was finding the kids in the school—there were only 26 of them, but they were from grades one to 9—a bit of a challenge. But she was managing, and she was determined to make this Christmas concert 'the best Christmas concert ever'!.

She knew that the children's contributions were usually augmented by those in the community who had specific talents, but these people, being suitably modest, usually waited to be asked and, being 'new', Miss Emma didn't know who they were. So she pumped her landlady for names of those in Saint Agatha who might have some musical talent, and Edon's name came up.

When she arrived at the farm and looked around, she smiled to herself as she remembered her grandfather's words: "You can always tell a good farmer. His barns are always bigger and better than his house."

She was just about to knock on the cabin door when it opened and Edon stepped out, almost running into her. It was an awkward moment, and Edon, who was a shy man, appeared to want nothing more than to get away from it, but, politely (as his mother had taught him), he invited her in.

Emma could see that Edon had obviously been heading somewhere when he opened the door, so she offered to go with him, and just talk as they walked.

She did all the talking, perhaps a bit desperately after a while, as Edon continued to stare at the ground and only communicate in nods and small sounds, and when they got to the barn, where the animals were housed for the winter, she gratefully accepted the offer of a seat on a bale of straw, as Edon got on with feeding his sheep.

Emma was quite comfortable with sheep. Her grandfather had been a sheep farmer, and she chatted knowledgably about them, as he worked.

'Wooly', the least sociable of Edon's sheep, came and put her head on Emma's knee, for a bit of a scratch under the chin, and when Jep did the same, on the other side, Emma laughed, and Edon looked up at her and smiled. And, to the shock of everyone in Saint Agatha who knew Edon, he agreed to play his flute for her in the Christmas concert.

While she watched the sheep, in the quiet of the warm barn, a 'great idea' sprouted in Miss Emma's brain: What if they had a 'real' Christmas pageant, with real sheep, and a real manger, and Joseph with Mary, on a real donkey? The donkey might be a bit tricky, though she did wonder about 'Brute', but look! She already knew where to find the sheep!

It was 20 below, the evening they all got together at Edon's farm, to create the pictures for the pageant, and the stars were glowing like real stars on real Christmas. The farm kids were comfortable with the animals, but the town kids, not so much. In fact, at least two of the 'shepherds' appeared to be terrified of their sheep.

Edon had a small steel grain silo in his yard. It was shaped like a cylinder with a cone on top and, with the sheep around it, it looked just like a spaceship had inadvertently gone off course, and landed in a field of sheep.

The Rev and Mrs. Rev had given permission for their new little 'Revlett' to play Baby Jesus, but Mrs. Rev balked at the idea of the baby being tucked away under a blanket, and carried, by 10-year-old 'Mary', in the freezing cold, on a 'donkey', into the barn where the baby was to be 'born', so that bit was played by a doll. But it was a real baby in the manger.

The shepherds looked a hefty lot, They had all their winter gear on under their shepherd's costumes (Old sheets with a slit cut for their heads, and tea towel headscarves, with pieces of rope for belts), with the wise men (there were four of them), in tinfoil crowns, and striped bathrobes.

But, you know, they did rather look like kings. They were so serious; so determined to do this right. They were four of the older boys, considerably bigger than their teacher, and they were usually far from serious, but, that night, they measured up, and Miss Emma was proud of them.

Most of the rest of the kids were angels; a whole 'host' of them, all shapes and sizes. Miss Emma couldn't believe they could look so sweet and innocent, when at least half of them had been mischievous brats that day, and pretty well every day. She was proud of them too.

Jep came and laid his head across Emma's knees, as she sat on a bag of grain, taking the pictures, and she talked to him, and ran her hand across his soft, sleek head.

And when 'Joseph', a tall, awkward, 15-year-old, appeared, leading the donkey (Mr. Watson's hairy little pony did look quite 'donkey-like'), with Mary and the not-yet-born baby on board, Miss Emma's eyes misted over.

I don't know that there were actually pigs and chickens in the real manger scene, but there were that night, as well as a couple of cats, and a duck, and Edon's neighbor's milk cow 'Loretta'. But it didn't really matter. The Nativity Scene was perfect.

At least for long enough to take the pictures.

Before Mary fell off the 'donkey, and the shepherds' started a snowball fight, and a couple of the littler angels, who had been looking a bit blue, told their teacher that they couldn't feel their feet anymore, and 'Baby Jesus' began to howl, cuz she was hungry.

Henry Watson took his cow, and 'the donkey', home, and the rest of them all herded the kids into Edon's small cabin, for hot chocolate, mostly courtesy of 'Lorretta', except for the chocolate part of course, and cookies their teacher had baked.

Jep was in his glory that night. Running from kid to kid, begging pats and bits of cookie. That night, he didn't seem old at all. And when Edon went out to move the sheep from the corral back into the barn, Jep leaped over the fence, just like he had when he was a pup; just like he had before he got old, and his old heart gave out, mid-leap, and he dropped into the snow.

Emma watched as Edon gathered the old dog into his arms, and carried him into the barn. He would bury him in the morning—and she waited outside until Edon came out, swiping at his eyes, and stood with her at the fence.

"It was a good way to go," was all he said, and Emma put her hand on his arm, as they leaned on the railing and stared up at the brilliant stars and the dancing northern lights. There was nothing more that needed to be said.

The Christmas concert was a huge success.

The 'Christmas pageant', projected on a bed sheet tacked to the wall in the church basement, with Bill (from 'Bill's Gas Bar and Beauty Emporium'), in his deep bass voice, reading the Christmas story, and Edon quietly playing the flute in the background, brought tears to the audience's eyes. Some cuz it was so moving, and some cuz some of the pictures were just so darn funny.

There were other things: Tap dancing; a play written by the kids, about a cat, and a mouse, and Santa. Nobody really got the point of it, but they all clapped and cheered when it was done.

Hellie and Wellie, the church caretakers, demonstrated their 'clog dancing' abilities, and Sergeant Bell played the fiddle, while they all stomped and clapped to the tunes. Two little grade-oners recited 'Twinkle Twinkle Little Star', with appropriate actions, and Mrs. Chadwell pounded out Christmas carols on the old, slightly out of tune, piano.

And they all sang: 'Here comes Santa Clause', or at least the first verse, over and over (cuz nobody can ever remember the rest of it), until Santa finally got his act together and DID come, and passed out little brown paper bags with a candy cane, and oranges, and nuts, and a couple of pieces of Mrs. Dillon's sugary fudge inside.

And you know, everybody there that night agreed: It was 'The best Christmas concert EVER'!.

And, after it was all over, Edon stayed to help Miss Emma clean up.

Ellie

It was 35 degrees below zero that day. 35 below, and it was Ellie's last day of work, before her maternity leave began.

(She had left it as long as he could, cuz she only got 3 months, and she wanted every minute of it after, not before. She had timed it that she would be stopping just before Christmas too, to take advantage of the few more holiday days, to add to the time.)

Actually, she thought it was likely closer to 40 below—Her thermometer, obviously a 'fair weather thermometer', had quit working—cuz her car's tires were squared off on the bottom, sitting there in the yard, and 'square tires' was one of the signs, along with the fact that your nostrils froze together when you breathed in, that it was 'too cold to be outside'.

The nose thing was happening too. But her clients needed her, and her car would likely start (she'd had the block heater plugged in), so she dragged on her mukluks, and her heavy coat, and, "Way we go!"

It shouldn't be too bad a day. The sunlight, actually still moonlight, was sparkling on the snow, the sky was crystal clear, and most of her clients booked for today shouldn't have any big surprises. Mostly she just wanted to check in on some of her regulars, to make sure everyone was settled and reasonably okay, before the fill-in nurse took over.

The car coughed, and whined a bit, and Ellie held her breath, cuz she really didn't know too much about cars. But then the engine caught, and grudgingly settled into a reasonable hum, as she pulled out onto the gravel road. Her first visit was to a 95-year-old couple who had lived, in a house they'd built themselves, ever since they had immigrated to Canada from Scandinavia, and 'moved up north', via ox cart, almost 75 years before.

They still managed on their own, with their little old dog Burr, who demanded a daily walk even at 35 below, keeping them mobile. Ellie always thought of them as 'true pioneers'.

It was early in the morning, only 5:30 am, and the snow was dry and crisp. It 'squeaked' under her tires, another sign of extreme cold, as the crystals flew up in front of the headlights of the car. The Eriksens didn't live far, and they were always up well before six.

Her second 'client' was more than 2½ hours away, and it wasn't actually a person; it was a place: The community health unit on a tiny First Nation's reserve. Ellie checked in on them regularly to make sure there were no problems bigger than they could handle, and dropped off the supplies they needed. The trunk of her car was full.

She usually enjoyed the long trek to get there, through the morning wilderness, on the raised road, edged with wide ditches like long black trenches on either side of her, in the sparse light of dawn, between walls of gigantic evergreens. It was like a meditation, that drive, and she was always kind of sorry when the trek ended.

This day though, she was a bit less relaxed than usual. Her seatbelt seemed tight at times, and she tugged at it, to loosen the pressure, and rubbed her belly now and then, to relieve the pinch.

(It still seemed unbelievable to her that there could actually be a small, living, human being in there! Like one of those Russian stacking dolls.)

Today it was more like a 'wilderness' out there than ever. It was obvious she was the first on the road; that she was 'breaking ground'. It reminded her of being the first kid to make footprints in a virgin field of snow. She had always loved that.

There was a fair amount of snow down too, but her tires were good, and she had time to spare, so no need to rush.

When she came around a corner, she abruptly realized she was not the only one on the road after all, and she slammed on her brakes, and the rear end of the car fish-tailed, but then straightened.

A moose, young but still considerably bigger than her entire car, was 'sauntering' down the middle of the road. There was no other way to describe it, and she checked her watch, and shrugged, put the car into low gear, and followed slowly behind him.

There was no way to get past, and he didn't appear to even notice her presence, just out for his morning constitutional, and as she watched him, she started to laugh. He did remind her of a loose-limbed teenager. Her nephew walked just like that!

It was another 15 minutes before the moose decided to abandon the easy way, and veered off, across the ditch and into the woods, and Ellie was able to continue her journey, and deliver her supplies.

On the way back, she got behind a 'chip truck', on the narrow road.

You would think following behind one of these huge, impossible-to-pass vehicles would have been a pain, but Ellie loved chip trucks.

The pines grew slowly, way up here in this cold climate, and their sap was tightly compressed into thin rings in the trees, so when it was released by the chipper, it burst out into the air. It smelled amazing, and the scent easily got through to her, even inside the car. It was Ellie's favorite 'perfume', and she was sorry when the vehicle turned off on to a side road, and the sweet, lingering aroma gradually faded.

Ellie never did find her third client of the day. His directions read: 'Turn right across from the red barn, then left at the old schoolhouse, and go about a mile down the road, just past Old Freddy Ryan's dock. You can't miss it'!

But it turned out, she discovered later, that the red barn had been painted blue, the schoolhouse had long since been demolished, and there was no possibility 'Old Freddy's dock' could ever have been seen from the road. Not only that, but 'Old Freddy' himself ("Bless his heart, poor soul"), had passed on ("Must be a good ten years ago now dear!").

Her fourth client lived, with a daughter and son-in-law, in a low house, surrounded by forest, 'over the big bridge, not far from the railroad track', just the other side of town. She was so wizened and tiny, she reminded Ellie of a little bird, tucked into a wheelchair way too big for her.

She didn't seem to notice it though. In fact, she didn't seem to notice anything, and, these days, she seldom spoke, or reacted to anything, except, again like a little bird, she opened her mouth, and swallowed, when her loving family fed her.

They didn't mind. She had loved them, and they still loved her, and when Ellie held her hand, she sometimes laid her own fragile hand on top, like a small blessing.

It was quiet there, peaceful, as they all watched the snow, big flakes now, coming down gently, outside the big picture window, and the woman's family began to talk about the lady, about her life, her love of nature, and the poetry she had written, there in the middle of the woods, before she wasn't able to write, or think, anymore.

"There was one poem," her daughter smiled, "It was my favorite. She called it 'Wild Birds'. I wonder if it's still in there 'somewhere'," and she leaned forward and gazed into the blank eyes: "Mom, Mom?" There was no flicker of recognition. "Do you remember 'Wild Birds', Mom? 'Wild Birds'?"

But there was no answering spark in the tired eyes, and the watchers sighed, almost in unison, and sat back and sipped their coffee and, gradually, began to speak of other things, as Ellie started to gather her gear.

But, as Ellie struggled up out of the low chair, the little lady in the wheelchair began to speak, at first softly, hesitantly, and then with growing confidence, as she gazed out into the snowy sky:

"I'd never really seen the sky

or glanced a peek of heaven,

until I saw the wild birds, the beauty they've been given—"

It was a long poem, and every word rang clear, like a bell, as her listeners almost held their breath, right to the very end.

Then the light in the eyes faded, and the frail lady was, yet again, just a small, tired, bird in a wheelchair.

Silent tears slid, unnoticed, down the listener's cheeks, as Ellie finished pulling on her coat, and they accompanied her out, and they whispered: "Thank you, and Merry Christmas."

Ellie's next client was 'a crotchety old guy'. (Ellie didn't call him that, but everyone else did) who lived all alone in an old house that should have long ago been condemned.

I suppose he could have been called a 'recluse'. He was certainly shy, maybe even more than that, and his neighbors, who attempted to check on him every once in a while but never made it past the front door, were concerned about him.

They had contacted his doctor who had, in turn, contacted Ellie, and asked her to drop in, and do some tests, to see how his brain was working. Cuz the only way anyone was ever going to get him out of that house was to carry him out, probably kicking and screaming, on the doctor's orders.

Ellie knocked. There was no answer, but Ellie knew he was in there cuz there was smoke coming out the chimney, so she persisted and, eventually, the door opened a crack, just enough for one eye to peer through.

"Wha duh yuh want?"

"The doctor sent me," and Ellie explained her errand.

"Interferin' young punk! Not you, Miss. I mean my damn doctor!" (His doctor was close to retirement age.) "You can come in if yuh want. I know yer only doin' yer job!" and the door opened enough to let her through, and then slammed shut behind her.

There wasn't much light in the house, and what there was, was obscured by piles of papers, and magazines, and books, on the floor, the tables, the couches, everywhere.

One of the stacks had a cat on top of it who, typical of cats, gave Ellie one sullen, baleful look, decided she wasn't worth the effort, turned his rump toward her, on his precarious perch, and pretended she, and he, were not even there.

Except for his tail, hanging down, swinging back and forth like a metronome, in front of the pile of books.

The gaunt old man, dressed in faded jogging pants and a raggedy flannel shirt, swept his arm across one of the easy chairs to clear it, and then sat down, in what was obviously 'his chair', across from her, and he just sat there, staring.

Ellie did the same, and, eventually, the old man started to chuckle.

"Yuh got me, Miss! Would yuh like a cuppa tea? The kettle's here somewhere. Orange Pekoe? Or one of them fancy ones in the little boxes my niece sends me? So. What'd yuh want me tuh do?"

The 'thinking test' went well. In fact, the old man aced every part of it.

"So, why do you live here, all by yourself?" Ellie asked him, as she put away her papers.

"It's my home! Where else would I live? One of them fancy retirement places that cost a fortune, with a bunch of stuck up people I don't even know? I'd have to get dressed up every day! (He shivered) Tuh tell yuh the truth Miss, I'd just as soon die, and besides, I'm not 'all by myself'! I got Snoopy here," and he pointed to the cat.

Ellie nodded. She may not have agreed, but she did understand, and they chatted a bit, then she heaved herself out of the chair, and put her hand down to the floor, to lift her bag.

"You want your cat back?"

(The surly character of the first few moments had snuck down, and insinuated himself, unnoticed, into the bag, and was now sound asleep, purring in his dreams.)

"Yeah, I'd miss him I guess, even if he is an old reprobate. You want 'im?" He helped her into her coat, and escorted her to the door. "You come back again sometime, Miss! And don't forget to bring that new baby with yuh!"

Ellie's last client of the day, her name was 'Christina'—Ellie had always loved that name—was dying. Her daughter, 'from away', lived with her now, in her cozy little cottage about a mile outside Saint Agatha.

Christina had been dying for quite a while, without much pain, but inexorably, and when Ellie got there, she realized this might be the day.

The woman seemed lost in her large bed; restless, tossing and turning. Different than usual, and Ellie and the woman's daughter Joanne agreed that she would likely be more comfortable in a hospital bed.

But it was Christmas Eve – Ellie had almost forgotten that – and when she phoned the medical equipment dealer, to arrange for a bed to come, Ellie was told there was 'No way'! that could happen.; That they were 'run off their feet', and there was no one left who could make the delivery before they closed at 6 pm. "So sorry!"

So Ellie and Joanne rolled blankets into bolsters, and tried to surround the woman in the bed, to make her feel more secure, and they took turns holding, and rocking, her. Even the family dog, an enormous, elderly bullmastiff, who had always been gentle and welcoming, seemed disturbed and distressed, and snapped at Ellie, something he had never done before, and so got himself locked in the back bedroom, to provide a background accompaniment of very loud, very mournful howling, that went on and on.

It was almost funny, if it hadn't been so not funny, and Ellie and the woman's daughter shared a wry smile, and rolled their eyes, and Ellie phoned her husband, to let him know that she wouldn't likely be making it home in time for Christmas Eve at St. Aggies, and for him to go on without her.

But at 7:30, a van rolled into the yard, and a man hopped out, and began unlatching the back doors of the vehicle. It was the 'bed guy'. There was 'No way'!, he was going to leave anyone stranded, on Christmas Eve, and he brought in the parts, and gaily put the bed together, with Ellie and Joanne, in the background, providing 'helpful advice', and the three of them laughing together, while he worked.

The minute Joanne's mom was transferred into the hospital bed, she settled, comfortable and secure, and went to sleep.

They let the dog out of the back room, and he immediately came and laid his huge head on Ellie's knees, gazing up at her soulfully, as if to apologize for his previous behavior, and Ellie and Joanne hugged, and wished each other 'Merry Christmas', and Ellie made it home in time for Christmas Eve at St. Aggies.

A few hours later, just past midnight, Christina died, peacefully, in her sleep, and, on Christmas Day, Ellie had her baby. A little girl. And they decided to call her, 'Christina'.

Mary and the Baby

It was a few minutes after midnight, Christmas Eve. Still, clear, and crisp. The traditional Christmas Eve service at St. Aggies had just ended, and the warmth of all those 'Merry Christmas' and 'Goodnights' still hung in the air, while the people shuffled sleepily home to their beds.

Wellie was holding his coat closed. He had a gap at the front where two buttons were missing, and the cold air seemed determined to get at him through that gap, as he and Hellie started a final check on the premises, before going home to their apartment across the street, for a cup of hot apple cider, and then to hit the hay.

Hellie was doing the front, and Wellie the back, but when Wellie got to the side door, where they usually would have met, Hellie wasn't there, so he continued on round, and found Hellie standing, looking stunned, at the front entry, staring down at a cardboard box in the corner of the top step.

"What's up, Hell? Something wrong?"

But Hellie just looked at him, his eyes wide, and pointed to the box. Wellie frowned, and reached down to fold back the blanket that was shoved snugly in and around the edges at the top, and they were so engrossed by the sight which met them, that they didn't even notice the thin shadow, from behind a tree across the street, slip silently away.

"Good Lord! It's a baby! What's a baby doing here?"

"Maybe it's from God, and He sent it down, for Christmas." Hellie's voice sounded strange; like a small boy, awed by a weird and wondrous sight.

But Wellie always had his feet, and his head, firmly grounded on solid earth.

"From heaven, you mean? Not unless there's a Whoamart in heaven, which I seriously doubt," and he pointed to the tag on the blanket.

"So where did it come from then?" Hellie was still whispering.

"He."

"He what?"

"He's a 'he'."

"Oh. How do—No. Never mind. So what do we do with him? Take him to the town office, or the hospital, or the police?"

"Nah. Nothing much open tonight, and he doesn't seem sick or anything." The baby had managed to free his hand and was making a grab for Wellie's silvery beard—"I guess we just take him home."

"Take him home? You mean to our apartment?"

"Yeah well, we can't leave him here, can we? Though I must admit I never did think you and I'd ever be seen carrying a baby across our doorstep. Did you?"

Wellie gathered up the box with the baby in it, and shoved it under his arm, as they headed across the street through the slush.

The next morning, around 7 o'clock, the knock on the door Wellie had been expecting, came, and a thin teenage girl stood, stomping the snow off her sneakers, on the welcome mat in the hall outside their apartment.

"I guess likely you've been expecting me?" She avoided looking at them, and appeared ready to run.

Wellie stood back and motioned her in.

"Where's Jessie? Is he okay?" She looked around anxiously.

"Jessie—" Wellie smiled at her, for the first time, and pointed to the cardboard box wedged securely in the corner of the couch, where Hellie sat, with his arm protectively across the top, as a small foot appeared, and Hellie captured it, and tucked it back under the fluffy blue blanket—"is just fine."

And the girl rushed over, and lifted the baby out of his box, and snuggled him in her arms.

"I just didn't know what else to do!" she sobbed, "I don't have anyone else!"

"His father?"

"He has no father!" The girl sounded angry. Defiant. And Wellie pressed his lips together and looked resigned, while Hellie just nodded, as if he hadn't expected any other answer.

"What's your name?"

"My name is Marylou, but most people just call me Mary." (Hellie raised his eyebrows at his brother.) "And this is Jessie."

She tickled the baby, and he laughed; a joyful gurgle that reminded the boys of swallows chuckling.

"I knew someone would find him, you know. It being Christmas Eve and all."

"But what if we hadn't?"

"I was just across the street, watching. I wouldn't have left him there!"

"So why then?"

And the whole story came out: A mistaken 'love'. An angry parent, who 'wouldn't have anything more to do with her', and yelled that she 'had made her bed, she'd better just go lie in it'!

(And the boys began to realize how young this girl actually was.)

She had tried to get a job, and did manage to secure a casual, part-time position.

"At Whoamart?"

"Yeah. How did you know?"

Hellie lifted the edge of the blanket and showed her the tag.

"Do you need to pay for it?" Wellie asked gently.

"I will."

And he left it at that.

"But I don't make enough money to pay for our room, and for food, and someone to babysit Jessie while I'm working, and I didn't know where to turn!", and the girl broke down again.

"Can you sew?"

"What?" The girl frowned, and swiped her tears away with her fist.

"Can you sew? We need someone to fix our clothes, and do hemming and stuff like that."

Hellie lifted his leg and showed her his pants, with a couple of inches at the bottom held up by a row of safety pins, and a rip in the side seam.

"Sure. I can sew. My mother taught me before she left. I can fix that for you, no problem. No charge," and she smiled wetly at them. "But nobody else is going to pay me enough to keep us both going!" and she hugged the baby again.

"Oh. You'd be surprised."

The next day an advertisement appeared on the St. Aggies' bulletin board, and in 'The Tattler', and in the windows of both Joe's Gas Bar *and* his Beauty Emporium, as well as on the wall at the Manor, and at 'Mr. Ho's Chinese Food Restaurant and Laundry', and bewildered neighbors watched as Hellie lugged an old, antique, sewing machine, which very much resembled the one Mrs.

Chadwell usually displayed in her parlor window, into Hellie and Wellie's apartment.

Marylou continued to work her shifts at Whoamart, but when they all found out how good she was with a sewing machine, she actually had all the work she could handle.

She did her sewing at Hellie and Wellie's, so they could watch over Jessie, and they were assisted by Mr. Rooney and Thug, who also 'Jessie-sat', usually in their snug little office in the basement at St. Aggies, while she did her hours at the store.

Eventually, once everyone realized how skilled she was, Marylou was offered a full-time job, doing sewing and mending, for Mr. Ho's Laundry. and pretty soon everybody in Saint Agatha got used to the sight, just like they got used to most everything else.

Still, you'd have to admit, the first time you saw the two, identical, aging, bearded, 'confirmed old bachelors', pushing a baby carriage down the street, it did give you pause.

Wooly and Friends

It was a rainy, misty, nasty morning, when Edon went to check on the sheep and the count was one less than it should have been: 29 instead of 30. He recounted three times, then sighed. Of course, it was 'Wooly'. It was always Wooly. The sheep with not only an especially thick coat, but 'wooly-headed' as well.

He made sure the rest of the sheep were well-corralled, let his wife know the story, called the dog, and trudged off into the deep woods, at the edge of his small, hacked-out-of-the-forest farm. He knew which way that sheep had likely gone. The way she always went, when she 'escaped'.

(Wooly was a major-league escape artist. He respected her for that; often he had no idea how she managed it. But there were times, like today, when he did have a vision of her as 'mutton pie'.)

She was likely headed for 'the meadow', which was a small patch of lush grass and wild flowers, tucked in a niche between a couple of rocky outcrops, with a small stream flowing through. He often headed there himself, to do a bit of fishing, or when he needed to think, so he could understand the lure of the place.

It was quite a ways from his homestead, and sometimes other animals; big ones, who also had a taste for mutton, went there as well, so Edon would have really preferred his sheep avoid the place. But how do you tell a sheep what or what not to do, once they get an idea into their wooly heads!

The dog, they had called her Fini, bounded around him. She was a new dog, still a puppy really, and a bit wooly-headed herself, although, with a lot of patient training, she was shaping up.

Fini was excited by the fresh new sights and smells, and just glad to be out on a jaunt with her master, and she forged ahead, checking out every trail and every interesting scent she found, but returning when Edon gave the shrill whistle which was her signal to 'check in', and do what she was told.

When they finally got to the meadow, there was no sign of the sheep, so Edon decided, as there was lots of daylight left, he may as well look a bit further afield, and he called in the pup, as they headed deeper into the woods.

It was a part of the land Edon had never been in before, and the forest got thicker and darker, as they got closer to the cliffs, and Fini suddenly darted off to the side, and began furiously barking.

Edon broke into a run, calling the dog. He didn't even see the body on the ground, until he almost fell over it. The man was unconscious, with bleeding cuts, and darkening bruises, and Edon knelt down beside him. Fini kept trying to get past but Edon pushed her away, and carefully raised the wounded man's head, and he opened his eyes.

They were deep brown eyes, and his hair was black, tied back with a strip of leather.

"Who are you?" They both said it at the same time, and the man on the ground grinned. He was really not much more than a boy.

"My name's Charlie," and they introduced themselves.

"What are you doing here?" Again, they both said it at the same time, and the young man chuckled again, and carefully moved himself up into a sitting position, wincing as he pulled himself back to lean against a tree.

"I was looking for my sheep, and I found you instead. Well, actually, my dog found you."

"Likely the wolves got your sheep by now."

"Wolves? I bet you it's that pack that was hanging around last winter. Nearly got some of my sheep then, and looks like they almost got you today."

"Nah. They were only playing with me. If they had wanted to eat me, I wouldn't be here. They just wanted to get rid of me, and I lost my head and ran. I never should have come out here on my own anyway, especially without my gun, but I heard there's a guy in town paying the big bucks for pine mushrooms, and I wanted some of those big bucks in my pocket, and I didn't want to share any. Serves me right.

"By the time I noticed them, the whole pack was around me. They're tricky; I didn't even hear them come. But likely I was thinking about becoming a rich man, 'n likely I was in their territory without an invitation. But the look of them lookin' at me, sizing me up, kinda freaked me out, 'n I just started to run. A couple of miles maybe. Seemed longer.

"I musta bin' pretty good entertainment, cuz they just loped along and kept up to me easy, while I yelled, and stumbled, and fell over half a dozen dead trees." He looked ruefully at his bleeding arms and legs. "I guess that last tumble was a good one. I musta hit my head.

"Then when I opened my eyes, I was staring into yours. Blue eyes. I thought maybe you were a spirit, and I was dead". The boy chuckled again.

"But my head hurt. Still does" He blinked and grimaced "and I didn't think my head would hurt, if I was dead. Hey! Look here though!" And he dug into the leather bag slung around his waist, and showed Edon what was inside. Six large pine mushrooms. "I made $12.00 on the way out!"

Edon smiled and shook his head, and helped the young man, or tried to help him, to his feet. But it appeared cuts and bruises, and a headache, were not the whole story. It looked like a broken ankle could be added to the list.

"Well," Edon shrugged, "we may as well make a start before it gets dark," and with his arm around the young man's waist, and one of Charlie's slung across Edon's shoulders, they started the long trek back home to the boy's village.

"How come you speak English so good? Better than me."

"So well."

"What?"

"'So well'. Not 'so good'. I went to residential school. They beat it into me. Well, to be fair, not ALL of them beat it into me, but some did. I ran away. Ran just like wolves were after me (He smirked), and I made it home and my father met them at the door, with a rifle, when they came to take me back, so I guess they decided maybe I wasn't worth the trouble, and left me there. What about you? Where are you from?"

It took quite a while to get Charlie back home, and by the time they got there they were friends, and Charlie invited Edon and his wife to come to the village for a feast, in Edon's honor, the next week.

It was dark by the time Edon and Fini made it back to the farm, and Edon's wife Emma was anxiously peering out the door, with a lantern in her hand.

But when Edon stopped to look in on his sheep, there was 'Wooly', back over the fence, back in the corral, placidly chewing her cud. She looked up at him, stopped chewing for a moment, decided he was boring, and bent her head to reach for another mouthful of hay.

Rebecca

It just kept raining and raining, and raining some more. Most places it wouldn't have mattered; might even have been welcomed, but like a lot of First Nation's Peoples, Rebecca's Saint Agatha Band had been given a piece of 'the land no one else wanted', as a 'gift' from the government.

In this case, a piece of marsh—'Swamp', Rebecca called it, only without the alligators ('See! There were some positive things'!) so they were actually 'Swamp People', and she shook her head wryly at the thought.

Her neighbors were great. That was another good thing.

Rebecca always tried to think of the good things, as she stared out the window at the rain. She looked across the road, at the farmer's; her neighbor's, yard: A cow was standing on top of the rack of hay, like 'the king of the castle', placidly chewing, while the rest of the cattle stood in the mud.

Smart cow!, she thought.

Rebecca lived with her family; her husband, their three kids, her sister, and their parents, in their house on the reserve. The size was not too bad, but there was only one bathroom, for 8 people, and only one fan in that bathroom, so, on this swampy land, and with 8 people having showers, there was always mold in the house; a continuing 'battle of the mold', and her kids were sick a lot, likely because of that.

But it was 'their house', the house they had been 'given', so they stuck with it, black mold and all.

As she gazed out into the rain, Rebecca smiled as she thought of the girl who had come to see them last week. A nice girl, a bit too serious though, from Ottawa, or Toronto, or somewhere 'official' like that, in a shiny big car.

Rebecca had been planting a rose, out front, when the girl came.

Came to study their 'cultural practices'. She wondered what the girl's own 'cultural practices' were, but she'd been too polite to ask.

Charlie, Rebecca's brother, who was a pretty funny guy, came rushing in during the visit, with his rifle over his shoulder, and told them he'd heard there was a buck down here in the yard, and he'd run home to get his gun. But now he realized it was just a 'Buick'! His eyes danced, and he winked at his sister, over the girl's bent head – Rebecca just shook her own head, and rolled her eyes at him, as the girl industriously wrote it all down.

"Your roses are lovely!" the girl had said, as she looked admiringly at Rebecca's rose bed, on the way back out to the car. "How do you make them bloom like that?"

"I put a fish, and a banana peel, in the soil under them, when I plant them," Rebecca replied calmly, as she patted the dirt down, around her latest rose.

The pen and pad came out again. "And is that a secret passed down from your ancestors?" The girl's pen hovered over the paper.

"Nah," Rebecca smiled, "I read it in Harrowsmith."

***

"Terrible joke. Buck and Buick. Where'd that come from?!"

"Yeah, I know. I just wanted to meet her, and it's the best I could come up with on the spur of the moment. I was gonna use that old 'Indian Car' joke, Uncle Sam told me."

"No way! That joke's so old, it's growing a beard! Even your dog doesn't laugh at it anymore. And what's with Grandpa's gun? I thought you threw that thing away years ago."

"No. I still had it behind the door. It's not loaded. Doesn't work anyway. I was just going for the manly caveman look. You know, slung over my shoulder like that."

"Yeah well, it didn't work. You wanta stay for supper?"

"Accordin' to what you're havin'."

"You'll eat what you're given. Take those boots off though, unless you want to scrub the floor…and leave that old gun outside!"

First Encounter

All he could see was a flowered bottom, sticking out of the encircling bed. It stood out because the flowers on the dress were blue – Forget-me-nots perhaps – in the surrounding sea of rippling yellow daffodils.

Wellie averted his eyes. Good heavens! There were two of them! One in either direction.

He didn't know where to look. So he looked up at the sky, and started to whistle, as if he was just moseying along, in the park perhaps, enjoying the birdies. But, not watching where he was going, his foot strayed off the edge of the sidewalk, and he lost his balance, and fell, sprawling, face down, onto the grass.

He found himself being lifted, one on either side, to his feet, by two surprisingly strong females. His embarrassment made him angry, and he shook himself free, straightened up, and stalked off down the street, slapping at his knees, to clear the dirt off his jeans.

The two gardeners watched him go, then burst into hysterical laughter, which reduced them to tears, as they supported each other, and they, eventually, returned to their weeding, though a little spurt of lingering amusement did escape, every now and then, while they worked.

Wellie pretended not to hear.

But Wellie was not without a sense of humor himself, and as he walked away, under that beard, where no one could see, a rebellious twitch, at the corner of his lips, betrayed him.

Malcolm MacPherson

Malcolm MacPherson (sometimes called 'Monty', by his friends) loved a good funeral. They gave such nice hugs at funerals. Winnie had always given him nice hugs, but, since Winnie was gone, he didn't get much in the way of hugs these days.

If he attached himself to the end of the line of mourners, he found that nobody really noticed him. They were all just so glad to have gotten through the ordeal, and often, they gave him an extra warm squeeze, just for that reason.

He always wore his black suit to funerals. The one his kids had bought him for Winnie's funeral. It was getting a bit threadbare though—Malcolm went to quite a lot of funerals—and he was thinking it might be time to look for a new one at the Mission Thrift Shop.

The music was good too, at funerals, if a bit somber. Sometimes they even had bagpipes, and Malcolm's Scottish roots tingled at the sound, even if those Scottish roots were stretched thin after 6 or 7 generations in Canada. He liked the sermons too. He went to funerals at all different churches; he did not discriminate. He didn't even care if he couldn't understand the language.

In fact, Malcolm MacPherson was probably Saint Agatha's foremost authority on which ministers/priests/rabbis/imams were the best speakers in town, if anyone thought to ask him, or wanted to know.

It was interesting, educational really, to find out about people's lives, when family and friends said their bits at funerals, and Monty particularly got a kick out of the funerals for those they all knew were actually horrible people, and the multitude of pure lies which could, and did, get produced for the occasion; when everyone there knew it was all just a bunch of hooey.

Malcolm didn't go to every funeral in town. You had to pick and choose these things. He never went to young people's funerals; they were just too sad. But he always went to old people's. There was less chance of being recognized there, and, every once in a while, he had even known the person.

Sometimes, if they were really old, there were hardly any people there at all, so he felt like he was 'doing his duty'.

His kids would likely have been shocked, possibly even appalled, if they had known about all this, but Malcolm didn't see any harm in it. After all, the 'guest of honor' was dead, so they obviously didn't mind.

Then there was the food. There wasn't always food, but St. Aggies, and a couple of others, often had 'funeral receptions' after the burial.

Malcolm disappeared for the burial. He felt that was a private affair, and besides, it did seem a bit 'final', if you know what I mean. Personally, he planned on being buried in a cardboard box, or maybe have his ashes scattered off the CN tower, unless his son would climb one of the Rocky mountains, and do it there; a nice thought, but not something he could actually ever see happening.

But after the burial, Monty quietly reappeared for the food, and a cup of tea. The ladies of St. Aggie's did make a particularly good cup of tea, and everyone seemed to produce their best delicacies for funeral receptions. Monty especially enjoyed Mrs. Bailey's sandwiches, with the grated carrot and cream cheese filling, and sometimes families even ordered in the local favorite; broasted chicken, which happened to be Malcolm MacPherson's favorite as well.

He 'circulated' during the funeral receptions, and then left early, and if anyone wondered who he was, or why he was there in the first place, they were too polite, at funerals, to ask.

It was different at weddings. You could usually get away with going to the ceremony.—Malcolm added a flashy tie to the black suit, for those occasions—but the wedding receptions were another matter.

For one thing, unless it was a huge affair, everyone knew everyone else, except maybe when one side of the couple's family was from Australia, or Ohio, or some other foreign place like that, and then you had to fake the accent, which Monty wasn't particularly good at.

The other thing was that there were usually place names on the tables and, at some point, everyone had to sit down somewhere, unless you wanted to spend at least part of your time in the bathroom.

So, after a couple of trial runs, Malcolm decided weddings were just too much trouble, even though he did love the dancing, and he stuck with funerals.

In fact, between the music, and the educational opportunities, the socialization, the food, and the hugs, (especially the hugs) Malcolm

MacPherson's very favorite thing, and something he really looked forward to, was a good funeral.

Just as long as it wasn't his own.

Oliver—The Musical (Act Two)

Occasionally the stars align, and the right people, the right place, and the right time, come together. Such was the case, that spring, at St. Aggies.

The pandemic was finally over, sort of, and everyone was sick to death of talking to themselves, and singing along with the TV commercials, and wondering who on earth that person with the mask on, who'd just yelled, "Hello!" to them from two aisles over at the grocery store, actually was.

Nobody ever did remember who had the bright idea that it might be fun to 'do a musical', but it was time to 'live a little', at least until the next wave hit, and being part of 'a musical' sounded like just the thing.

People came and went in Saint Agatha but, that year, there happened to be a lot of 'musical people' in town. Thus, when the word got around that there might be the possibility of St. Aggies hosting 'a production', and there would be a get-together to discuss this possibility, the response was almost overwhelming: 56 people showed up for that first, tentative, 'dip your toe in the water' meeting: Two choir directors, a voice instructor, the high school bandleader, a random bunch of musicians who, combined, played an astonishing variety of different instruments. Even Mrs. Chadwell, St. Aggie's rather bad-tempered organist, was there.

Artists, carpenters, electricians, a veterinarian, 'the Girls' and Jim and Lennie from the Beauty Emporium, a police officer, two kindergarten teachers, one mechanic ('and a partridge in a pear tree').

A troop of 'weird people' (Mrs. Chadwell's words), who had previously been involved in 'theater', wandered in (late), plus a whole bunch of others, of all ages, who had never before set foot on a stage, but just thought it might be fun.

Hellie and Wellie came: "Just tuh see what's up," and they even brought Mr. Rooney and Thug along.

It's a good job the Chairman of St. Aggie's board was there, cuz it was chaos, but he quickly 'whipped them into shape', or at least got them all to sit down and shut up, and then handed the mike over to the Rev, who had had the foresight to come heavily armed with a big box of magic markers and his stand-up flip chart.

(He had assumed he wouldn't require anything more lethal. This was Canada after all so, thank God, he probably shouldn't need a gun, and besides, he didn't own one anyway.)

It certainly looked like there was no question of interest in the project, so the next question was: "What Musical did they want to tackle?" and with limited funds for things like production rights and costumes, and limited options for space, since St. Aggies was the only place in town with a stage, what was actually possible?

A committee was formed, to investigate the options, and then they all had coffee, and Timbits, and everybody went home.

It took a couple of weeks to sort it all out but by the time they met again, the stage was set, so to speak, and 'OLIVER' appeared to be the best fit (and the cheapest) of the musicals considered.

A few of this motley crew, which had quickly expanded to a motely crowd, pulled some chairs aside into a corner, and wrote down the names of those they thought would be best to manage the different bits of the production, and possibly fit some of the acting roles, and this 'document', written on the back of a recycled brown paper bag, was then presented to, and approved by, almost everyone.

Notes from a Brown Paper Bag:

(With side comments from *'The Production Team',* sitting over in the corner.*)*

Music:

Choir directors
Voice instructor
Mrs. Chadwell (St. Aggies organist)—*'She's gonna be trouble!'*
School band teacher, etc.?
(Mrs. Chadwell, strongly, felt that she should be the boss of the music, but she, eventually, agreed to be in charge of 'the more difficult pieces'—Which

only goes to show the Rev's excellent negotiation skills, and prevented the breakdown of the entire affair before it even got started.)

Publicity:

Mrs. Pickett (Saint Agatha's tireless town gossip).
'That woman can spread news—even when it's all fluff—faster and further than anyone else I know!'

Hair and Makeup:

Jim and Lennie and 'the Girls' (From 'Bill's Gas Bar and Beauty Emporium').

Head of Costuming:

Marylou (with Jessie in tow)

Cast Director:

The Rev.
 'He's a pretty good judge of character.'
 'Yeah, and he can talk almost anybody into almost anything.'
 'And he says he was in OLIVER in high school, so he should know the thing inside out.'

Small Animal Control:

Docky (A father of 4, and the town vet).
(This job involved dealing with Mr. Rooney—and Thug, in case he snuck in, which was highly likely—as well as the management, feeding, and watering of all the 'wretched urchins', including Marylou's Jessie, and any other minions who showed up at practices.)

Procurement:

Mrs. Wakita?
  '*Good idea! She knows everybody in town!*'

"What's 'Procurement'?" Hellie whispered.
"Finding stuff."
"Ah."

Undertaker:

Mr. Unger (Saint Agatha's local undertaker)
  Note: '*Refused. Said it would be "bad for business". Will lend us a (used?) coffin though.*'

(So they ended up casting Malcolm MacPherson for the role, cuz he already had a black suit.)

Undertaker's Wife:

Mrs. Unger
'*That woman has probably never screamed in her life, and she has to scream and fall backward into a coffin!*'
  '*Likely need a lot of practice.*'

Wretched Urchins:

School kids?
(Two days after the meeting, a whole pack of bedraggled children including Evan, talking a mile a minute, and Ada and Nala, from 'Bill's Gas Bar and Beauty Emporium', all in tattered hand-me-downs, showed up at the church door.

It appeared the first thing the Rev had done was to send a note out to Saint Agatha's two schools, and the Sunday Schools, to recruit: "Wretched urchins! The more the merrier!"

They did end up having to cut it off at 35 though, cuz if there were more than that, some wretched urchin would most likely end up falling off the stage, but, after a 'strike', complete with signs, by the 'over 35s' and their mothers, the wretched urchins ended up alternating performances, which was just as well, cuz by the time the show was over, it was WAY past their bedtimes.)

Thieves and Pickpockets/Artful Dodger

The Aggravations?

(The teen 'Aggravations' did make quite credible thieves and pickpockets, and doubled as 'policemen' when needed, and Jack, as the cocky 'Artful Dodger' fit perfectly into both roles, smirking broadly all the while.

(Note: Mrs. Henley gladly lent 'her kids' some of her ragged clothes for the play, and when these somehow 'got lost', she accepted newer replacements the teens told her they had 'found around home').

Policemen

Sergeant Bell?

(It was no surprise when Sergeant Dingwell Bell – His friends called him "Ding" – from the RCMP constabulary just across the corner, tried out, and was approved, as the 'Chief of Police'. He was 'a natural', and even came with his own (decommissioned) old uniform—which was a good thing cuz he was a big man, and Marylou and her costume people were having enough trouble as it was.

His old uniform was a bit snug, but he managed, and it rather added to his 'persona'. His 'policemen' turned out to be quite convincing too, probably because half of them actually were police officers. (Sergeant Bell had commandeered the three 'newbies' from the station.).

Nancy

Ask at Teen Center?

('Nancy', recruited from the teen help center downtown, was, in reality, as well as in the fiction of the play, a 'runaway', from a family who didn't deserve her. She was being assisted by the staff at the center to find somewhere she would fit in, and Saint Agatha, at the moment anyway, appeared to be it.

She was sweet, and she didn't really have to fake the lost, fragile quality the Rev had imagined for their 'Nancy'. It was her own look, before she had started to find herself.

She couldn't really sing, at least not at first, but like the Rev said: "Sometimes talent is born, and sometimes it's made," and he confidently handed her over to their choir directors and voice instructor.)

Bill Sykes

"I can't think of anybody in town that bad. Can you?"

(Using a bit of 'poetic license', the Rev finally decided to cast both Hellie and Wellie as 'Bill Sykes', the truly evil villain of the show, and 'The Sykes Boys' became the stuff of nightmares, until their makeup came off, and everyone realized it was 'just Hellie and Wellie'.

Even Mr. Rooney got involved and, with a bit of theatrical 'dirt' smeared here and there, made a most disreputable-looking 'hound', for 'The Boys'. Thug had tried out too, and lots of people thought he would have been great for the part, but he didn't make the cut, cuz he refused to do what anybody wanted him to do.)

* * *

By the end of another two weeks, the Rev had managed to fill pretty well all the needed roles, except for the two most important: 'Fagin', the sleazy and despicable taskmaster of the child criminals, and 'Oliver', the child star of the show.

The Rev wanted these to be 'perfect', and he saw them clearly in his mind. But, in spite of lots of tryouts, 'perfect' had not yet shown up, and the Rev was feeling a bit discouraged about it. Not yet without hope, but getting there.

Talking to the 'visitors' at the Mission was part of the Rev's daily routine. He enjoyed meeting all the different people who came there, for such a variety of reasons, and he felt like he could, at least sometimes, be helpful, even if it was only to provide a listening ear.

195

That morning he was being listened to himself, over a cup of coffee, describing his search for 'The Perfect Fagin', and the portrait in his mind, to Gwynn, one of the regulars at the mission, who had been involved in shows himself, in his younger, more stable days.

Gwynn was describing some of these times, when he abruptly went silent, reached out and clutched the Rev's arm, and pointed, and the Rev turned and saw him: 'The Perfect Fagin', standing in the Mission doorway.

He was thin, and tall, even though he was stooped over so he looked less tall than he really was, and he had lank, gray hair, sprouting out from the edges of a mostly-bald head, and thick, shaggy eyebrows, over startling, almost-colorless, gray eyes. ("Like a wolf!" Gwynn whispered.)

He wore a saggy, sad, brown overcoat, and a long, faded-gray, knitted scarf, slung across his skinny neck. He even shuffled as he walked, likely only because his shoes were too big for his feet, but still, it added to the image, and he was flicking his startling eyes here and there, across the room, 'casing the joint'.

"Look Rev," Gwynn breathed out the words. "He's even got a twitch in one eye!"

There was no question about it. He was perfect; 'The Perfect Fagin'. But what was he like really, and would he want to play the part?

The Rev had found that most of the people he met at the Mission were good people. Good people with troubles, and it was the troubles that needed sorting out, rather than the people themselves.

He beckoned to the man, to come sit with them, and grabbed another cup of coffee, and held the cream jug over it. The man nodded, and then sat down across the table, as the Rev handed him the cup, and pointed to the sugar bowl.

It was more than a bit awkward, getting to the point, but, as they talked, and although he was a bit vague on where he came from, and how he got there ('Hopped a train from somewhere' was all they got), it became obvious that this was 'a good guy'. That he was just another person who had tripped, and fallen through the cracks.

It was also obvious that Gwynn was getting impatient. Impatient enough that he finally burst out: "Oh, come ON, Rev! Are you gonna ask him or not?"

The man frowned, his unruly eyebrows almost covering his eyes, and he stiffened, and sat back in his chair: "Ask me what?"

"The Rev is looking for someone to play Fagin, in 'Oliver', and we both think you're perfect, that's what. Right, Rev?"

The man's eyes widened, and one bushy eyebrow rose: "You want me to play that disgusting old crook, in your show?"

"Um. Well. Yes, actually." The Rev stuttered to a stop, looked down into the dregs of his coffee, and then glanced up, sideways, at the man. "I don't mean it as an insult or anything, it's just—"

But the man held up his hand. "I'd love to!" he said, and his thin lips twisted in something at least resembling a smile. "As a matter of fact, I've done quite a bit of acting in my time, and I've always wanted to play that role."

"Lordy, Rev! Look at that! He's even got a couple of teeth missing, just like me. He really is PERFECT!"

"One down. One to go," the Rev commented to his wife, who had been following the drama over the past couple of weeks. "But where on earth are we going to find the perfect Oliver?"

Michael Jacob Gregory Findlay, who had been invited for supper, was sitting on the floor, entertaining the Revlett, and singing a sweet little lullaby to her, as usual, as he pushed her in her baby swing.

It is funny how people sometimes can't see, or hear, what's right in front of their noses, but, this time, as the Rev, and Mrs. Rev looked up from the scene on the floor, the light finally came on, and their eyes met.

And they smiled.

Timmy Titmouse

"So little Timmy Titmouse never got justice after all then?"

"That's the whole point of the story, Sir. Timmy Titmouse was guilty. He did the thing."

"No! Not little Timmy! He was guilty after all? I don't believe it!"

"It's true, Sir."

"Well, I'll be darned. Mice just ain't what they used to be are they, Sergeant Bell?"

"No, they are not, Sir, at least not all of them. I'm sure all mice are not painted with the same brush though, Sir, even if this one was a bit of a rotter."

"No, I suppose not. But still, it is a disappointment. He seemed like such a nice little chap."

"You can't always tell, Sir. Sometimes they can be sneaky little beggars."

"True. That's true. Fooled me in all those bedtime stories, I'll tell you that. I think perhaps I'll not tell the kids."

"Yes. Best not, Sir, if you think it might upset them."

"Do you think you could maybe change the ending?"

"Change his personality, you mean?"

"Yeah. Just soften it up a bit. Give him a break?"

"No, Sir, I couldn't do that. That'd be a lie, wouldn't it, Sir? And besides, 'Once a rotter, always a rotter'."

(Sergeant Bell wrote children's stories, as a hobby. He was a big man. Big in every way; like Santa Claus, only bigger. Some people, especially the 'bad guys', were scared of him, cuz even if he was a gentle giant most of the time, he had no tolerance for crime.)

"By the way, Sergeant, I always thought a titmouse was some kind of a bird?"

"Not this time, Sir. Definitely a mouse, and you can't always tell with last names, can you, Sir? I once knew a fellow with the last name of 'Good' and he wasn't good at all."

"Yes. I suppose you're right there, Sergeant Bell. Still, it is surprising how often last names do fit though. Sometimes, they're right on!"

The two police officers, absorbed in their conversation, passed out of earshot, and the puzzled-looking man on the hard bench, in handcuffs, caught red-handed in Whoamart, with a pocketful of expensive things he hadn't paid for, shivered.

His last name was 'Goner'.

The 'Memoire'

The Boys had, for some reason, recently decided that their brains were 'going to mush', and they should do something about it; something to 'improve their minds', so they joined a new 'writer's group' which had just started up at St. Aggies.

Neither of them had actually ever 'written anything' before, except when they were at school of course but, even then, only when they hadn't been able come up with an excuse to get out of it.

(Part of the reason for this unaccountable enthusiasm for such an uncharacteristic endeavor may have had something to do with the 'mentors' of the group, but more about that another time.)

The first 'assignment' was to write a 'memoire'. So Hellie and Wellie enthusiastically went down to Dollarama, and bought a big package of pencils ('Free sharpener included!'), a couple of erasers, and half a dozen pads of paper, and got right down to it:

"What is a 'Memoire' anyway?"

"No idea. Something like a memory, maybe?"

"Yeah. That sounds right. We should be able to do that, ay? You go first Boot, and I'll write 'er down."

"All right." Wellie settled back into his chair, and closed his eyes.

"It was a dark and stormy night."

"What! You're going to start with: 'It was a dark and stormy night?' Nobody actually ever says that, you know."

"Yes, they do so!"

"When then? When do they actually say that?"

"When it's a dark and stormy night. And besides, I'm not saying it, I'm writing it. Well, actually you're writing it. So get on with it and stop whining.

"You don't like the way I was gonna start it, I'll start it different. Besides, it was actually the mornin'. So: Once upon a time—"

"'Once upon a time? Once upon a time!' Is this a fairy tale?"

"Will you stop interruptin', or we'll never get this done! All right then, I'll just jump right in:

"Once a year me 'n Sammy used to go moose huntin'. Sometimes we even saw a moose, but bein' as we were both such bad shots, he was safe enough."

"Well, one day we were out in this marshy place, in our little boat—We called her 'Nellie'—that we always took with us in the back of the truck. We had some sandwiches, and a thermos of coffee, and we were just layin' back, with our fishin' lines out, not catchin' anything, but we really didn't care, when this big bull moose come out of the woods, the other side of the bulrushes."

"He was tops 30 yards away, and he was big. Man! Biggest I ever saw. Even bigger than that Bruce that comes to watch the soccer games.

"Well, it seemed an awful shame to shoot him, and the idea of us maybe missin' a good shot, which was likely, and just hurtin' him instead, didn't sit right either, so we stayed there quiet, just watchin' him, as he ate his way toward us.

"Then Sammy got this funny look in his eyes. Sam always talked about the time he went 'out west', 'n played at bein' a cowboy, before he smartened up 'n come back home, 'n settled down."

["Shorten it up a bit, will yuh Boot? My hand's startin' tuh cramp."

"You cannot 'shorten up' a piece of fine literature!"

"Yeah, yeah. Alright, just carry on then, Shakespeare. Only take a breath now 'n then, tuh give me a chance tuh catch up. 'N if I lose the use of my right hand, maybe even my whole arm, we'll all know who to blame."

"Are you done belly-aching? MAY I continue?"

"Hey! Don't go all hoity-toity on me! Okay, drive on, Wellington!"]

"So anyways, Sammy got this funny look in his eyes, and he grabbed the rope we always kept in the bottom of the boat, 'n, slow, slow, he stood up, 'n he started to swing that rope, real easy, back and forth.

"I had no idea what he was up to 'til that minute, 'n neither did the moose.

"To tell you the truth, I think both of us got the point at the very same time, cuz the moose's head came up, and his eyes bulged, just the same as mine did, the very second Sammy threw that rope, and lassoed that moose.

"Seems to me there was kind of a little break in time there, when everything just stopped; 'When time stood still', likely they'd say in a book, before all hell broke loose.

"That moose was sure not happy about bein' lassoed like that, especially right in the middle of his breakfast, and he gave this big sort of bawling, snorting sound, 'n he tore off back into the bush.

"Sammy lost his balance and fell back into the boat, but still hangin' on to that rope like grim death, with me holdin' on fer dear life to Sammy, 'n to Nellie's side, while she bucked and rocked like crazy in the water.

"She was just a light little boat, aluminum, so she skimmed across the water pretty good, though she got stuck in the mud for a minute there, at the edge of the bank, 'n nearly up-ended."

["Slow down! Yer talkin' too fast!"

"Oops. Sorry. Got a little excited there.

Now where was I before I was so rudely interrupted?"

"Stuck in the mud."]

"Right. Well, even when the boat smacked into the bull rushes 'n the weeds 'n stuff, it wasn't too bad, but when we hit the woods, we were in big trouble.

"I don't know why Sammy didn't just let go of the rope. Likely he just never thought of it, or he was too busy still playin' cowboy, or maybe the rope got caught somewhere on the boat, I don't know.

"But for whatever reason, he didn't, and the last thing I remember was us hittin' a big old pine tree, 'n Nellie's front end just sort of rearing up, like she was trying to climb it, and Sammy 'n me landing in the brambles at the bottom, 'n the picture of that moose, plunging like a mad thing through the bush, dragging poor Nellie, crashing back and forth, from tree to tree, behind him, until they both disappeared into the mornin' mist.

"We only ever found a few pieces of the boat, 'n my good thermos, lookin' like the moose had sat on it, and maybe kicked it a couple of times too, just for good measure, 'n the rope, with a bit of the front of the boat caught in it, way up in a tree.

"It took us a while to get back to the truck. Sammy's arm was bruised up pretty good; turned out it was broken.

"But you know the thing he was maddest about, was losin' his favorite fishin' hat, cuz he said it always brought him luck. Though I'd say it didn't work too good that day, 'n served him right!

"We did end up with a great story though, and I bet that moose had a good one too, to tell his missus, when he finally made it home.

"'N that's the last time we ever went moose-huntin'."

"Whoa, Boot! (Hellie shook his hand to restore the circulation). This is a pretty good story, even if it is all just a pack 'o lies!"

"Tis not a pack 'o lies."

"Tis so. You never did all that!"

"Not me. A fella at the park told me it. I just memorized it, and yuh know, I think I told it better than him!"

"Hey, that's not right then! This is supposed tuh be a 'memoire'. It has to be about you."

"About me? Nobody told me that. You just said it had to be a memory. You never said it had to be MY memory."

"Well, yeah. That's why it's called a 'MEmoire'."

"Well now. I suppose I could pretend it was about me. Nobody'd know the difference, do you think?"

"So then it *would* be just a pack 'o lies?"

"Yeah."

"Okay, I can live with that. Carry on then," and Hellie shook his hand in the air again, licked the end of his pencil, and poised it expectantly over the pad of paper.

"What do you mean: 'Carry on'? I'm done! That was the end of the story."

"Oh! Okay. I'll just write 'The End' here at the bottom then, 'n that's that!"

The End.

***

["So what about your Memoire, Hellie?"

Hellie had dropped in early to the church office, for a coffee and a chat with the Rev, and was just getting ready to leave.

"Nah. To tell you the truth, Rev" (he leaned forward, boosted himself out of the chair, and headed for the door), "I think I'm more a poet than a writer," and he blushed—or at least that's what the Rev thought it was. It was hard to tell, with all that hair in the way.—"In fact, I'm thinkin' I might try my hand at writin' a 'Love poem'."

And Hellie turned and disappeared down the hall, while the Rev sat, with his mouth open, and watched him go.]

Oliver—The Musical
Spotlights and Sidelines

It was finally opening night for: 'OLIVER-The Musical'!.

There are two directions for the word 'finally': The positive, as in: "Yay! This day is finally here!" and the negative, as in: "Oh no! This day has finally come! I'm going to die!"

The cast of OLIVER, frantically getting ready in the basement at St. Aggies, alternated between the two.

Part of the Rev's job in the production could be described as 'smoothing the waters', which was sort of a cross between trouble-shooter, and referee, or perhaps 'lion-tamer', in the case of 'Fagin' and Mrs. Chadwell, the St. Aggie's organist. Fagin was a teaser, and a practical joker, and very skilled at it too, and Mrs. Chadwell was particularly susceptible.

At the moment though, the Rev was standing back, leaning on the stair rail, watching the choir.

The St. Aggies choir members, who doubled as 'back up singers', and 'townspeople', as OLIVER required, were presently 'in a state': Running back and forth for no reason, hunting for things that were not lost, calling to each other in high, excited voices.

(The choir always reminded the Rev of a bunch of birds, though he certainly would never have told them that. Budgies actually, when they had their blue gowns on. Like the budgies he had seen one time in a pet shop, with their wings clipped, all in a big box together, meeting and greeting and chirping away at each other, then rushing on to the next cluster of birds, to do the same thing all over again.)

He smiled, as he watched them fondly. At the moment, they may have looked like a flock of flustered birdies, but they were HIS flock of flustered birdies.

I'll not describe the show to you. Those of you who have seen it will know, and those who haven't seen it should.

The Saint Agatha Tattler used words like 'Spectacular' and 'Amazing', and 'Extraordinary' and, by the end of the run OLIVER even made it to: "A triumph!"

But the guy who owns the paper was the brother of OLIVER's Stage Manager, and the brother-in-law of the lady who took the tickets at the door (and who also made 'extraordinary' pecan butter tarts at Christmastime, and gave them out to all her relatives), so you may need to keep those things in mind, and take these accolades with a grain of salt.

Personally, I would say: 'pretty good' would be quite accurate, and maybe even on the low side.

St. Aggie's amateur troupe did their best to create the pictures, and the sounds, and send them out to the avid 'theater-goers', on the other side of the footlights, and, like all such productions, some of it was just passable; some bits were not quite what was expected—Like when Mr. Rooney, as 'The Hound', just couldn't hold it in a minute longer, and peed on the, obviously authentic-looking, streetlamp in the middle of the stage, while the audience hooted with laughter – and some moments were amazing, like Nancy's solo: 'As Long as He needs Me', sung alone in the spotlight, sobbing, on her knees on the floor, in her glad rags, after one of the 'Sykes Boys' had (theatrically) viciously slapped her.

Nancy's amazing voice, soaring to the rafters of the old church, left hardly a dry eye in the house.

And then there was Lillian, from the St. Aggies choir, pelting out bar songs, as the slightly inebriated barmaid behind the counter, adding just the right note (or not!) to the rambunctious gang choruses.

The St. Aggies' Mission folk made up the enthusiastic, and mildly rowdy, 'patrons of the arts', for the dress rehearsal, with Gwynn in 'the best seat in the house', in honor of his role in procuring 'The Perfect Fagin' for the show.

The St. Aggies' stage was not large, and it was hard to know what to do with all those actors, so none of them disappeared over the edge during the larger street scenes, until someone—Mrs. Chadwell always claimed it was she—had the bright idea of using the entire 'theater' as a stage, and they did. So, each night, the audience members were surrounded with, and infiltrated by, 'wretched urchins', in every corner, sitting on the floor, begging, playing dice, etc., while many of the rest of the cast, sitting among the crowd, gradually 'leaked out', on to the stage, as required:

"Excuse me, dearies. Can yuh not all just clump up a bit, and let me through? They're needin' me bad up there!"

"Just move yer big feet a tad, Love, if yuh don't mind. I'm tryin' me best tuh get past yuh."

It 'worked a treat' and the audience loved it.

Gumdrop

They called her 'Gumdrop' because of the bright pink 'beanie' she always wore, perched on the top of her head, to cover a patch of thinning hair, and also because she was very round, and very large, and kind of 'squishy-looking'.

She would have liked to be less large. She faced blatant prejudice, bordering on verbal abuse, every day, because of it, and she had tried, must be dozens of times, to change her body. But it was hard, and after a while, impossible, to make any real progress.

She worked as a night 'watchwoman' at Tims. It was not an easy job cuz it was like working in one big temptation factory, and because the job required her to be on her feet for 8 solid hours in a row.

After a while, she just got so tired of it all; tired and angry, with what her grandmother called 'her lot in life' that, though she actually had quite a sunny personality, some people also started calling her 'The Grouch'.

She did have one small beacon of light, in her daily grind: Every morning, on her way home from work, she dropped in at Sundown Manor, on the other side of town, to visit her grandmother, and sing to her. Singing was her joy; perhaps her only joy, at the moment. She had made her living from it, when she was younger, as an opera singer.

The people at the Manor got to know when she was coming, and would start to gather round, as did the staff if they weren't too busy, and beg her to, "Give us a song, Marie! Give us a song!"

And she would 'give them a song', like a small, personal gift, every day, before she went home to sleep through to her next shift at Tims.

When she heard about OLIVER, she wondered if, maybe, she could possibly be involved, even if it was only to do some small thing, like clean up after practices? Simply to be close to the music.

But she knew, in her heart, that they probably wouldn't want her. Certainly not anywhere near the stage!

Her grandma could tell something was on Marie's mind – Grandmas can always tell—and gradually that something was teased out into the light. Her grandmother thought it was a great idea, and encouraged her to: "Go! Go this very day, before you change your mind!"

It turned out to be the best thing Marie had done in a long time. Even though it was tricky juggling her work hours and she was often exhausted by the end of her day, just being part of it lifted her up, made her thoughts lighter, opened up her world. Just being around the songs, even if she wasn't singing them.

The 'clean up crew' had no idea Marie could sing, until one day they heard her unconsciously joining in with the choruses, at practice.

"What on earth are you doing down here, stacking chairs, when you should be up there!" and they, almost literally, dragged her out of her self-imposed exile, onto the stage, and into 'the streets' of OLIVER.

When the show run was over, and the bows, and shouts of, "Bravo! Bravo!" were long gone, 'Gumdrop' didn't really look any different than she had before. Except when you saw her face: Instead of defeat there, it seemed to shine, like the glow from a precious jewel, and she no longer sat alone, far from others.

Instead, they gathered around her, as if they were drawn to the light, as they coaxed her to: "Give us a song, Gumdrop! Give us a song!"

["That's terrible! Calling that woman 'Gumdrop'!"

"What on earth are you talking about? Why is it so terrible? We call her 'Gumdrop', because she's so sweet!"].

The 'Outing'

Bethany Wakita, newly licensed, braved the craters in Mrs. Henley's long, rocky laneway, driving her mother's shiny new Cadillac, to pick up Mrs. Henley for 'an outing': Opening night of 'OLIVER'.

And Mrs. Henley laughed so hard (even in places which were not really meant to be funny) that the teen 'Aggravations' just had to take her out for ice cream after the show, to 'settle her down', before they dropped her back off at her home.

And, surprisingly, Bethany's mother never did seem to notice the dents in the back bumper of her brand-new car.

Olivia

Dan loved Olivia. At least three or four times a week. She knew he did love her, cuz he told her so, at least three or four times a week. No one had ever really loved her before, at least not the way Dan did. And she loved Dan.

And if she didn't feel like loving him, he sometimes hit her.

Of course he did! It was his right, cuz she was 'his girl'; 'Dan's Girl'.

Sometimes he asked Olivia to do other things, with other men. She didn't really want to, but she did it. She'd do anything for Dan.

Dan had other girls too, of course. Men were like that; they 'had their needs', as Dan would say. But Olivia knew she was Dan's 'Main Girl', and she was proud of that, and besides, if he hit her, afterwards he always said he was sorry, and sometimes he even bought her a little present, and she'd say she was sorry too, and then they'd be okay, and Dan and she would walk down the street together, with Dan's arm across her shoulders, and she would feel happy again.

On her birthday, her 17th birthday, 'Dan's girls' all got together and bought her a ticket, for opening night, to go see the musical at St. Aggies. Olivia had never been to a musical before and she loved music, and they joked that her name was so much like the name of the show that it was 'karma'; meant to be!

She had never been in the church before either, and she'd always wondered what it looked like inside. She even wore Dan's latest present; a cheap bright pink feather 'boa', with some tendency to molt, to celebrate the occasion.

It was a wonderful show. She laughed, and she even cried, especially when they were teaching that poor little boy to steal and do other things he shouldn't; to do 'anything for them'! Couldn't he see they were using him? That they didn't really love him? Olivia knew it was only a show, not real, but still!

Dan's arm felt heavy across her shoulders, on the back of her seat—Funny how she had never noticed that before – so she shrugged herself out from under the weight, and told him she had to go to the washroom.

She left the boa behind on her chair.

Olivia seemed to be gone for an unusually long time.

But Dan didn't really notice.

Li Ho

I don't know how they managed; those men. To make their way halfway across the world, across a wicked ocean, leaving their wives and families behind (to follow 'later', 'sometime', 'if things worked out'.) 'Things' must have been pretty desperate back home, on the other side of that ocean, for those men to come at all. And for what?

To build a railroad, to extend all the way across this huge land, through vast forests, and lakes, and muskeg; over mountains, and across dry 'bad lands', which really were bad, all on the whim of what seemed to them to be a 'crazy man's dream', to unite a country.

Under baking sun, through pouring rain, and freezing blizzards, and swarms of bloodthirsty black flies, they worked. Some learned the new language; a very difficult and different language from their own, and took on 'western culture', as best they could, and some did not, or could not.

An alien race in a strange land. Sometimes treated, by bosses and fellow-laborers, without respect. Called names, and worse, as if they actually were unwelcome aliens, from another planet, rather than just another branch of the same human family.

By the time the railroad was completed, many of them had died and, literally, become part of that 'crazy man's dream'. But others survived, and Li Ho was one of these.

(His actual name was Ho Li, with his surname first, as was his tradition, but the foreman at the work camp said: "You can't be called 'Holy' around here! We'll call you 'Lee Ho'," and that was that.)

There were two things the rest did respect about those men: They did like to be clean, and they made 'great food', so, as small towns popped up along the path of the railway, pretty well every one of these towns boasted one 'Chinese food place', usually with a few other groceries, and things like fortune cookies, piled at the end of the counter, and one 'Chinese laundry', sometimes both in the same building. And the owners became part of the community. Though, often, they seemed to remain, still, somehow apart.

That's how 'Mr. Ho's Chinese Food Restaurant and Laundry' came about, and, after a few years expanded into 'Mr. Ho's Grocery' as well, just down the street from St. Aggies; 'kitty-corner' to the police station.

Mr. Ho eventually was able to afford to bring over his wife, after 5 years of separation, and then his mother and father, who all helped out at the restaurant and laundry.

It was hard work, from before dawn to well after dark, with no time for anything else, or anyone else really, except the family.

The Ho's had two children, a boy and a girl ("Born Canadian!" Mr. Ho always proudly declared), and these two children went to school with the rest of the kids in Saint Agatha, and then one of them went to university, then on to a job in 'the big city', while the other took over and became 'The Boss', at 'Mr. Ho's', while Mr. Ho and his wife, in their turn, got older, and became the 'helpers', and still lived 'in the back'.

When the announcement appeared in the Saint Agatha Tattler, that there was to be a meeting in the basement at St. Aggies, to discuss the idea of putting on a musical, Mr. Ho decided to go, and he tried out for the role of a 'street vendor' (and 'extra policeman'), and he got the part!

It was a proud day for the Ho's, that opening performance of 'OLIVER'. The whole family was there, even the elders, who were pretty old by then, and had to be helped down the aisle to their seats, and when the curtains parted, and they saw Mr. Ho, standing beside his 'street vendor cart', dressed in his costume and grinning from ear to ear, they all shot to their feet and cheered, and so did everyone else in the audience (even though some of them weren't exactly sure what they were cheering about.) and Lee Ho, the 'stranger in a strange land', finally felt like he was 'home'.

Bella Bell

"Daddy! Daddy!"

OLIVER abruptly came to a halt, and the 'Chief of Police' did too, right in the middle of his big (actually his only) line in the play, and he went down on his knees at the edge of the platform, and put his hand over his eyes, to peer out into the dark audience.

"Bella?"

(Sergeant Bell had two daughters: Gracie, who was 8, and 5-year-old Isabella. Most of the family called her Izzy, but her dad called her 'Bella'.)

Sergeant Bell's small daughter, skillfully evading her mother's reach, charged up the aisle, climbed awkwardly onto the stage, and launched herself into her father's arms.

"Daddy! I HAVE to show you something!" and she opened her fist and held it to his face. "It's a tooth! A real one! It just fell out of my mouth! I wanted you to see it before the Tooth Fairy got it."

"No! Really? A tooth? And it fell out of your mouth, just like that?"

(The 14-year-old 'Lighting Man', catching the moment, moved the spotlight a fraction to the right and suddenly it appeared as if Sergeant Bell and his daughter were the only important people on the stage, which, in a way, they were.)

"Well, *actually,* it was sort of wiggly, and then I wiggled it a bit more and then there it was, in my hand! Isn't that 'MAZING? Do you think it's a 'mircle' Daddy?"

"I do, and on your birthday too! Would you like us to sing you the birthday polka?"

"Yeah. Okay," Bella whispered, as she became aware of all the people around her, looking at her and, suddenly shy, buried her face in her father's neck.

Sergeant Bell motioned to Mrs. Chadwell on the piano and to the 'orchestra', and then the cast, and the whole audience, joined in a rousing, and reasonably musical, rendition of: 'Happy Birthday to Bella'.

Mrs. Wakita slipped onto the stage and handed Sergeant Bell two small, tattered coats—"I betcha she 'procured' those!" Hellie whispered to his brother—and then she spoke softly in Sergeant Bell's ear, and he beckoned for Gracie to come up too, so the two little girls could join the rest of the 'wretched urchins', for the remainder of the show, and OLIVER resumed, as if nothing had happened to interrupt it at all.

It was a birthday Bella Bell, and her sister Gracie, would never, ever, forget.

'The Girls'

Identical twins are not uncommon, but they're not that common either. 'one in 250', according to the people who know, and even though the chances of having identical twins apparently does not run in families, Marion and Ruth's family had had a set of identical triplets and three pairs of identical twins in 6 generations, and Marion and Ruth were the latest.

They were dressed alike when they were little, and everyone had always commented on how 'cute' they were, which becomes irritating around 11 or 12, when the girls started hoping for 'beautiful', rather than 'cute', or, at the very least 'pretty'.

Marion and Ruth (They were always referred to in that order, cuz Marion had beaten Ruth by three minutes in the grand entry) were not beautiful; maybe not even 'pretty' in the ordinary way, but they were 'interesting-looking', as they had heard a local 'old bachelor' commenting to their mother, one day when they were 13 or so:

"Yuh know, your girls ain't pretty, but they ARE interesting-lookin'."

He thought he was giving them a compliment but, at 13, the girls considered it a deadly insult, and they never did forgive that man.

They were quite identical; even their father couldn't really tell them apart, although he pretended he could.

Their teachers, and even their boyfriends, didn't have a chance, which led to numerous tricks and embarrassing moments, and, in spite of the boyfriends, they never married. There just didn't seem to be any need. After all, they had each other.

When 'the girls' retired from teaching, they found they had had enough of big city life and they decided to move to a small town; 'any small town'. So they got out their map of Canada, linked their index fingers together, closed their eyes, and pointed.

Their linked fingers landed on: 'Saint Agatha'.

Which explains why, the middle of that summer, Marion and Ruth moved to the little yellow house, with the flower garden out front, three houses up from St. Aggies.

For quite a while, because they alternated chores like grocery shopping and gassing up the car, their neighbors didn't even realize there were actually two of them. And their first real, 'dress up' outing, was to 'the theater', a couple of months later, for closing night of 'OLIVER-The Musical', at the church just down the street.

They loved the show, glitches and all, and they even quietly commented to each other that those rough, tough, 'Sykes Boys', were 'actually quite romantic looking'!

(Words which certainly had never been applied to Hellie and Wellie ever before.)

Oliver

Nobody in their right mind is going to voluntarily call one small boy four names in a row, unless his father is there to make them do it, and since his father, in this instance, didn't appear to notice, or care, if his son was involved in 'that musical nonsense', Michael Jacob Gregory Findlay had become

'Oliver' from the first moment he stepped into the role, and after the show, other than his father, nobody in Saint Agatha would ever call him anything but 'Oliver' again.

Oliver looked down into the cheering crowd, after the last encore of the last show, and abruptly leaped off the stage and raced up the aisle.

"Dad! You came!" and he hugged his father fiercely. "Did you like it?"

His father hugged him stiffly back, then patted his son awkwardly on the shoulder, and detached himself from the embrace.

"You did fine, son, just fine."

And he turned and walked back up toward the exit door, leaving Oliver and his mom, dancing around and chattering about the show, in the aisle.

"Well"—The Rev, who had been watching from the wings, sighed, and pressed his lips together—"I suppose we can't expect 'mircles', but I guess at least it's a start."

***

It was over! Finally over!

There had been talk of 'taking it on the road'. Just to Harrow, the next small town a half dozen kilometers away – but everybody knew it was just talk. Still, it was nice to have been asked.

The last 'Hurrahs!'; The last big hugs (Mr. MacPherson hadn't felt the need to go to a funeral, for hugs, for months!); The last case of the jitters; The last time the 'wretched urchins' would be allowed up so far past their bedtimes.

The last of the burgers and hot dogs, donated by Pete, of 'Pete's Burgers', had been devoured at 'the cast party'.

The chairs had been stacked, and the floors swept, and tomorrow Bill, of 'Bill's Gas Bar and Beauty Emporium', would come with his old pickup, and take away the lights and the rental props, and the last 'bits and pieces' of OLIVER would be gone; Gone, but not forgotten, and St. Aggies would return to 'normal'. Normal, but not quite the same.

The Rev was feeling relieved, but also kind of melancholy, and very, very tired ("Zosted!" as Bella Bell would say).

In fact, the Rev was so tired, by the time he walked out the door that night, that he was seeing double, and he rubbed his hand wearily across his eyes: Two identical 'Sykes Boys', and two identical ladies! and he giggled to himself.

213

But then he frowned: If he was seeing double, shouldn't there be four Sykes Boys?

Then he closed his eyes, and shook his head from side to side, to clear his brain, and took himself off home to bed.

***

'Fagin' had had a wonderful time doing the show. Everybody loved him, except maybe Mrs. Chadwell, and he had become the unofficial 'Wise Papa Bear' to them all, so when he walked away, after that final cast party, they all figured they would be seeing him around again, lots.

But they never did. He disappeared into the night, and none of them ever saw him again. They all missed him, even Mrs. Chadwell, though she would have never admitted it, and the Rev realized, sadly, that their 'Perfect Fagin' had likely just 'hopped another train to somewhere'.

***

'Nancy' became a regular visitor at St. Aggies, dropping in for long talks with the Rev, or coffee and some of those chocolate mint Girl Guide cookies (her favorite) with 'her boys', in their church basement lair, and she became a very welcome, and much needed, member of the St. Aggie's choir.

She got a job with the 'Girls'—several of whom were well past 'girl' stage, and two of whom were men— at 'the Beauty Emporium', and when Mrs. Chadwell surprised everybody by deciding she was a bit lonely, now that the musical was over, and that she planned on fixing up her basement as a permanent 'Pied-a'-terre' ("French words do sound so lovely, compared to English, don't they dear!") and wanted a 'nice quiet girl' to live there, she asked 'Nancy', whose real name actually was Nancy, if she would care to move in, and Nancy agreed.

***

"So! What musical are we doing next year, Rev?"

The Rev looked up from his desk, and then leaned back in his chair, which promptly almost tipped him over backward again, as usual.

214

"Next year?"

He propped his chin in his hands, and stared off, out the window.

"Don't know.

But grab a brown paper bag from behind the door there, and maybe we'll start figuring something out!"

***

Lexi's Dream

Lexi had a dream. I suppose he had more than one dream, I don't know, but this was his big dream.

He had never really had a home. His family were refugees from somewhere they were not wanted. There are many people like that, you know. Nothing they'd done, or said. It's like they were 'born despised', through no fault of their own, and they had run from that, to a land which may not have openly welcomed them, but at least tolerated them, to build a life.

It was a life of struggle, but there was usually food, in the forests and rivers, and the means to make shelter, at least in the summer, and in the cold seasons, they moved from town to town, doing the jobs no other people wanted to do, living in places, and buildings, no one else wanted to live in. Managing.

Lexi had never gone to school, but he was bright and he picked up the language of this new land, and the skills which helped the family survive, and wherever he went, he would look, usually standing on a hill, shading his eyes, for his dream, and then sadly shake his head, when he didn't find it.

But he knew it was out there somewhere, and he knew that, someday, he would find it.

Then one day he did. There it was, in a small jewel of a valley, between two hills covered with scarlet and golden maples, with a river running through, and the sun sparkling off the water, into the distance. He knew it when he saw it.

So he built a little cabin, in the shelter of the side of the hill, from logs he cut himself, bit by bit, month by month, until the day he carved a door, from a single slab of pine, with his name chiseled out into the wood, and he walked in, and shut that door, and sat down on a chair he had made himself, at a table he had made himself, and Lexi knew he finally had his dream: A home that he could call his own.

He didn't even notice the three men standing at the top of the hill ('His hill'), looking out into the distance too, just like Lexi had done.

They were big men. Not physically bigger than Lexi, but more powerful, and they too had a dream, bigger than Lexi's. They dreamed they would build a dam. A huge, 'amazing' dam, with 'amazing technology', which would 'serve the people', and 'move them all into the future'—and, quite possibly, make these three men a lot of money, which may well have been the biggest part of these three big men's 'Amazing dream'.

They never even noticed Lexi's tiny home, there in the valley, tucked into the edge of the hill below them; it blended so well into the land around it. And if they had, they likely wouldn't have cared much anyway.

Constable Kaminski

Gus Kaminski was a good police officer. Conscientious and hardworking. Proud of finally completing his training, of being a 'Constable' now, instead of merely a lowly 'Cadet'.

He had been taught, during cadet training, that he should stay a bit apart, a bit aloof, from the general folk in the places where he would be working; to 'maintain his distance'. So he did.

It made for a bit of a lonely life.

Of course, there were the other officers at the station, which included two other 'new guys' like him. They were friendly, but not, at least not yet, really 'friends'. He did miss his family, and his girlfriend, on the other side of the country. He had never really realized just how big Canada was, and, sometimes, he felt homesick.

But he had known this would be part of the job, before he signed up, so those times, especially in the long dark winter evenings of that part of the country, when it was the worst, he just had to tell himself to: 'Suck it up', and he volunteered for extra shifts.

He did, every once in a while, go to church, at St. Aggies, but again, he 'maintained his distance, as he should', and his work made him a pretty irregular attender anyway.

When Sergeant Bell asked him to be part of 'Oliver', he would have refused, but the request seemed pretty close to an order, and he shrugged and, determined to 'do his duty', he gave in.

Sergeant Bell told him he needed to get out there, to 'get to know the people', even though Gus was not really convinced this was a good, or even a 'proper', thing to do, and he had his own opinion of Sergeant Bell's obvious tendency to 'mix in with the crowd', but he kept that opinion to himself. So Gus made for a bit of a 'stiff' policeman character, in the play ('and properly so'!).

In spite of his feelings, and although he would not have admitted it, even to himself, Constable Kaminski began to rather like the practices, though he tried hard to think of them as 'duty' rather than 'fun'.

He also discovered he had 'a voice', which he had never known before. He had never sung before, and it was actually a bit of a shock and, against his better judgement, he began to enjoy himself.

The day, a couple of months later, when Henry Watson called him up and invited him for 'a little fishing trip' he and Edon and Charlie were planning, Gus initially refused.

But Constable Kaminski did love fishing. He always used to go with his dad and his brothers, and he had brought his gear with him, when he was assigned to work in Saint Agatha. So when Henry met him again at Bill's Gas Bar and Beauty Emporium—they were both getting haircuts—later that week, and the invitation was repeated, he impulsively (and wrongly, he felt later) agreed and, in spite of himself, he started to look forward to the next Saturday.

The four of them talked about everything, that Saturday, like people do when they're fishing: About farming, and wolves, and their families, and about the three big men who seemed to be hanging around Saint Agatha, and had even been seen 'snooping around' on Charlie's family's traditional land. But mostly, they just sat, quiet, watching the water and the birds, or talking about fish.

Gus caught a lot of fish that day, and he tried to convince Henry, and Edon, and Charlie, to take them home, but they had caught lots too, so they told him to just give them away, if he didn't want them for himself.

"To your friends," they had said, but Constable Kaminski didn't really think he had 'friends' in Saint Agatha.

"So to whom?"

That was the question which loomed large in his mind, as he drove home in his car smelling, not unpleasantly, of clay, and trees, and very fresh fish.

To 'the guys at the station', for sure, but there were more fish than that, and some of the guys were fishermen themselves anyway.

The situation was not really worrying, there was a bit of time to figure it out, but not much; the fish were fresh right now, but they wouldn't stay that way for long, and, after dropping off a couple of the larger salmon to the chef at The Mission, and one to a delighted 'Mrs. Rev', and one to Malcolm MacPherson, who just happened to be walking down the sidewalk—and attempted to give Constable Kaminski a thank you hug, through the car window—Gus was starting to get a bit desperate, and 'FISH' filled his thoughts, as well as his back seat.

So he found himself 'randomly flinging fish', at people he barely knew, through his car window, and since this vision of himself started to strike him funny, the friendly, laughing face of Constable Kaminski was a face most of the people in Saint Agatha had never seen before. He even took fish to play practice, and dropped one off on Mrs. Chadwell's front step, even though he didn't even particularly like Mrs. Chadwell!

Finally, he ran the last one out to Mrs. Henley, who initially saw the police car come into her yard and refused entry, and told him, through a roughly mended gap in her front door, that she was, "Innocent!" and asked him if she "needed to call her lawyer?" (Mrs. Henley did not actually have 'a lawyer') until she understood why he was there, and invited him in, for a cookie and a cup of tea.

Since there seemed no way he could decline without hurting her feelings, he accepted the invitation and, in spite of the fact that the cookies were stale and the tea weak, Constable Kaminski found himself enjoying the visit, and liking this lady, and promising her he would 'come again'.

Christmas was a-comin', and Constable Kaminski was not looking forward to it. Some of the other guys had family close by, but his own family was far away, and the time, and the cost – his salary barely covered food and lodging— was simply too much for him to even consider, so he tried to 'throw himself into his work', and not think about it at all.

"Just as well," he told himself. "The job comes first! I don't have time to go. They need me here. I'd rather stay here anyway!"

And, you know, he almost convinced himself.

It was about a week and a half before Christmas when Chief Superintendent Jacob called out that he wanted to see: "Constable Kaminski! In his office. Now!" and, grim-faced, he handed Gus an envelope.

Gus' heart sank. Obviously, he had done something wrong; something really bad, by the look of it, though he had no idea what that something might have been.

"Sit!" The Chief ordered, and Gus closed his eyes, and even swayed a bit.

Being a police officer was all he had ever wanted to be, and now it appeared that dream was to come to an end, when it had barely started.

He dropped into the chair the Superintendent had indicated, his legs weak, grateful to sit down.

"So open it!" the Chief Superintendent ordered, pointing to the envelope in Gus' hand, and Constable Kaminski did as he was told.

Inside was an Air Canada ticket; a return ticket, for the other side of the country, where his family, and his girlfriend, lived, and $369.75 in cash, for 'spending money', from 'Your Friends in Saint Agatha'.

"Better start packing!" the Super smiled.

and Constable Kaminski started to cry.

Sergeant Stinky

Sergeant Bell did have a particular soft spot for animals, especially wounded animals, and in his job he encountered wounded animals pretty regularly: Deer; raccoons, (Raccoons should NEVER try to cross the road!); squirrels, especially in the fall when they were too busy collecting nuts to pay much attention to cars; Cats, dogs, hawks, and, often, skunks, and he was a major contributor to the 'Damaged Animal Drop-off Program', at the local Humane Society.

His wife was used to her husband bringing home 'the wounded'. They had a 2½ legged dog, named 'Bungie'; an old crow with a broken wing, which never did heal, who 'walked' up trees, instead of flying there; two cats with only one pair of eyes between them; and 'Bunny', a totally benign, and also totally blind, gray rabbit, who appeared to actually enjoy being wrapped up in 'blankies', and carted around in an old wagon, by Sergeant Bell's two small daughters.

Sergeant Bell didn't often hit any animals himself; he was a very careful driver. But sometimes, there was just no help for it, and one day, when he was racing to the scene of an accident, an entire family of skunks; a mom with three kits, chose the wrong moment to decide to brave the trek across the Trans-Canada, and Sergeant Bell, who did slam on his brakes to try to swerve around them, and almost ended up in the ditch because of it, only managed to avoid one.

One of the kits, barely old enough to toddle, was still alive, and Sergeant Bell popped it into a pocket, turned on his siren, and made it to his destination in time.

But when he got home that evening, and showed his wife what was in his pocket, she made it clear that she drew the line at skunks.

"But they don't spray when they're little! And he's SO cute! Don't you think?"

Usually that worked, but not this time.

"Okay. It can stay until it gets old enough to spray. But no way! Not even one minute past that!"

So 'Stinky' joined the menagerie, but only for a while!

Stinky never sprayed, but, true to his word, Sergeant Bell, when the little skunk was about 4 months old, took him to see 'Docky', and the vet examined him, very, very carefully, and declared that he was pretty sure the car had hit the little fella after all, and had done enough damage that 'that bit' was permanently out of order.

Sergeant Bell's wife was pretty mellow, having lived with Sergeant Bell for more than ten years, but when she said, "No way!" that's when the door shut, and skunks, even if vets were 'pretty sure' they couldn't spray, hit that door.

So there was nothing else to be done; a skunk without the ability to spray was a sitting duck, so to speak, so Sergeant Bell felt there was no alternative.

The skunk would just have to live at the police station.

Stinky, renamed 'Sergeant Stinky', due to his elevation in status, actually turned out to be more asset than liability at the station: He was a great mouser, and he kept the elderly building pretty well free of rodents, even taking on a rat now and then, if it was necessary, and the sight of a skunk sauntering across the room in front of an ornery criminal, who of course did not realize that this particular skunk was 'scent-free', generally reduced the miscreant to a stammering, and controllable, state.

One night though, two of the officers brought in a particularly nasty local tough, who made it clear he had no intention of staying for the night.

He was 'drunk as a skunk' (No slur against skunks intended), so 'talking him down' wasn't working, and he was becoming more belligerent and abusive every minute, instead of less.

Skunks are generally nocturnal animals, so 'Sergeant Stinky' was up and about, but he was used to a relatively quiet life at the station, and he was in the middle of his midnight, cat food, dinner, in the back office, and I guess he didn't appreciate the kafuffle, so he waddled out the office door and across the room, and stood looking—'glaring', I suppose you could say, if you can tell that in a skunk—at this disheveled human being, roaring and swinging his fists, and being a serious irritant, to man and beast.

The man did notice the skunk, but he had been in that station, plenty of times, before, so he just started to jeer: "Yeah, yeah. None of you are worth nuthin'! Even your damn stupid skunk can't even spray!" and he leaned over and poked his finger in said skunk's direction.

Now it is highly unlikely that Stinky understood the words. The tones? Maybe. Anyway, for whatever reason, he had obviously had enough. He turned his back on this disgusting individual, who was making all that noise as well as interrupting his dinner, and he lifted his tail, and he let him have it. Smack in the kisser!

It appeared Sergeant Stinky was a 'fully functional' skunk, after all.

(It took the officers and cleaning staff at the RCMP station 3 days, and a lot of vinegar, tomato juice, baking soda, peroxide, and dish soap, to clear out the smell, but they really didn't mind.)

Sergeant Bell, still chuckling, was describing the incident to his wife the next morning, at breakfast time (His uniform was in a pile, on the grass, in the back yard).

"So, looks like you were right, my love! Sergeant Stinky CAN spray! If he really wants to.

He just has to be properly motivated, that's all."

Uncle Jake

Usually Uncle Jake spent Saturday afternoon with his buddies, down at the pool hall, but today he had been 'invited out to dine', so he was standing in front of the mirror hung on the back of his wardrobe door, trying to decide what to wear.

The wardrobe was the only piece of furniture in his bedroom, other than the bed. The rest of his small apartment was similarly spartan. It was a 'no frills apartment', by choice. A 'man's apartment', Uncle Jake always thought of it, as he thought of himself as a 'man's man'.

But today he had been invited out to dine, by a lady. Two ladies actually; they came as a set, and he was trying his best to 'dress to impress'. He finally chose the blue tie.

He only had two ties, and the other one was red, with a picture of a charging bull in the middle of it. A friend had picked it up for him, as a joke, at some rodeo, after Jake had made a quite spectacular blunder during the bull-riding competition, and ended up in hospital.

He chuckled at the thought, and put on the plain blue one, slipped on his good shoes instead of his cowboy boots, even though they pinched a bit, took a final look at himself in the mirror, and rubbed his chin to check for a smooth shave. It was a while since he had shaved at all. Usually he wore a beard. Then he nodded at his reflection, grabbed his hat, and headed out the door.

He met the girls at their home, and they each slipped a dainty hand through one of his elbows, as they looked him up and down, liked what they saw, and smiled up at him, and his heart—or at least that's what he figured it must be. It seemed to be in the right general area anyway—did a flip-flop.

It was a lovely afternoon, and he gave barely a thought to the boys down at the pool hall, as the three of them strolled down the lane. They had handed Jake a basket, which he held in front of him, with both hands (since his elbows were occupied.)

He was hungry. He was hoping it was something major in that basket, but he had his doubts. The girls hadn't told him where they were going to dine, or what they were going to dine on. They had just asked him to show up. So he had.

It seemed to be quite a long walk. He should have ditched the good shoes and worn the cowboy boots, but, as the girls chattered at him on either side, and they all laughed together, he didn't really feel the pinch.

Finally, it appeared they had reached their destination, and the girls formally seated him, under the green awning of a huge chestnut tree, while they perched across from him, spreading their skirts carefully around them, and opened the basket.

They explained that they had 'tea' and 'crumpets', although they weren't actually sure what 'crumpets' were, and neither was he, and a huge birthday cake, "since it WAS his birthday after all," with fairy icing made of rainbows and cream.

There was a lot of giggling – not from Jake of course, cuz he was a man, and men don't giggle, though he did come close – and after they had eaten the entire birthday cake, and the tea, and every single one of the crumpets as well, they all sat back on the blanket, which had done double-duty as a tablecloth, and discussed the pictures in the clouds, and the best places to find wild strawberries, and other important topics, until the afternoon sun got lower, and the shadows got longer, and it was time to go.

"So! Did you enjoy dining out with us?"

"Oh! Ladies! It was exquisite. And the cake! He kissed his fingers to the sky – I have never tasted anything more wonderful! So light! And the crumpets! I am totally filled up! I couldn't eat another thing! Not another bite!"

"Oh, Uncle Jake! You big silly! You know it was all pretend! Now come on back home with us—and don't forget the basket! You're the man, so you have to carry it!—Mom has a REAL birthday cake ready for you when we get there. Hurry up!"

And Uncle Jake slung the basket over his arm, and grabbed his two nieces, ages 6 and 7, by the hands, as they headed back down the path, swinging their arms, and skipping.

(Well, Uncle Jake didn't skip. There ARE some things a real man feels he simply CANNOT do!).

"Will there be crumpets?"

"No. No crumpets."

"Ah. Too bad. I've grown rather fond of crumpets. Whatever they are."

The Gift

"You know, you've got a gift!" his grandmother always told him, when he gave her one of his carvings, this time a small, carefully but crudely-cut bit of shiny stone, as she held it up in her hand, to catch the light, and thanked him with a hug.

"I'll make you a better one sometime. I just need to practice."

"Yes. 'Practice makes perfect', you know—"Jo's grandmother was proud of her English, and she 'practiced' on him regularly—"Maybe, someday, you will be great, and people will know your name, and ask for your carvings, and treasure them all over the world!"

Jo smiled at her. He didn't say it, but he doubted her words. Maybe in 'his world'; the run-down, crowded street where he lived with his grandmother, but not likely much further in 'the world' than that. Still, his street would be a start.

Jo was only 12, but he was 'the man of the house'. His grandmother always called him that, proudly, when she introduced him to someone new, even though this 'man of the house' was even smaller than she was, and she was quite small.

But 'size isn't everything', as his grandmother always said.

She was full of such 'sayings'. She got them from an old book she had found in a second hand shop, when she was trying to learn to read English, and she spouted them at him, and at anyone else who happened to be nearby, regularly.

Jo and his grandmother lived in a tiny, cramped apartment, at the end of an alley, in 'the bad part of town'. Not that any part of that particular town was that great, though there were a few people who did pretty well, and had big houses, sometimes even with pools, which Jo thought was foolish anyway, cuz all you had to do to go for a swim was to walk down the street to the docks, or the beach!

But whatever. "Different strokes for different folks," as his grandmother would say, and besides, every once in a while Jo would get a job cleaning one of those pools, so he certainly didn't mind anyone having one.

Mostly, Jo did whatever jobs came along; whatever jobs 'kept food on the table': Delivering packages, for one of the shops; Gathering up branches after a storm came through; cleaning floors or washing dishes in one of the local restaurants (and taking home leftovers!), when one of the regular staff was off sick.

Jo wasn't old enough to be a real 'employee' yet, but the rules were a bit 'loose' on all that around here, so he grabbed what jobs he could get. His grandmother took in washing, and made place mats, from old material she found at the dump, and labeled them: 'New Material Only' ("After all, it IS new, to me!"), and sold them on the corner, to the tourists.

So, between the two of them, they managed. There wasn't much time for carving; Jo was usually pretty exhausted by the end of the day, but he collected odd pieces of wood wherever he went, or sometimes one of the builders sold him a scrap piece he liked, for a few pennies, and stones and shells from the beach were free.

He liked carving shells the best, because they cost nothing, and they changed colors, from white, to mauve, to purple, as he carved through the layers, and he practiced 'his gift' on them, whenever he got the chance. He knew he would never be 'great', but his 'gift' was a gift to him as well, because he loved doing it.

Sometimes his carvings took him a long time; days, even weeks, to complete, but 'If you can't do something right, don't do it at all', so he didn't mind. If he wanted to 'do one right', and it took him weeks, then that's the way it was, and his carvings improved; his 'gift' sharpened into a 'skill', and the people on his street began to recognize 'one of Jo's', as better than a lot of the others.

So when a man came to town, looking for 'Carvers', to carve shells 'for sale all over the world', Jo, who was now old enough to be 'officially' hired, applied for the job. So excited to finally be able to be paid for something he loved to do!

Dozens of others applied too, and every one of them was hired.

When Jo showed up for work, his face lit with joy, that first morning, and all the new 'carvers' were gathered together in a big warehouse room, with barrels of seashells, they were told what their 'carving' would be, and the joy went out of Jo's eyes, and reality set in.

Jo, and everyone else, was to carve the shells, with words mostly. Sometimes the names of towns, or countries: 'Welcome to London' or 'I visited CANADA'! or 'USA forever'!, or simple designs like maple leaves, or hearts, or even skulls and crossbones.

They had ten minutes, maybe 15 if there were many letters, to 'do' each shell, and they would be paid a few pennies for each 'carving'.

Jo took a deep breath, and sighed.

"Well. 'Beggars can't be choosers'," as his grandmother would say, and he had never had to be a 'beggar' yet, and neither had his grandmother, and he wasn't about to ever let that happen, if he could help it. So he grabbed one of the tools the man supplied, and pulled his stool over to a barrel of shells, and started to carve.

But, every once in a while, usually at the end of a day, when he'd met his quota, Jo carved a shell the way HE wanted it, even if it took him a long time and he ended up leaving late, or tucking that particular shell into some hidden corner, to complete the next day, or the next week.

And when it was 'perfect', he hid it among the other shells, in the 'COMPLETED' barrel, and he smiled as he thought of someone who would appreciate it, in some far off country, finding it, and maybe catching their breath, because they thought it so beautiful; a 'treasure', and taking it home, to put in a 'place of honor' in their home, or maybe, to give it as a gift, to someone they loved.

***

'The Fair' was coming to Saint Agatha! It was a rodeo really; the first 'Real Rodeo' Saint Agatha had ever had, with a parade, and bareback riding, and chuck-wagon races, and carnival rides, and vendors 'from all over the world'!.

'Everyone', including the Rev, and his wife, and their little daughter, went to the fair, and they all bought 'cowboy hats', so they would look like 'Real Cowboys'. (Even though the actual 'Real Cowboys' called them all, 'Drug store cowboys', cuz the drug store on the corner by the Manor sold the hats, and sold out too, for weeks before the fair.)

They wandered the grounds, eating sticky candied apples; helping the two little girls beside them in the stands scream for 'Uncle Jake' to "Hang on!"; Cheering for 'Queenie', Mrs. Chadwell's pig, to win the prize in the 'best-dressed pig' competition (and she would have won it too, if she hadn't tried to bite the judge!), and savoring the scents of cotton candy, and onions frying for the hot dogs, and the smell of the horses; marveling at the size of the huge, prize-winning zucchini Hellie and Wellie had produced in their minuscule community garden plot, back behind the church.

And when they came upon a vendor, selling 'SHELL CARVINGS! Direct from THE TROPICS!' The Rev absent-mindedly dug through the shells in the barrel, as he took in the sights and sounds around him.

They were a bit of a disappointment, those "SHELL CARVINGS!". Most of them just said: 'SAINT AGATHA' on them, or had a rough maple leaf, or sometimes a horseshoe, carved into them, but he kept on digging, and his gaze focused, as he drew a shell out from the barrel, and lifted it up to catch the light.

It was a picture, delicately carved through layers and shades of pearls and purples, of a pair of cranes, each poised on one leg, among the beach grasses, silhouetted against the waves, and the setting sun. He caught his breath, then breathed out the words: "It's beautiful!" as he held it out for his wife, and their little one, to see.

It was only $4.00. But 'Four dollars is four dollars', as his grandmother would say, so he put it back in the barrel, and they moved on.

It was still there when his wife, who 'just needed a few minutes to find the Little Cowgirl's Room', rushed back to the vendor's tent.

And a couple of months later, it was the gift the Rev got to open on Christmas Eve, and the one he loved the most, from 'The one who loved him the most', and it was given a place of honor, this 'treasure', on his desk in his office at St. Aggies, so he could look at it, every day, just, because it was so beautiful.

Nick

It wasn't Nick's fault. That's the first thing that needs to be said – Though, truth be told, if your house was the one that got broken into, it's likely you wouldn't care whether it was his fault or not – it was actually his mother's fault.

Now, let's be clear, I'm not big on people's mothers getting the blame for everything their kids do. In this case though, it was true.

Nick had broken into every vacant house in Saint Agatha, and a couple of the nearby communities too, over the last three years. Only in the winter though, or sometimes, in the late fall, or early spring, if the weather was particularly nasty.

He was good at it. He never got caught. Close though, a couple of times, and usually people didn't even realize that their house had in fact been broken into. Maybe they noticed that their lock was left unlocked (and blamed their wife, or their husband), or they were surprised they hadn't remembered that they were nearly out of bread, or peanut butter, or milk, but they never clued in that the shower had been used.

Nick always cleaned up after himself. Like I said, Nick was really good at it. But after a while, it kind of added up.

Nick was only 13 when it started; the first time his mother locked him out of the house. She didn't hate him or anything. In fact, she always said he was a 'good kid'. But she just couldn't be bothered with him anymore. She just had better things to do.

Most of the 'better things' involved drugs and, more and more often, she simply forgot Nick's existence. He never tried to break into his own house. Not sure why. Maybe there wasn't anything there worth breaking in for, or maybe it just seemed wrong to him.

It was 'no big deal' in the summer. He could live in the woods, or by the water, in the summer, and he got skilled at that too. Nick was quick at figuring out things, and good with his hands. But winter was different.

Nick did go to school, off and on; had learned to read and write and all that, before things went bad (or 'worse', I suppose you could say.)

He was actually quite smart, and his teachers really missed him every time his "parents had to move away for a new job", and he'd decided he'd better 'disappear', until he appeared again, at a different school, sometimes even with a different variation of his name, somewhere else.

But as he grew, it got harder to hide, to 'stay under the radar', and get lost among the rest, cuz he grew a lot. By the time he was 14 or so, he was big. Really big. Six feet tall, at least, unlike most of the other boys whose genes would kick in later, and he was strong too.

Maybe he was like his dad. He always wondered about that. He had never met his dad.

(So, I suppose the situation he was in was just as much his dad's fault as his mother's, so there you go!).

He also had curly, curly hair. Like an 'afro', only blond. That must have been from his dad too. All in all, he started to 'stand out' in a crowd. So he stopped going to school.

It got hard, almost impossible some days, into weeks, just getting enough to eat, so the times his mother left the door open for him—and they both pretended nothing had ever happened, as if everything was 'normal', until the next time she locked him out—he 'hoarded' food from the house, mostly things that wouldn't go bad, and hid them here and there, in some of his secret 'caches' in the woods, and his mother would complain about how she "could NOT understand how one kid could eat so much!".

Sometimes she lasted for a couple of weeks, and Nick's life would return to some version of 'normal', but then, out of the blue, he would come 'home' to find himself locked out, and alone, again.

(Nick understood exactly what they meant, in books, when they talked about 'that sinking feeling', cuz he felt it every time that happened.)

Nick liked books. He spent a lot of time at the library, when he was not doing odd jobs, or simply trying to stay alive. It was warm there, and he could sink into a book, and, for a time, be somewhere else. He never took books out of the library. Where would he keep them safe? And it was important to him, to keep them safe.

Then one day, finally, something good happened to Nick. That was at the library too.

"Nick? Is that you?" and Nick dragged himself, reluctantly, out of his book, and looked up.

"It *is* you! Whoa! You're big!"

It was a girl, about his age. A girl he didn't recognize, but obviously she had recognized him, which was not good.

"It's Beth, Bethany. You remember? You were in my class, in grade seven, until you moved away."

He did remember her, but he wasn't about to tell her that.

"Nah. The Name's Cal."

(He'd always liked that name; always wanted to be called 'Cal'. It sounded 'cool' in his ears.)

"It is not!"

It was as if she could see right through him; Right through the bubble he had so carefully constructed around himself, and it made him angry. It made him feel unsafe. So he got up from his seat at the table, gave her a rough shove out of his way, and stalked through the door. He stayed away, across the street, in the park, for more than an hour, watching the ducks, but by then he figured it was safe to go back.

(It had been a good book, and he hoped nobody else had taken it out, before he'd had the chance to finish it.)

"Here's your book. I put a marker there, at your page."

God! Would this girl not just leave him alone? He glared up at her and she laughed. She was not supposed to laugh! She was supposed to back off, maybe even be scared of him. He knew he was big, and he had actually practiced, in front of a mirror, because it didn't come naturally to him, looking 'mean!' It worked on most people, when he needed it to, but apparently, it wasn't working very well on her.

Maybe it was 'Karma' or something, but Nick's first 'bad thing' happened that day too. (He didn't actually consider the rest of his messy life 'bad', like maybe the rest of us would have. It was 'just life'.)

The police were not blind, or deaf, and they had listened to plenty of stories in town, from people who were 'Just wondering if maybe their house might have been broken into?', over the last couple of years, and the officers had tried to 'keep an eye on things', in the neighborhoods where these musings seemed most common.

They had particularly centered on a couple of houses where the owners were away regularly, and which had produced more than one of these reports. That evening, their vigilance paid off, and Nick's luck failed, or close anyway.

They caught him, just climbing through the window, at the back of one of these houses.

Actually, 'almost caught him' would be more accurate, but they did see him. He was hard to miss, and hard to not recognize, if they ever saw him again. So Nick had to 'lay low', in the woods, for a couple of weeks.

It was a cold, and a hungry time, and Nick, eventually, risked a visit to the Mission at St. Aggies, to at least get one hot meal under his belt, before he vanished again.

The Rev saw him there, but didn't approach him cuz, head down, hood up, his body language screamed that he didn't want to be approached, possibly didn't even want to be noticed. So the Rev pretended he didn't notice him, but he did 'see' him.

Nick went to prison on his 16th birthday. To the 'Big Boy's Prison' (the local term) 'up north'.

It seemed a long drive. Long in lots of ways, and when the police car finally turned into the driveway, and Nick could actually see the place, it looked, on that rainy evening in late November, like a fortress; a foreboding, grim 'Chateau d'if', in his mind. (He had recently been reading 'The Count of Monte Cristo', in the library.)

Like a huge, stone, tomb, and he was, at that moment, Edmond Dantes, about to be entombed in it, and he panicked.

Nick hadn't panicked very often in his short life, even though he had had plenty of opportunities, but, when he did, it was spectacular.

Basically, by the time they got him out of it, Nick had taken the inside of the police car apart.

The Rev went to the prison now and then, when he was asked. He generally went on the bus, which gradually dispersed the other passengers along the way, until it was just he, and the bus driver, and a couple of the wives, or sisters, or mothers, of inmates, left to make the last bit of the journey. The Rev always thought of it as 'The Sad Bus', as if even the air on the bus seemed to be heavy with grief.

St. Aggie's choir sometimes made the trip to the prison too, at Christmas time, to sing carols, and take cookies, for the inmates.

By and large, the choir members (and presumably, the inmates) enjoyed the visit, although that may not be the right word. It was more that they felt it was a good thing, 'the right thing' to do.

Still, the singers did all feel quietly relieved, when the last gate clanged shut behind them, and they were on the outside of it.

On one of the Rev's visits, he noticed Nick, sitting on a bench in the exercise yard.

He looked familiar, and the Rev felt sure he should know him, and racked his brain for that elusive image, until he finally recognized the boy, seen only once, but still remembered, at the Mission. He did look different; older, and his bush of curls had been shorn down to a mere shadow of yellow fuzz.

The Rev walked over to him and sat down and, this time, Nick didn't mind. After that, the Rev visited him every time he came to the prison to see someone else, and there were some days, he came just for Nick.

The Rev wasn't Nick's only visitor. He had one other: Sometimes, Beth came too. Eventually, Nick told the Rev his story—He had already told Bethany—and the two of them felt the same way, and thought the same thoughts: They had to get Nick out of there, and they had to make sure he never ended up there again.

It was 'only 6 months', but it was the longest 6 months of Nick's life, and it seemed like years to him. Way worse than having no home. He had always had 'freedom' before, even if it was sometimes a scary type of freedom, and this did not feel like any kind of a 'home' anyway, even if he did have a bed, and food. Instead it felt like a cage, with everyone looking at him, all the time. Judging him, hating him, or trying to get at him, one way or another.

The Rev and Beth came together, that final day, to pick Nick up, and when the last steel door banged shut behind him, and he was on the outside of it, Nick started to sob. It embarrassed him, but he just couldn't stop the tears from coming.

Beth's father was a carpenter, and Nick, when he had been able to get odd jobs before, loved working with wood. He loved the smell of it, and the feel of it. So Beth convinced her father to take him on, at least for a while and 'See how things work out'.

It didn't take much convincing, and, in a matter of weeks, the 'Jailbird' changed to 'My apprentice', and eventually to 'My daughter's boyfriend' and, in a couple of years, to: "Come meet Nick! My son-in-law!"

The Huckleberry Patch

I knew I was truly part of the family the day my new in-laws told me how to find the secret, family, huckleberry patch.

Huckleberries won't grow just anywhere, you know. The soil has to be sandy, and the land high, so the sun can get at them, and the woods around them, and the land beneath them have to have just the right mix of earth and air and water.

The other thing though, is that bears REALLY like huckleberries too, and bears don't like to share. So there is a certain 'technique' to picking huckleberries. First, you have to get there, over a series of pot-holed, poorly-kept, seldom-used logging roads; over terrifying 'bridges' (an honorary name only, not actually an accurate description, due to the frequency of chunks of missing timber, allowing views of the crashing rapids below).

If your vehicle makes it that far, without all the screws loosening and the dash falling off, then you have to tackle the long trek at the end, through ancient mosquito/tick/blackfly-ridden wilderness/back of nowhere/primeval forest. (The words vary, according to who's talking.)

And since you never know if a bear, or several bears – who can be very sneaky in spite of their size – may very well be 'picking berries' on the other side of the same hunk of huckleberry bush which also looked good to you, you'll need to make enough noise, the whole time, to scare them off.

Sometimes a radio works—maybe the CBC, maybe the rock station, or country and western, according to the bear's taste. Personally, I always found Rap works pretty well—but cuz radios, in the 'wilderness', use up batteries, and your cell phone won't work there, mostly everybody just sings.

I had never sung. My parents, my siblings, never sang. We were a whole big family of 'non-singers'. Even humming was pushing it, and generally earned some comment like: "What IS that weird noise? Are there bees around here?"

So being expected to 'sing', with my new family, was a bit daunting. But the thought of huckleberry muffins is highly motivating, so I did my best.

I'm not sure whether it's good singing, or bad singing, or just singing in general that the bears don't like, or maybe it was just my singing, but anyway, it seemed to work, and I usually filled my ice cream bucket with the best of them, and ate my share of huckleberry pie, and huckleberry muffins, without guilt.

I hadn't actually ever encountered a bear in 'our huckleberry patch', so I suppose I grew a bit complacent. It was a good patch, scattered here and there among the trees, over quite a stretch of territory, so sometimes you felt quite 'alone with nature', even though you really weren't cuz some relative was always 'just up the road', working on his or her bucket too.

Anyway, that day, I forgot to sing. It wasn't a habit with me yet, I suppose, coming from a different kind of family, and when I heard a bit of rustling in '*my* huckleberry patch', I didn't pay much attention. I likely thought it was cute little bunny or something.

Certainly my initial reaction was not to automatically break into song, which was too bad, cuz when that bear stood up on his hind legs, (Bears look REALLY big when they do that, by the way, WAY bigger than bunnies.) to check out who was messing around in '*his* huckleberry patch', it was not a nice surprise.

We looked at each other and I seemed to see a kind of speculative: "Do I eat him now, or save him for later?" look in that bear's eyes, before my recent training finally kicked in and I abruptly burst into the first song that came to mind.

(And not just sang. I danced too. Also something I wasn't used to doing.)

"Skinna marinki dinky dee. Skinna marinki doo! I LOVE YOU! I love you in the morning! And in the afternoon! I love you in the evening! Underneath the MOON, etc., etc…" with lots of arm actions in the 'I LOVE YOU'! parts, and jumping around, in the other bits. And it did the job.

For a few seconds, though it seemed a lot longer, that bear just looked at me, and he frowned (I never knew before that a bear could frown, except maybe Yogi Bear on TV), and then his eyes widened, and I guess he decided the berries weren't worth the risk, cuz he took off.

(Good job it was a black bear. A grizzly likely would have stood his ground and suffered through it for the tasty reward at the end; me, not the berries…or maybe he would have just joined in on the actions.)

'The relatives' never let me forget it:

"Whooh. Just like a one-man-band!"

"The volume! The finesse!"

"You were pretty good! You should share your talent with the world, not just with some mangy old bear!"

"Yeah, man! You really should join a choir!"

So I did, 'n I bin singin' in the choir, at St. Aggies, ever since. I guess I never would be singing at all, if I hadn't liked huckleberries so much, even better than that bear.

And tomorrow, after the wedding—Well, maybe I'll wait until after the honeymoon—I'll do my bit for the next generation, and share the 'secrets of the family huckleberry patch', with Nick, my new son-in law.

A Horrible Fate

"By the way, did you hear what's happening at St. Aggies on Saturday?"

"No. What?"

"Hellie and Wellie are getting married!"

"Getting married? I thought they were brothers!"

***

Everybody in Saint Agatha came to the wedding. 'Widely attended', the *Tattler* reported.

Most came because they were friends, but quite a few came because, until they saw it with their own eyes, they wouldn't have believed it was true: Hellie and Wellie, the most confirmed of all confirmed bachelors in Saint Agatha, were getting married!

"Can you believe those girls agreeing to marry Hellie and Wellie?"

"Well, I suppose there's no accounting for taste."

"Certainly not my cup of tea, that's for sure!" and she shivered artistically.

If they hadn't been such a perfectly matched pair everyone in town had known for years, no one would have recognized 'The Boys': Scrubbed to within an inch of their lives, beards shaved and hair trimmed (by Bill himself, at 'BILL'S GAS BAR and BEAUTY EMPORIUM'), black tuxedos, top hats, silver-tipped walking sticks. The lot. Like a cross between 007s, and two English gentlemen out on the town.

When they took their places at the front of St. Aggies, an audible sigh seemed to ripple through the gathering. Perhaps a sigh of regret, of missed opportunity, from some of the older women in the congregation?

And, as they passed the pew, leading their new wives triumphantly back down the aisle, one of these disappointed females turned to the another and whispered, a trifle too loudly: "Well! Personally, I don't know how the boys are going to tell them apart, to figure out who's who, on their honeymoons," and her friend snickered.

Hellie and Wellie, who both had excellent hearing, now that all that hair over their ears was gone, stopped stock still, causing a bit of a pile-up behind, and stared at the two ladies in amazement.

Then they spoke, simultaneously, like in a long-practiced pantomime: "What on earth do your mean?" and they gazed lovingly at their respective brides. "They don't look a BIT alike!"

***

When the couples emerged from the church and stepped into their horse-drawn carriage, a mob of bedraggled children erupted from behind St. Aggie's cornerstone pillars, hooting and whistling and holding their hands up in the air pleadingly, begging for pennies.

It was the 'wretched urchins', dressed in their Oliver costumes, complete with filthy faces and bare feet, and one of them was leading a bedraggled 'mongrel', with only three legs, on a worn old rope lead.

Mr. Rooney jumped into the carriage, and settled down on the seat, grinning, if dogs can grin, which we all know they can, and panting happily, between the couples, as 'The Boys' threw handfuls of pennies, and nickels and dimes, into the air.

***

The wedding cake, a typical airy fantasy of icing rosebuds, lovey-doves and lace, had been created by Frank, the pastry chef at the Mission.

Frank, in spite of his usual stolid appearance, did possess a spark of puckish humor, so instead of the expected 4 small figures; two brides and two grooms, on top of the cake, there appeared to be only three: two brides and one groom.

But, if you looked closer, you could see the fourth figure; the second groom, hanging partway down the back of the cake, being hauled up to the top via a thin liquorish rope attached to his waist, by the other three.

There was no way of telling which of the two grooms this figure represented, both of the plastic groom figures (from Dollarama) being identical, so the identity of this apparently rather reluctant husband remained forever an object of amused speculation for the guests at the reception.

241

"Egypt! They're going to Egypt for their honeymoon! Look here! It says it right here, in *The Tattle*," and she gave it a shake, as if it was the newspaper's fault.

"Yes, I heard that. Apparently Hellie's always wanted to ride a camel."

"What! Could he not have done that somewhere more civilized? Like Toronto. Toronto has some sort of a zoo, doesn't it? Surely they could have rigged up something there for him, so they didn't have to go gallivanting off to some filthy foreign place, halfway across the earth!" Mrs. Winters sniffed.

"I just don't understand WHAT this world is coming to, Emily! I just don't!"

Clive

"Yes, Ma'am. That is our alligator – the name's Jeff, by the way, and this is my wife June – oh, yeah, he's friendly. You can pet him if you want. We call him 'Clive' after my Uncle Clive. He has no teeth either. They were probably removed when he was a baby. The alligator's I mean, not Uncle Clive's. Uncle Clive probably lost his cuz of all that chewing tobacco, and I'd guess likely he never did own a toothbrush.

"I think it wasn't very nice; removing his teeth." (I'm talking about the alligator again now. We'll just leave Uncle Clive alone, from here on, which is likely just the way Uncle Clive would prefer it.)

"Don't you think it was kind of mean? Takin' out all his teeth? Like really, what else does an alligator get to do for fun? You'd think they could have at least left him a couple. I suppose Clive was likely flushed down the toilet—which, by the way, must be a pretty nasty way to go—when he started to grow too big for his owners, in New York or Toronto or somewheres like that, where people don't think.

"What did they suppose he was gonna do? Stay a 'cutsie little baby alligator' forever? When we found him, in a ditch on the side of the road, (Heaven only knows how he got there!) we knew he wasn't just any alligator. For one thing, there's not a lot of alligators in Canada, and for the other thing, he had a collar on, which is, again, not something I would say a normal alligator would generally wear.

"He's a great 'watchdog', though I suppose 'watch alligator' would be the proper term, but it is a bit of a mouthful. I mean what burglar in their right mind is gonna face down a full-grown alligator.—They don't know he has no teeth—just to steal your TV, or your computer, or something?

"Must be quite a shock, poor things, when they climb over the fence, though it does make me smile when I think about it. Everybody round here is used to Clive by now. We keep him on a leash (We replaced his collar with that studded one. Looks more 'macho', don't you think?) when we take him for walks and such.

"They don't allow him to come in the grocery store with us anymore, which I can understand, and I can see why they're not killed on us leaving him tied up outside either. Likely a bit of a deterrent to customers.

"So we usually just take him for walks. More like 'strolls'; Clive 'strolls', on the sidewalk, or in the park, and sometimes, on Sundays, we stop at 'Bill's Burger's' in the St. Aggie's parking lot, before church lets out, and pick him up a couple dozen burgers (Clive does love his burgers! But no pickles!) and he can swallow them whole.

"The other dogs in town kinda like him, though it took them a while. I suspect he doesn't smell like a dog. A fish, maybe? I've never actually smelled him, up that close, to know. But they all seem to be 'buds' now, and we often have quite a crew, all with wagging tails, except for Clive, of course, along for the trip.

"Clive is too big for the car now, so we can't take him for rides, except in Uncle Clive's old truck.—There you go! There's 'Uncle Clive' again! He does tend to crop up—He seems to enjoy it. Hangs his head over the tailgate, with his mouth open, to catch the wind. The alligator. Not Uncle Clive. Uncle Clive stays home.

"We don't generally take him in the house; he tends to take down the furniture, but in the winter, he stays on a really, really big dog bed, in the back porch. We did keep him in the front porch for a while at first, but he seemed to freak out the mail lady.

"He sleeps a lot in the winter anyway, all cozy under a big quilt Aunt Evelyn made for him. Then Uncle Clive decided he wanted a quilt too, so she had to make another one. Likely, they both spend most of the winter snuggled up under one of Aunt Evelyn's quilts, just not the same one. And sometimes, in the winter, Clive likes to watch television. We don't let him watch 'Alligator Hunters'.

"In the summer, he pretty well lives in our pool. It does discourage the local teenagers from sneakin' in for a midnight swim, which I really wouldn't mind them doin', every once in a while. We don't swim in it much ourselves anymore either cuz Clive does like to 'play with you' in the water.

"He spends a lot of the summertime in the garden too. We have a big garden. We call it 'The Everglades', just to make him feel at home, and we never have to worry about squirrels, or rats, or bunnies, or raccoons, or even the neighborhood cats. Clive takes care of that. Just gulps 'em down. Likely thinks they're burgers, though I suppose they all might taste a bit different. But you know what they say: 'Variety is the spice of life!'

"We did talk about finding Clive a girlfriend cuz, in the spring, he was roaring at the moon a lot, so likely he was lonely for female companionship, and the neighbors were starting to complain, seeing as their windows were crackin', but he eventually got over it, so we didn't end up getting him a girlfriend after all, which is probably just as well.

"Yeah, sure. You can take our picture. Clive doesn't mind, but I woulda worn a better shirt, if I hadda known. Clive likes to keep his mouth shut for pictures. Likely he's embarrassed about the no teeth thing, but I don't really see any reason he should be shy. He does have lovely eyes."

The Park

The Guy in the Tree

Boomer Park wasn't that big a park. It did have a bit of a beach, at the edge of the pond that froze in the winter, for skating, and it had kind of a practice soccer field, at one end, for kids, and dogs, and anyone else who just wanted to mess around with a ball and not tick off the 'Serious Soccer Players' in the big field. And the geese tended to avoid it, which was nice.

I'm not sure why they avoided it. Maybe cuz of the dogs, or maybe cuz it was used so much the grass wasn't as lush as it was on the 'official' patch next door. The park had a little stage too, for anyone who wanted to air their views to anyone who wanted to listen, and it made a great 'venue' for aspiring, usually seven-year-old 'entertainers'.

It also had lots of trees, and benches, and a set of swings and stuff, like any good park should have, and everybody figured it was pretty safe.

But there was this guy who lived in a tree. Not like Tarzan or anything; he was just a guy. Maybe 30 or so. The tree was a big one; old, and in the summer, when the leaves were out full, there was no way you could have ever seen this guy, unless he wanted to be seen, which he didn't.

His sister knew he lived in that tree, and sometimes she left him packages; cookies and stuff, behind a bush at the bottom, and they would be gone the next morning when she checked, but even she hardly ever saw him. I'm not sure where he went in the winter, cuz he obviously couldn't live in the tree then. Maybe he was one of those people who slept in a tent, in the scrubland, back behind St. Aggies, and ate at the mission, when it was cold.

The park security fella must have known he was up there, but then maybe he didn't, or if he did, maybe he was just keeping his mouth shut, cuz the guy in the tree didn't seem to be doing anyone any harm.

I think maybe he wasn't just antisocial. I think maybe there might have been more to it than that, but like I said, he didn't seem to bother anybody, so nobody bothered him. In fact, nobody else even knew there was, or ever had been, a guy in a tree, in that park.

Until one day, something bad happened under that tree, or almost happened.

Little Bella Bell and her family were on the beach, enjoying the day, and Sergeant Bell was lying on a blanket on the sand, soaking up the sun, with his wife sitting nearby, chatting with him, and Gracie and Bella were busy making a castle, out of sand and sticks, just down the way.

None of them even noticed Bella wandering off, following a rabbit, until suddenly, they realized she wasn't there anymore. She wasn't anywhere. A parent's worst fear had become real.

Actually, Bella was somewhere; She was in the bushes, under a tree, in the arms of a man with his hand over her mouth, stroking her hair, and whispering to her, to try to keep her quiet.

It wasn't just any old tree though. It was the tree with the guy in it. And the guy could see, and hear, everything that was going on in the bushes below him, at the bottom of 'his tree', and, even though it went against every illogical fear, and every overwhelming urge for secrecy and self-preservation he had, he knew he had to do something about it. And he did.

When the guy at the bottom of the tree leaned over, to peek through the branches, to see what was happening back at the beach, the guy in the tree made his move, and dropped like a stone; like an avenging angel, straight out of heaven, and landed smack on top of the man at the bottom of the tree, missing Bella by well-calculated inches.

Bella, for some reason, wasn't at all scared of the guy from the tree—She certainly had been scared of the guy at the bottom of the tree—and she clung to him, and became calm, even chatty, as they walked, holding hands, across the park, back toward her frantic family on the beach.

The guy at the bottom of the tree was still unconscious when they all got back to him, although, too bad for him, he did come around in time to realize what had happened, and to face Sergeant Bell who, being a good RCMP officer, did his best to control himself, and not rip the man into tiny little pieces (which was his first inclination), before the rest of the officers showed up, and took the man away.

It would be nice to say the guy in the tree, who refused to tell anyone his name, became just a regular guy, and got himself a regular life, and maybe even became an 'honorary uncle' or something, to the Bells. But actually the guy in the tree just found himself another tree, in another, more secluded, part of the park, and 'laid low', until the fuss died down and everyone forgot about him again.

Except the Bells. The Bells never forgot him, and every night, little Bella Bell, even when she got older, would finish off her prayers with: "and please bless the guy in the tree."

***

Drive On

I rub, and rub, and rub, her hand. Nothing. So I rub, and rub again. Maybe a twitch? Or maybe just my imagination. Still, I go at it again, and rub, and rub. Her eyes flicker open. Blank, then fearful, then confused, and then she closes them again. So I rub her hand again.

"Stop that." (So I do.) "Why were you doing that?"

"Cuz I thought maybe you were dead. You looked dead."

"Ah." The word was like a sigh, expelled on the air.

"You must have fainted. I've never seen anyone in a faint before."

She snorted. That's the only word for it.

"How ladylike," she said, and she laughed, mockingly, at herself, there on the ground, with her eyes still shut. She was definitely alive.

"I'll go away now then, as long as you're alright?"

"Don't go. Not just yet."

So we sit there for a bit. Well, I sit there, and she lies there.

"It must be pretty uncomfortable, lying there on the ground."

"No. I don't mind. I can feel it. Like I'm 'grounded',"—and she laughs again, but, this time, it is a laugh. Not a great laugh, but healthier.—"Why the hand thing?"

"Well, I could reach it, and it didn't seem quite polite to rub your foot, and besides, you have shoes on."

She opened her eyes. They were deep brown, like the best dark chocolate; 'Dutch Boys Chocolate' brown, and she smiled.

"Oooh! Fancy chair."

"Um, latest model. High tech. 'The Mercedes' of wheelchairs."

"I like Porches myself."

248

"Nah. Not as comfortable, but not bad. Mine's over there," and I swing my arm randomly in the air.

She laughed again; a real laugh this time, and began to struggle to her feet. I couldn't help her. I would very much have liked to help her.

"I hate this wheelchair!" It just came out, in a burst. I hadn't meant to say it.

"I know. I'm sure you do."

"Maybe we'll meet again. Don't know where. Don't know when."

"You're supposed to sing it," and she sang it back. She had a nice voice.

"Hmm. Not bad! Are you, by any chance, 'In the Theater'?" I attempted to say it in very 'English' tones.

"Yes. I am actually. Selling popcorn." It was my turn to laugh. "Next time, don't rub my hand."

"Oh. Why not?"

"Bit weird."

"Ah. Then next time, don't faint."

"Right. I don't know why I did this time."

"I do. No breakfast."

"Um. Could be."

I 'walked her' to her car. She was still a bit wobbly, but okay, and she kept her hand on the back of my chair, for support.

"Nice car."

It was a beat up old Mini that looked older than she did.

"Thanks. I left the Porsche at home today; 'Slumming it', you know."

"Yes, I've done that. Makes for a change."

She got in the car, and it started, reluctantly, with a roar, and a cough of smoke, from its rear end.

"Sorry. It's not a very polite car."

"No. I can see that."

"I come here, to the park, on Thursdays, by the way, at lunch time."

"Ah. Okay. I'll bring the sandwiches next time then?"

"Okay, and I'll bring the popcorn."

***

In general, Saint Agatha was a pretty law-abiding little town in spite of its rough roots, but, recently, the RCMP had been receiving a spate of complaints about thefts, mainly of small things; watches, jewelry, a few wallets, centering mostly around Boomer Park, mostly at the beach by the pond, so Sergeant Bell was sent out, on an 'undercover assignment', to suss it out.

It was hard to picture Sergeant Bell 'undercover'. It would take a big blankie to hide him, but with his wife, and his little daughters, and his bright red Wiley E. Coyote shorts his wife had given him for his birthday, he blended in reasonably well, on a summer Sunday afternoon.

'The Revs', were there as well, walking their dog and cat.

It was not actually 'their' dog and cat; It was actually Mr. Rooney and Thug. The Revs were 'babysitting' while Hellie and Wellie were away, in Egypt, on their honeymoons, and it was really only Mr. Rooney who was 'walking'. With Thug, it was more like 'taking him for a drag'.

But the Rev was determined to keep full control over his two charges, while their owners were away. Mostly due to the trauma of a dream he had had, about Hellie and Wellie returning home to the news that their precious pets had disappeared.

His dream, more a nightmare really, had involved a lot of shouting and brandishing of deadly weapons, though the Rev was sure that would never have really happened. He just wasn't taking any chances.

There was a yell, from down the beach, from a bather who had just come out of the water. "Hey! Where's my wallet?" and Sergeant Bell sprang to his feet, spun in a circle, with his hands shading his eyes, to survey the area, and spotted the culprit, sprinting swiftly and silently toward the woods.

Sergeant Bell took off (He was surprisingly fleet for one so large), and disappeared into the trees. He returned, out of breath but triumphant, about 20 minutes later, talking on his cell phone with one hand, and holding the 'perpetrator of the crime', by the scruff of the neck, in the other.

It was a fox, and the constable was on the phone to the Wildlife people, directing them to 'come take 'er away'!

They found quite a 'stash' there in the woods, in the thief's den: Dozens of watches and pieces of jewelry (apparently she—It was a 'she': There were two 'junior apprentices' there as well—liked shiny things.) plus at least 70 golf balls, 'Likely from that new mini golf place, down by Mr. Ho's'. They assumed she had mistaken the golf balls for eggs, which must have been frustrating – and seven wallets. All top quality leather ('The girl knows her stuff!'), pretty well chewed up, but with most of the cash and credit cards intact.

It appeared the fox wasn't in it for the money.

"Good you caught her before she had time to teach those 'wretched urchins' her thieving ways, ay?" the Rev commented, as the two friends stood together watching the white van, with the three foxes in it, disappear down the road.

"Hey Ding! I wanted to tell you something: Jeff asked me the other day if I would baptize Clive."

"What! The alligator? Are you kidding?"

"Nope. He said he'd heard I'd baptized Mrs. Chadwell's pig—Which I did NOT, by the way—and he was wondering if I would 'do Clive'."

"No! So what did you say?"

"I told him I couldn't, cuz Clive wouldn't fit through any of the church doors."

"Good one."

Sergeant Bell looked down at the golf balls in his hands, and he laughed.

"Saint Agatha sure is a funny old place sometimes, isn't it?"

"Yeah", The Rev gazed around him, and smiled, "But you know, I do love this town."

Epilogue

The sun was going down and St. Aggie's stained glass windows reflected rainbow colors onto the tops of the cars that drifted by that lazy Sunday evening. Four people; two couples, were sitting, on either side of the church's front steps, looking like matching figurine bookends.

They weren't saying anything. They were just licking their ice cream cones—A new Dairy Freeze had just opened up down the street—and watching the sunset.

One of the men finished the last bit of his cone, sighed contentedly, rested his hand on the top of his dog's head, and put his other arm around his wife's waist, as she bent her head to his shoulder.

"Well Hell, I can't say it wasn't a lovely honeymoon, but it sure is good to be home!"

"Yeah…and yuh know what else, Boot?"

(Hellie smiled at Ruth, sitting beside him, with Thug on her lap.)

"For a 'Horrible Fate', this really isn't that bad!"